SECOND
CHANCE

PATRICIA MORTON

Second Chance

First published 2019 by Patricia Morton
Copyright © 2019 Patricia Morton

ISBN: 978 1 78645 324 2

Cover Design: Debbie McGowan

Typesetting/Formatting:
Beaten Track Publishing
www.beatentrackpublishing.com

CONTENTS

LIVERPOOL 2012

CHAPTER 1

Friday 9th November

CAROLE OPENED THE rusty gate. It creaked indignantly after being left in peace for so long. The front garden of the old Victorian house had turned into a jungle. Brambles carrying the dried-up remains of unpicked blackberries swarmed everywhere, crying almost accusingly at their rejection. She slammed the gate and rushed up to the front door before critical eyes behind the lace curtains next door could catch sight of her. The neighbours had never liked them, two women living together! *I suppose they wanted a nice family next door,* she thought bitterly. Her foot caught in a bramble and she nearly shot headlong up the steps. It would have been funny in a film but not now. She turned the key and the front door opened into the dark hall. She very nearly shouted to tell Paula she was home but stopped herself just in time.

The house seemed to echo in spite of the carpets. After four weeks of neglect dust lay thickly everywhere. She went into the kitchen. The silence was as loud as an orchestra. The table was in its usual place near the window, covered by the yellow plastic cloth Paula had bought to save washing. She sat down on the painted chair which rocked dangerously. It should have gone to the tip years ago!

1

Once the funeral was over she'd gone straight to the B&B in Southport. The truth was she had run away like a terrified child. The four weeks she had spent there had given her plenty of time to think objectively about the past. She looked back with mounting horror at her teaching career and then doing what Paula had planned for them in the holidays and at weekends. She had spent too much time lying on the bed in the B&B, staring at the ancient flowery wallpaper until the pink and yellow daisies turned into multiple copies of Paula's face. Was she planning the next part of Carole's life from the grave? Then the landlady had started to give her questioning looks. The summer season was well over. Florid-faced Mrs Smith wanted her out so she could close up for the winter and depart on her cruise to the Canaries with her sun cream and glittery new clothes. It was time to go home and face the house and the silence.

With a start Carole remembered the food in the boot of the car parked outside. Some of it was frozen stuff. She ran back down the hall, sneezing as her feet banged on the dusty carpet and hauled the bags out of the boot and into the house. She was glad to have at least something to distract her from the problem of what to do with the rest of her life without her friend.

As she dumped her case down in the bedroom she caught sight of herself in the mirror and stopped dead in her tracks. The long mirror had been there for years yet she'd hardly noticed it. She stared at the person standing there as though it was someone else. The face that looked back at her wasn't too bad in spite of a few wrinkles. Her grey hair was a bit untidy and her pleated skirt and jumper were out of date but still in good condition. The lace-up shoes had been repaired a few times but, as Paula would have said, why buy new ones when the others are not worn out?

She suddenly smelt burning and remembered the fish fingers under the grill. They were patterned black and yellow and just about edible. The baked beans were about to dry up in the pan. She grabbed the handle then dropped the pan with a shriek. The metal handle was boiling hot. She looked at the yellow plastic tablecloth with distaste, as though seeing it for the first time. Its rather slimy surface squeaked as she pushed her plate away a little. It was Friday. They had always had fish on a Friday. Paula's idea!

A wave of nausea rippled through her. There was no way she was going to eat this. It would have to go into the fridge for another time. Paula would at least be proud of her. 'Waste not, want not' had been her philosophy. Damn Paula! A heart attack was a heartless way to go. She could have laughed at the pun but she wasn't in that kind of mood. Time had run out for her or had it? Was it too late to make a new life for herself?

The fish fingers and beans were safely stored in the fridge. She walked out into the November night, slamming the door behind her and pulling her old camel coat up close to her neck. It was only six o'clock but already pitch-dark. As she approached the shops, lights surged up out of the darkness like fireworks. She passed a fish and chip shop full of people waiting patiently in a long queue. The other shops were just as busy, everyone going through the usual weekend routines. The hairdressers were chopping and washing under hastily installed paper decorations and wafting red and yellow balloons. Christmas was coming. Pippa's Pizzas loomed ahead at the end of the block. It was the very last building. After that there was an unending void of blackness and now drizzling rain. She stopped and stared through the door. It looked so welcoming.

'Excuse me.'

She jumped, suddenly realising that she was blocking the doorway. A young woman with two small children was trying to get past her. Blushing slightly she moved to one side. The woman joined the queue; her shoulders slumped as though she was carrying a heavy invisible rucksack. The little boy and girl hopped up and down like two wooden puppets in competition with each other. There were a lot of people waiting. Fed up, the boy poked the little girl and, like Punch and Judy, they started fighting. It was an uneven battle. She grabbed hold of her mum's coat, tears running down her cheeks.

Carole suddenly found herself in the queue as though some invisible force had pushed her towards the children. She saw the problem and politely asked if she could give them the two takeaway menus she had just picked up. The mother, skinny and pallid like an anorexic teenager, looked at her in surprise and then nodded with a smile. The children started looking at the pictures. The queue went down. Carole started to panic. What on earth was she going to order?

Almost as though she had read her mind the girl turned to her. 'Kids! They hate waiting for things. Thanks for the menus. I wouldn't have thought of that. I'm all in. I could do with an early night.'

'You're welcome. I used to teach little kids. Mind you, you never get to be an expert, well sometimes it works!' A warm glow of relief flooded through Carole. She had practically joined a family. Nobody would know she wasn't with them. She felt almost normal.

'I'm Jenny by the way,' she said, tossing her blond hair off her face. 'And this is Eva and James. They always have the same thing, the Margarita. What are you having?'

'I don't know. I've never eaten pizza.'

'Really!' Jenny's cornflower blue eyes opened wide with astonishment.

'What do you recommend?' Carole asked her. It seemed a good question, as the pizza menu inside her head was completely blank and the children had the real ones.

'The one the children like is probably the best to start with. You can always go upmarket later.' She laughed.

Carole smiled and nodded, keeping her thoughts inside. She didn't think there was much upmarket about the place. However, she decided to follow Jenny's advice.

'Would you like to sit with us? The children would like that. They don't have any grandparents. Oh, I'm sorry. Perhaps you're too young to be a granny,' she added hastily.

'I'd love to,' Carole exclaimed, really meaning it. 'I don't have any grandchildren. Thanks for the loan.'

In spite of the queue, they were soon sitting at a table with the pizzas. It was like being part of a family. A wave of sadness rippled through Carole as a man's face came into her mind uninvited. The years had blunted the outline of the image but he was still there after thirty-five years, reminding her of what might have been. She still had the same dream. He was waving to her across a beach edged with pine trees. She was young again and running towards him, her long blond hair blowing in the wind. It was hard running in the water. The sand was soft. When she got to the place where he had been waving, he wasn't there. There was only space and silence among the trees.

'Carole. Why have your hands got all those funny lines on them?'

She came back to reality with a jump.

'Eva! Don't make personal remarks,' Jenny exclaimed, brushing her rather windswept hair out of her eyes.

Eva's face crumpled. Carole came to her rescue.

'It's OK, Eva. When you get old your skin gets wrinkles.'

'I'm four. How old are you?'

Jenny gasped. 'Eva, you don't ask people how old they are. It's rude.'

Carole chuckled. 'It's all right, Eva. I don't mind telling you. I'm sixty-one. I'm fifty-seven years older than you.'

'And you're fifty-five years older than me,' piped James, his solemn round eyes fixed firmly on Carole's round glasses.

'And you're a clever clogs,' laughed Carole, starting on her pizza. The pastry was warm and soft, the bubbly cheese and tomato rising like small volcanoes across a sunny desert. It was the most delicious thing she had ever eaten, a hundred times better than the fish fingers. Why had she never known there was a world outside that house of theirs?

Half an hour later the table was strewn with lemonade bottles, crumbs and crumpled paper serviettes. It was time to go.

'Thanks for keeping us company.' Jenny smiled, looking almost tearful. 'We're usually on our own here. I'm a single parent. It's not what you think,' she added defensively, two red patches growing on her cheeks. 'He walked out on me. It's just us three now.'

Carole was tempted to instantly offer her services as an adoptive granny but caution got the better of her. 'I expect we'll meet again.' She smiled. 'I'll be back!'

'See you next week.' James grinned. 'I'll bring my new Lego robot to show you.'

'I'll bring my new doll,' Eva added, not to be outdone. 'She's called Poppy and she's got pink high heels and a pink dress to match.'

Carole sighed, caught between the pink sexist issue and her own beige lace-up shoes. 'Maybe.' She smiled. 'I don't know where I'll be next Friday but I might come. See you soon, anyway.'

She walked away from the lights, off into a blackness that was a combination of the bleak November night and her own rapidly deteriorating mood. On her way home, everyone she passed seemed to be with someone else. They all had their heads together or arms round each other, laughing and talking. She pulled her headscarf tightly round her face but the rain drenched her, the November night engulfing her in a vacuum.

The house loomed ahead. She would be glad to get away from all those people, all that togetherness. She opened her bag, took off her black leather gloves and felt for the key. She always kept it in a little compartment designed for mobile phones. It was empty. Scrabbling in the bag she caught her fingernail on the zip and a large piece tore off. Her heart was thumping so fast, like an out-of-control funeral bell. She hardly noticed the pain or the sticky blood running down her finger. She must have left the key in the kitchen on the table or at the pizza place.

She stood helplessly in front of the door. She would have to break the window. Thank goodness they didn't have an alarm. They'd never needed one. Stumbling through the rusty wrought iron gate, she felt her way down the side of the house. The paving stones were mossy and covered with weeds growing in between the slabs. She tiptoed gingerly, as though walking on ice. Who would know if she fell down and hit her head? And who would care? She firmly dismissed the dismal thoughts and carried on. The door at the back had a glass window. The key was in the lock so it would be easy. She picked up a rock then stopped. The nosy neighbours next door would hear the noise. What a pity they hadn't made friends with them and left a key. Paula had refused their offer of tea and cake when they moved there and now the relationship was set in stone. Maybe it was Paula's fault, not the neighbours. Nothing seemed straightforward.

She raised the rock above her head, took a deep breath then stopped, remembering something. Paula had left a key under one of the plant pots on the patio just in case! No asking the neighbours for help! But which one of a dozen possibilities? She felt under the first one, then the second, cursing the number of pots. Green slimy moss came off the icy cold clay pots and stuck to her hands. 'Ouch!' The fifth pot was full of dead nettles. She had grabbed a bunch in the darkness and now her fingers were fizzing. The tenth one was the mint. It had died down, the roots resting under the soil for the winter but underneath was something hard and pointed – the key!

Standing there soaked, bleeding and stung, she felt, nevertheless, an amazing sense of triumph. She turned the key in the lock and heard the other one fall out. Waves of warmth swept over her in spite of the cold. She staggered into the kitchen and, to her relief, saw the other key on the table. At least she hadn't left it at the pizza place. She put the two of them safely into her bag. Her life, such as it was, was at least returning to normal. After a hot bath she went to bed, still glowing. She wouldn't need a hot water bottle. She was shivering with a delicious excitement. She was still alive. Who knew what tomorrow would bring!

CHAPTER 2

Saturday 10th November
A Chance Encounter

CAROLE WOKE UP early as usual. The sun was shining through the flowered curtains, turning the old floral pattern into a wonderful meadow of multicoloured flowers. She lay there mentally walking through the field then looked around, her hands moving over the ancient eiderdown, up and down the stitched areas which formed small bumps like miniature hills. The anaglypta wallpaper had been painted a few times but the paint was peeling off in lots of places leaving spots of pink. Paula had chosen the pink. Carole chuckled to herself, thinking that perhaps her friend had been influenced by Barbara Cartland. Paula had never talked about her past but she couldn't imagine anyone less likely to have had a romantic affair like the heroines in her books. She'd always had her feet planted firmly on the ground, a million miles from the pink mist of daydreams.

She got out of bed, clutching her dressing gown around her in the icy cold and went down into the kitchen. She turned the radio on and jumped as a loud organ nearly deafened her. Oddly it was the Bach Toccata in D Minor. She recognised it as one of Paula's favourite pieces. She had always listened to Radio 3 and Carole had never objected, even though she would have preferred Radio 4 or Classic FM. The kitchen was so empty the music echoed like it would in a cathedral. As the massive chords soared into the space it was like the beginning of a horror film or a warning that a drama was about to take place. Chance would be a fine thing! She put the kettle on.

She turned on two gas rings to warm her up then poured out some cereal, only to realise she hadn't bought any milk. As she crunched the dry cereal she considered what she would do apart from buying some milk. The black coffee energised her. She needed a plan. The library! She would go to the library and borrow some books. There wasn't much on the television. Books had always been her way of escaping from humdrum reality. She would have liked to join the book group run by the library but Paula hadn't wanted to. She hadn't had the energy or the courage to go on her own so she'd taken the easy way out and just borrowed the new books that came in and sometimes asked the staff for recommendations. They were so helpful and friendly. They were like real friends.

Radio 3 was now playing chamber music. She sighed. She wasn't very keen on that and hoped it would soon be something less intellectual like Strauss waltzes or an aria from *La bohème*. She liked Puccini even though the operas always ended in tears. The music was so beautiful and easy to listen to. She liked them all apart from *Madame Butterfly*. She couldn't watch the end where the Japanese girl gave her child away to her ex lover and then killed herself. She had watched it once and the girl's grief had never left her. She was so affected by it and she knew why but didn't want to think about it. Young lovers dying didn't upset her a bit but the mother's dilemma – her sacrifice versus a better life for her child? That was different. She just wouldn't watch that opera again. The chamber music went on and on. She switched it off and got ready to go out, leaving the dirty dishes in the sink.

Traffic roared past her as she walked along the pavement. The world was on its way to work while she was free. She almost wished she was back teaching. Life at the school had been like belonging to a family. Little children were always the same. They never changed and she missed them. The area around her was too extensive, like floating in everlasting space. She tightened her fist, feeling her fingernails biting into the skin, remembering the little hands in hers.

The library was near the town centre, quite a walk away. She preferred to walk as parking was difficult and expensive. How often she heard people saying, 'Sorry! I can't stop. I've only got five minutes left in the car park.' With no car to worry about, the time was her own even though she wasn't sure quite what to do with it. She went through the library's massive carved stone archway. Two pillars decorated with stone roses on either side of the arched doorway had stood majestically for over a hundred years. They looked as though they were holding the whole literary world up. The door was propped open, the building a lovely example of Victorian quality and solidity. It was surrounded by a patchwork quilt of sixties concrete monsters and the latest twenty-first-century architectural delights that looked a bit like giant feathered birds about to fly off.

Inside it was quiet. It was a place where you never felt lonely as nobody was talking. Carole was at peace among the books. They were easier to deal with than people. They weren't domineering or aggressive or self-opinionated. Well, maybe they were a vehicle for people to get an audience and tell their readers what they thought about the world but you could always skip a few pages. Annoying people talked on and on about themselves. Some of them never asked questions so you knew all about them and they couldn't have written two lines about you. As she approached the bookshelves the bitter thoughts drifted away. She knew negative thoughts poisoned your mind and showed on your face. She might end up looking like the gargoyles in the cathedral if she didn't take herself in hand.

She went towards a shelf displaying the newest arrivals and selected one or two, noting who had made comments about them on the cover. She took them to the counter to have them stamped. They had a machine now so you could do it yourself but she liked the human contact. She couldn't talk to a machine. The woman behind the counter was about her age. Carole wondered if she could get a job in the library but quickly gave up the idea. That lady had been there for a while and probably had a qualification as a librarian. Anyway, she was too old to start again and then why should she? After all she had her pension. The world was her oyster, at least in theory! She put the freshly stamped books into her bag. There were several people behind her in a queue so the assistant had routinely stamped the books with a wordless smile.

She made her way out of the door with hesitant steps. She would go for a coffee then to the shops. The words of a pop song from long ago came into her mind 'Is that all there is? Is that all there is to life? Is that all there is?'

'Carole!'

She swung round. The voice came from a blond woman dressed in jeans and a faux sheepskin coat, open and revealing a smock top worn by pregnant women in the sixties but now fashionable for everybody. Well, nearly everybody. The person standing there was too old to be pregnant but, then again, with IVF you could never make assumptions any more. The eyes emerging from the lined face were wide with delight.

'How lovely to see you! You do remember me, don't you? Valerie,' she added helpfully, pulling her woolly hat down round her face.

'Valerie! How awful of me not to recognise you! You look so young in that outfit.'

'Thank you. I'm just comfy like this. Thank heaven for modern fashions!'

'What are you doing here? I thought everyone had gone apart from me.'

'We came back here two years ago from Birmingham. My mum died. You do remember her, don't you? She really liked you. She was always telling me how respectable you were, a good influence! She left us the house. We'd both retired so we sold up and moved back. The kids had gone so it was easy enough. I always missed Liverpool.' She chuckled, revealing a couple of gaps where teeth used to be.

Carole felt a surge of guilt. Valerie had been her best friend at Grammar School. They'd sat next to each other and struggled with mathematical equations and French translations. They had lost contact when Valerie had gone off to university where she had found a husband. That was what university was all about, her friend had always insisted. If you didn't find a man before the end of your course you were doomed to a life on the shelf. Well, that's what had happened to her. There had been no potential husbands at her all-girls' Teacher Training College or at the primary school where she had spent her life, only Michael and that was all so long ago.

'What about you? What have you been doing? I'm sorry we lost touch. Life was just very busy and not always very easy with kids.' An unexpected shadow fell across Valerie's face.

'Not much. I lived with a colleague I got friendly with when I was teaching. Her parents died in a car crash. They left her the family house so we shared it. She died recently and left it to me so I suppose I'm lucky in a way.'

Valerie's happy face took on an air of sadness as she listened.

'We got into a bit of a rut, the two of us. We were both too wrapped up in our work. I can see that now but at the time we were just too busy to notice. Teaching's like that, you know. It eats up your life! I retired last year and I'm at a bit of a loose end now. We had all kinds of plans but it didn't work out.'

Valerie looked sympathetic. 'Well, marriage isn't straightforward either so don't feel you've missed out that much. There were times when...' She stopped as though about to say something then thought better of it. 'I ended up in the Civil Service. I didn't want to teach and there didn't seem to be anything else to do with an English degree. I was glad to get out, I can tell you! What do you do now you've got your freedom?'

Carole felt like laughing. She made it sound as though she had just got out of prison. 'Not much at the moment. I went away after the funeral. I couldn't face the house. I've only just come back. I suppose we lived in each other's pockets. You just get into a routine and you don't even think about it. We used to go for walks, read books and watch TV. Nothing exciting really. Sometimes we went to visit gardens during the summer, you know the National Garden Scheme. People with nice gardens open them to the public.'

Valerie nodded uncomprehendingly.

'They make money for charity. Oh, and I still play the piano. I used to play for assembly. There was no one else to do it. The old piano in the front room still works OK. The piano tuner seemed to think it was quite good last time he came but I'm not what you'd call a pianist though!' She laughed, blushing as though she had been boasting.

Val listened solemnly, weighing up what kind of life her old friend must have been leading. 'Don't put yourself down. I remember you playing some really good things.'

Carole blushed with pleasure. A fresh wind of hope rippled briefly through her. 'Well I do still like music. Remember the prize-giving at the Phil? I played the violin in the orchestra. The string section sounded like a lot of cats on a wall. Perhaps it was my fault!'

Valerie giggled, like the schoolgirl she once was. 'Well, I do remember the screeching violins but I'm sure it wasn't your fault.'

'Thanks, Val. Perhaps it was the school violins.' She hesitated, thinking back to her life with Paula. 'We still go…went to the Phil quite a lot. It was a good night out. Paula was a bit more high-brow than me. Sometimes I went to the concerts for her and just sat there thinking about something interesting! But it was a nice feeling being with a lot of people.' Carole blushed uncomfortably. She wished she hadn't said that. She quickly changed the subject.

'How about you? What do you do to pass the time now you haven't got the Civil Service to keep you amused?' she laughed, relieved to turn the conversation in Valerie's direction.

'Jim and I joined the U3A a few months after we moved in here. I've really never looked back. It's great fun. There's always something to do. It gets me out of the house. '

Carole looked puzzled. It didn't mean anything to her. Her friend noticed the bewilderment and laughed. 'Haven't you heard of the University of the Third Age?'

'Don't tell me you've gone back to university at your age!'

'Oh. It's not like that. It's an organisation for older people who want to keep learning things, a kind of old people's club but one that isn't just for socialising. I shouldn't call it an old people's club. It's really not like that. You can pick up past skills like French conversation or learn some Italian before your holidays or join a choir or an exercise class. The sky's the limit. It stops you getting old before your time. At least I hope it does.'

'It certainly seems to be doing that for you,' Carole replied, admiringly. Valerie seemed so full of enthusiasm for the future and real excitement at all the possibilities. 'I really like your jacket. It suits you.'

Valerie smiled with pleasure. 'Thanks, Carole. Why don't you come along to the next coffee morning? It's on Monday in St. Andrew's church hall. You know where that is?'

Carole nodded. It wasn't that far from the library.

'You get a cheap coffee and a biscuit and you can pick up a newsletter and see what it's all about. I'll give you my phone number so we can keep in touch.'

'Here's mine.' Carole wrote it down on a spare bill she found in her bag. 'Yes. Let's keep in touch.'

As she opened the door the house suddenly seemed different, less faded and musty. How could that be? Nothing had changed. No cleaner had been in while she'd been out. Perhaps the world didn't really exist in its own right. Maybe it only existed inside people's heads. She put the shopping down on the kitchen table. At least she had remembered the milk. She put the bottle of sherry into the sideboard, feeling rather guilty. They had always had a glass on a Sunday but this time she had bought sweet sherry rather than the dry stuff. Her hand had approached the usual bottle and she had had to almost drag it away to the next shelf down, looking over her shoulder guiltily as though she was a shoplifter.

She had bought a frozen pizza with pepperoni pieces on the top. She wasn't sure she would like it but there wasn't much else left in the shop. Maybe everyone had bought them all for the weekend. She put it in the freezer compartment then got the fish fingers out of the fridge and put them in the oven. What a pity she hadn't got a microwave! She would eat them for lunch then go to the fish and chip shop tonight. Fish twice! So what? It was supposed to be good for you even if it did have five hundred calories worth of batter on it. She wasn't in the mood for cooking. She would get the fish and chips then start one of the library books. The new Kate Reynolds thriller looked interesting. Thank God for books! On Sunday she would go to the art gallery in the centre then eat her pizza. It would soon be Monday.

***

Carole put the television on and sat down to eat her breakfast. It was Sunday. She put her feet up on the couch. There was a debate going on about old people and what they should be doing with themselves. One rather self-satisfied woman had just sold half a dozen paintings. Her paintings, the ones she hadn't sold, all looked rather like the sort of thing a group of six-year-olds could knock up in ten minutes. At least she'd done something, Carole thought. 'Perhaps I could become a concert pianist or a violinist?' She almost laughed out loud at the thought. It was too late for that. You had to start when you were young. Anyway, she had been one of the screechers in the orchestra, not the next Stefan Grappelli. But maybe she could find something interesting to do at this new organisation.

She put away the breakfast things. She should make a list of jobs. Otherwise she would while away her time doing nothing. She sighed. One thing came to mind, that letter from the bank. Paula had always dealt with the finances. She had never even looked at the bank statements. Fortunately most of it was on standing order or direct debit but she knew there was a letter from the bank among the junk mail. That would be the first thing on the list. She took a piece of paper and wrote 'Bank Statement' at the top. That was the easy bit. Getting on with it was another matter! Lunch first then tackle it.

She watched the news, which was a series of murders, rapes, robberies and bombings, while she ate her lunch. When it finished she started watching a one star film. The time flowed by. She knew what she was doing but the envelope was lying there on the top of the pile. It was almost glowing or was it her imagination. Two words on a list! That's all she had done. She had put the envelope on the top of the pile to annoy herself. Why was she so bothered by this communication from the bank? There was no obvious answer but it made her nervous. She was venturing into Paula's territory and without any evidence a sixth sense told her to prepare herself for something unexpected. She shut down the television and grabbed the envelope, her hand shaking.

She tore it open, feeling angry with herself. She was on her own now and she would have to cope better than this. Surely Paula wouldn't have taken out a payday loan! She wasn't that sort, was she? Her whole body was shaking and her eyes filled with tears. Why on earth had she let herself be so dependent? She was paying a high price for not taking responsibility.

The first two sheets were requests to change insurance policies and offers of additional credit cards. They could go in the bin. The third sheet was the bank statement. At least there were no threats from the bank. She looked down the list of outgoings. Fortunately they were not in the red. She looked carefully at all the items on the statement. She would turn the heating down. The other items would just have to be paid.

She was about to heave a sigh of relief that things were all right after all when she noticed something unusual. There was something she didn't understand, a standing order for £300 made out to SAM 73. It was an incredible amount, more than the gas or electricity. What on earth had Paula bought? They were still solvent but it was unusual. They had always discussed any purchase and weighed up whether they could afford it.

Something in the back of her mind – was it fear of the unknown or just curiosity? – forced her towards the old desk where Paula had kept all her records. It was a shabby wooden writing desk, neither antique nor modern. The carved sloping lid opened to form a writing area spotted with ink, the grain raised from years of wear. There were no bits of paper stuffed into crevices. Everything was organised. She rifled through Paula's impeccable files and found the past bank statements going back two years. She held her breath, unable to believe her eyes. SAM 73 had been receiving £300 every month for the past two years, maybe longer! The bank statements didn't go back further than the past two years. Who or what was SAM 73? She had hoped to cross the bank statement off her list but now it would have to stay until the mystery was solved. One thing she did know was that SAM 73 wouldn't be getting any more money if she could help it.

CHAPTER 3

Monday 12th November
No Easy Answers

CAROLE HAD ARRANGED to meet Valerie outside St Andrew's church hall. The buffaloes were meeting at the water hole. One lone buffalo would be standing all alone to one side. The analogy was a bit extreme but that's how she felt. She hadn't wanted to go into a strange room with lots of people she didn't know. Valerie had been very understanding. Of course it was difficult. She had been with Jim on the first visit but it had still been a bit scary. Carole had been looking forward to it with real excitement but now the problem of the bank statement was threatening to spoil it all. She had had to sort it out so she could enjoy going to the coffee morning. She couldn't just shrug things off like some people.

She knew that Paula had used the bank's telephone service. She had heard her talking to a bank official from time to time. It was a good service. It meant you didn't have to waste time making appointments to see someone. As they didn't have a computer it was the next best thing and it didn't turn out to be as difficult as all that. The Phone Bank details were in the front of the file, solidly Sellotaped onto the inside of the cover. She hesitatingly dialled the number. A woman's voice answered, giving her own telephone number. She sounded very agitated. A child was crying in the background.

'I'm sorry. I've got the wrong number.'

The woman put the phone down without a word. Carole could sense the annoyance. She must have made a mistake. Her hand had been shaking so much. She tried again, being very careful, dreading hearing the same woman again.

This time she got through to the bank. Instead of a pleasant person saying hello it was an automated system. 'Welcome to Lloyds TSB. If you have an account with us please say or key in your account number.'

She froze. Where would it be? Of course, it was always on the bank statement. She slowly typed it into the phone, followed by the sort code as requested. She was beginning to feel rather pleased with herself and relaxed a little. Coping with things instead of running away gave you a good feeling. She had to key in her date of birth and a security number. It was all so easy after all or was it? She'd done what they asked but she didn't get through. Her ever lingering sense of inadequacy came back with a vengeance. The bank hated her and it was mutual. Then a more rational thought struck her. Of course! Her date of birth didn't match the security number. If she keyed in Paula's date of birth she would have to say that she wasn't Paula. They wouldn't accept that either. There was nothing for it. She would have to go to the bank after the U3A coffee morning and sort it all out.

In spite of not wanting to, she arrived early at St Andrew's church hall and stood awkwardly outside, uncomfortably remembering the buffalo analogy. It wasn't quite right anyway. Buffaloes all looked more or less the same whereas these people were all shapes and sizes and ages, dressed in a multitude of different styles. Some of them smiled at her, making her feel more and more alone. Then she heard a now familiar voice.

'Carole! I'm not late, am I?' It was Valerie, dressed in an even more exotic smock top embroidered with flowers and beads and large antique dangling earrings.

'No. I was early. I like your top. Where did you get it from?'

Valerie laughed, revealing just a little embarrassment. 'I got it from the charity shop near your house, you know, the one near the bus stop. Some people are a bit snobbish about charity shops but I don't care. You get some great bargains there and it's a contribution to Cancer Research as well.' After so many years away from Carole she didn't know which category she belonged to. Was she into expensive clothes shops like Magda from the choir or bargain shopping like herself? She hoped it was the latter. She didn't look as though she'd bought any clothes since the seventies so maybe it was irrelevant! 'Shall we go in and get a coffee? If we wait too long we won't get a seat.'

Valerie was right. There was only one empty table. They sat down, and then she went to get the coffee and biscuits, giving Carole time to look around. There were more women than men. The old fashioned women were all at least ten years older than her, maybe twenty in some cases. She smoothed out her pleated skirt, wishing she had put her dress on. She sighed. It wouldn't have made any difference. The dress was bubbly Crimplene and out of the ark. Valerie came back with two coffees and a few biscuits and distracted her from more uncomfortable thoughts.

'Hello, Val. Nice to see you.' A couple in their early sixties were towering over them. 'We've just got back from London. We've been round the art galleries and to a concert at the Albert Hall. They were playing Tchaikovsky's Fifth Symphony. It's one of our favourites.'

'You lucky things! I'd love a weekend in London,' Valerie exclaimed with obvious pleasure. 'Carole, this is Ruth and Ted.'

'Nice to meet you,' Carole replied shyly. 'I love that symphony too.'

'Ruth and Ted are in the U3A choir with me,' Valerie intervened. 'We're all music lovers, well all at different levels but it works OK. Ted's special. He's a tenor and tenors are in short supply.'

Ted grinned, obviously glad to be appreciated. He was tall with bright blue eyes that revealed a hint of mischief. 'I'm not Caruso or the next Pavarotti but the three of us do our best.

There are only three of us and one is hardly ever there. His wife's ill so we have to sing a bit louder to make up for him.'

Ruth was as tall as her husband. They both sat down on the spare chairs and it was a lot easier to talk. She was dressed in a very chic, almost timeless outfit, perhaps a bit too chic for a coffee morning, Carole thought. Unlike Valerie's out-of-time pregnancy smock, she was wearing a figure-hugging top adorned with a green ceramic necklace and matching earrings. The brown linen trousers looked expensive. She could have been a model! Carole would have been intimidated but the two people facing her were so warm and obviously interested in what they were doing she relaxed. She hated people who were out to impress you. Instinctively she knew that Ruth and Ted were not like that.

'Are you a singer?' Ted asked, directing the conversation in Carole's direction. 'We're always looking for new people for the choir. A few people have died lately.'

'Ted!' Ruth exclaimed. 'For heaven's sake! Carole doesn't want to be told about that.'

'Well, I know, but death's part of life, isn't it? It's all the more reason to make the most of every day. There's no point in worrying about it,' Ted added philosophically. 'What do you think, Carole?'

Carole smiled. Ted had a way of making you feel optimistic. 'You're right. As for the choir, yes, I used to sing in the school choir and then in the local music association choir but it was a long time ago. I think they disbanded soon after I left. Not because of me,' she added hastily. 'People just drifted away and nobody came to replace them. They used to rehearse on a Friday and I was tired after a week at work so I dropped out.'

'How about joining us?' Ruth intervened. 'We're just starting to rehearse Fauré's Requiem. It's our most ambitious project yet. We could do with someone with choral experience. Do you know it?'

Carole's eyes lit up. Know it? She certainly did. Then a cloud appeared in her mind. It was so beautiful but also had unhappy memories. But she was determined to put all that behind her and look forward the way Ted seemed to be living his life. She nodded. 'Yes, I've sung it twice. It's really so beautiful but it makes me want to cry,' she admitted. 'I nearly cried during the concert,' she chuckled, 'and I was in the front row! I just managed to stop myself by thinking about something ordinary – I think it was a mental picture of a chocolate cake!'

They all laughed. She sounded like a good addition.

'The rehearsal's in St Andrew's High School on Thursday at seven o'clock,' Valerie chimed into the conversation. She had been very quiet, watching how Carole seemed to be settling into the group so easily. 'Magda's the coordinator but the most important person is Robert. He's the expert and the conductor. He used to teach music so we're lucky to have him. We wouldn't be able to do much without him. You will come, won't you?'

Carole was a bit overwhelmed by the pace of events happening to her. She had only come for a coffee. In fact she hadn't even picked up a newsletter and now she was more or less part of the choir. She was going to say no, that she would wait a bit when she heard herself saying yes, she would come to the rehearsal and join the choir. She felt her cheeks burning but it was with pleasure, not embarrassment.

She glanced at her watch. It was midday and she really felt as though she ought to be going home for some lunch. Volunteers were clearing the tables and there was a sound of dishes being washed in the kitchen. Everyone was getting up. She quickly picked up a newsletter then the four of them made their way outside where an uncertain sun was shining through the clouds.

'See you on Thursday.' Ted waved, making his way towards a rather smart red sports car.

Valerie turned towards her friend, smiling with obvious pleasure.

'Well, I didn't think things would work out so well! Fancy you joining the choir! I knew you could read music, well you're a pianist, aren't you, but I didn't know you'd been in the local choir. You'll be really useful. Are you a soprano?'

Carole nodded, glowing from being called a pianist. She'd never thought of herself as anything quite so glamorous. 'Well, I was. People's voices can change, can't they? I hope I'm still a soprano. I like singing the tune!'

'So do I. It's easier too if you can reach the notes. If it's very high I've been known to open my mouth and mime. Don't tell anybody I said that.' Valerie laughed. 'They might throw me out.'

'They won't. Anyway they need the customers! Look, I've got to go now. I've got a nasty job to do at the bank. The sooner I face up to it the better.'

They went their separate ways, promising to meet again at the rehearsal on Thursday.

There was a queue in the bank. Carole wished she could have gone straight to a window. Unfortunately she had time to get more and more nervous. People seemed to have all kinds of difficulties that involved signing things, exchanging bags of what looked like loot from a cartoon and long negotiations involving lots of pieces of paper. After what seemed like an eternity it was her turn. She explained her situation as briefly as she could and the bank clerk informed her she would need an interview then disappeared through a door behind her. Minutes passed and the queue mounted behind Carole. The clerk came back eventually and told Carole to go through the door at the end of the room where someone would see her.

A young man of about thirty was sitting at the other side of an imposing desk.

'My name's George.' He smiled, shaking her hand. 'How can I help?'

He sounded like a robot. It was the kind of question you always heard when you rang up companies. These people had been through a training session and that's what they had been taught to say! He could have been her son if she had married somebody. She remembered Ted's comments and put the thought firmly out of her mind. She explained the situation she was in over Phone Bank and the mysterious standing order. He listened carefully, nodding sympathetically. He looked genuinely concerned as he listened, his hand supporting his chin, his brown eyes serious. As she finished her speech he smiled and relaxed a little.

'Well, I can give you a security number that will give you access to Phone Bank. Have you got any form of identification?'

She had brought her passport so that wasn't a problem but the SAM 73 situation was obviously more difficult. He looked a bit perplexed like officials do when their comfortable routine is suddenly disrupted. 'If someone takes money out of your account without permission, like your credit card might have been used by someone, a scam in other words, then we take responsibility. But this standing order was set up three years ago by Miss Jennings and she never questioned it. I can't really clarify what it might be. Maybe she bought something on credit although I don't recognise the company.'

Carole shook her head. 'Paula wouldn't have done that. She wasn't like that at all.'

The young man raised his eyebrows just a little. 'People don't tell their partners everything. You'd be surprised at some of the situations I deal with! Oh. I wasn't suggesting you were partners in that way,' he added, reddening slightly.

Carole blushed. 'What if we were?' she flashed angrily. 'We're not living in the dark ages. It's the twenty-first century, you know.'

'Sorry,' he said, awkwardly staring past her at some invisible object.

She and Paula had only been friends, not lovers. He was trying to be very politically correct. All he was doing was making her feel uncomfortable. 'What can I do about it then?' she asked him directly. 'I'm having to make economies. I can't just ignore this.'

He looked thoughtful then said rather slowly and carefully, 'If I were you I would cancel it. If it turns out to be a company they'll soon contact you. In fact whoever it is they are going to miss this money, aren't they? So you'll eventually get to know what it is that your friend set up. It doesn't go out of the account until the end of the month so you've got a bit of time before whoever it is misses it.'

Carole nodded. It sounded sensible. She agreed to have it cancelled, shook his hand again and left the bank, feeling a mixture of relief that the money was now safe but equally anxious about what on earth Paula had set up and what would happen at the end of the month.

CHAPTER 4

The Choir Rehearsal

IT HAD SEEMED a long time to Thursday but Carole had found a lot of routine things to do. Cleaning the house and organising the kitchen seemed more manageable with the prospect of the choir rehearsal beaming like a lighthouse in the darkness of her mind. With the business of the standing order on hold until the end of the month she felt relaxed, in fact almost happy. She has succeeded in curbing her anxiety and putting the issue of SAM 73 into a mental in tray for later. She would need to sort out Paula's belongings but it was too early for that. It was still two weeks to the end of November. It could all wait.

Once again she had arranged to meet Valerie outside the school hall. Meeting the choir and the conductor seemed more difficult than going to the coffee morning although she couldn't put her finger on why that should be. Perhaps it was a bit like going for a job interview. Fortunately Valerie was waiting for her and they went in together. Ruth and Ted were already there. Ruth was wearing a very glamorous skirt and expensive leather boots. A dark brown necklace and earrings complemented an embroidered beige jumper. Ted was dressed in the same comfortable corduroy jacket and rather threadbare trousers that he had worn at the coffee morning. His usual cheery self, he was busy laughing at some joke or other.

A tall woman who looked as though she had been out shopping with Ruth approached them. Her sharp brown eyes were carefully made up and her streaked auburn hair had been newly dyed at probably considerable cost. She towered over Carole in more ways than one!

'Carole. Let me introduce you to Magda. Magda, this is Carole. She would like to join the choir. Magda's the coordinator,' Valerie explained, as though that clarified everything. Carole was a bit bemused but didn't say anything.

'Oh, that's nice. We're always pleased to get new people.' She smirked. 'Can you read music?' She preened herself a little. 'This Fauré is going to be a challenge. Some of the choir can't and they'll find it difficult.'

Carole nodded. 'Yes, I can read music. In fact I know the Fauré a bit.'

'That'll be a help. Are you a member of the U3A?'

Carole shook her head. 'No, not yet. I haven't had time to join but I will do next week. The coffee morning seemed to go so quickly it was over before I could make a decision. I love the Fauré and I'd like to sing it again.' She suddenly remembered she was going to keep a low profile and now she'd used the word 'again'. Too bad!

'Well, you can stay for the rehearsal but you'll have to pay your subscription before the next one,' Magda retorted, rather sharply.

Carole felt almost as though she had been slapped by an old-fashioned teacher.

'Of course I will,' she replied quietly.

Robert, the conductor came over and smiled a welcoming smile, engendering a rush of relief in Carole.

'Hello. I'm Robert, your musical director. Well, I try to keep everyone singing in tune and together if possible. Are you going to join us?'

Carole nodded, noticing his very white even teeth – very unusual for someone in his sixties. Either they were false or he must have a good dentist! His white curly hair would have been blond when he was young but it was still beautiful, framing his face like the statue of a Greek god.

'Yes. I'll give it a go if that's all right with you. I've sung the Fauré before but it was a long time ago. I suppose you don't forget.

It'll probably come back once we start rehearsing, at least I hope so,' she added optimistically.

'Don't worry about it. I'm sure you'll be fine,' he replied. He pushed back the sleeve of his comfortable jumper and checked a rather ancient watch. 'We ought to get started. There's a lot to get through before the concert. I hope you enjoy yourself and decide to stay. Oh! You'll need a copy of the music. There's a pile over there. Take one and sign your name on the list and write the number. You'll find it inside.'

Carole went over to the table and helped herself to a copy of the music, overflowing with admiration at Robert's immaculate English. He sounded just like a Shakespearean actor. She noticed Magda staring at her with something verging on hostility as she picked up her illegal copy. After all, she was an interloper, wasn't she? A gatecrasher at the party! She had already decided that, come what may, she would definitely join the choir. They took up their positions ready to start. Carole joined the sopranos, mentally keeping her fingers crossed that she could still reach the high notes. The person next to her was small and dark, somewhat on the heavy side. She was cheerful and friendly.

'Hi,' she whispered, 'I'm Maureen. It's nice to see a new face. Hope you enjoy it!'

'I'm Carole. I'm a bit nervous. I hope I don't make a mess of it.'

'Don't worry. We're only amateurs. You'll be OK, I'm sure.'

Carole sighed, wondering if she would still be able to sing. It had been so long.

'We'll sing through without the solos,' Robert informed them. 'Just keep going and we'll see how we get on. Don't worry about making mistakes. We can sort all that out later.'

Carole relaxed a bit. There was no pressure to achieve at the moment. Just keep going! She could manage that.

Robert raised his baton and a diminutive chap on a keyboard started to play the introduction. It wasn't a very big keyboard but it made a startling sound. It was just like a church organ. Amazing! They started to sing very quietly. *Requiem eternum* – eternal rest they all sang. She looked across at the men on the opposite side and in her mind's eye she saw Michael standing there. That's where she had met him for the first time. She had joined the local choir and there he was singing the opening bars of the Fauré. It was like a re-enactment of the past. It had been an instant attraction for both of them, something that probably happens very rarely in life, something very precious. She was aware that the words came naturally to her. She hadn't forgotten the Fauré. How could she?

As the music soared upwards she breathed deeply and sang loudly out into space. It had been such a short relationship, only three months. He hadn't told her that the first time they met he had already bought his ticket to Australia. His mind was set on a far horizon and he wasn't going to change his plans. His job as a quantity surveyor was already in place. He was going to Sydney and he didn't ask her to go with him. Time had played a nasty trick on them both.

She remembered the night they had gone back to his flat after the cinema. She had grown up being told that sex before marriage was wrong, that you would not be respected if you gave in. But the pounding of her heart and the aching need had proved too much. Was it love? She didn't know. They had both simply lost control, overcome by the kind of passion that had no respect for upbringing or moral education. He was probably either sorry or embarrassed. He never came to the choir again. It had been a memory to last a lifetime. She didn't regret it and still experienced the same intense pleasure after all that time. It was a parting gift. She never saw him again. He would be an Aussie now, maybe singing in the Sydney Opera House. Or maybe not!

The men were singing their part now, echoing the introduction. With a start she came back into the present, realising that Robert was staring at her somewhat quizzically. Had she stopped singing? She looked down at the music and realised she had lost her place. Was she on the right page? She didn't know and couldn't start leafing her way through looking for the right place. It would be too obvious that she hadn't been paying attention. She took a quick glance at Maureen's copy and realised with great relief that she was still on the same page. How could she have covered three months of her life in half a page of music? She found the place on the page and kept going.

She was determined to not let her thoughts wander again and worked hard at singing the rest of the work. She found that she hadn't forgotten it and was at least as good as most of the other sopranos. Magda was in front of her and she had quite a good voice. There were a couple of others who seemed to be keeping everybody together. She knew from past experience that you needed a certain number of good singers to support the rest! They made it to the end without faltering too much. Robert looked pleased with their effort.

'Well, that's not bad for a start! We can build on that next week. Magda, have a good practice at your solo. We'll hear it next time.'

'Carole, you've got a really good voice,' Maureen said quietly. 'You'll be a great help to us sopranos and you'll keep me going when I get lost.'

Carole laughed with pleasure. 'That's really nice of you but you know I was the one who lost the place. I looked at yours to see where we were up to. I'm just happy to jog along like I did last time I sang this. I'm not a star, just one of the crowd!'

'Don't you believe it! You've got potential,' Maureen replied, solemnly, as she collected her things.

Valerie had been on the back row quite a way away from Carole. She was waiting for her near the door.

'Did it go OK?' she asked, anxiously. She was obviously keen for her friend to join.

Carole nodded happily 'Yes, it was fine but I'm not sure about Magda. She's a bit of a cold fish. I don't think she likes me very much.'

Valerie's smile vanished and she nodded. 'Well, we've all got problems but she's probably got more than her fair share. She went through a nasty divorce two years ago. Her daughter's in Scotland and she doesn't see her or the grandchildren. I don't know why. Her son lives at home with her. He's in his thirties and he's got some sort of emotional problem. He signs on but he never seems to get any work. It's a chicken-and-egg situation. You don't know whether she's caused the problems or maybe she's been unlucky. Life's a real lottery, isn't it.' Valerie sighed. 'Anyway, she's a good organiser and she gets a buzz out of that but she isn't exactly popular!'

'Is she singing the solo?'

Valerie nodded. 'She's been having singing lessons. She volunteered to sing the solo. I don't know how she'll get on. We'll know next week when she gets her chance to shine! I hope she does OK. She needs to succeed at something. Well, we all do, don't we?'

Carole nodded, revising slightly her opinion of Magda. She hoped she'd be good. At the last performance all those years ago, it had been beautifully sung by a small boy soprano with a voice like an angel. Magda would have to be pretty good to match that.

On Friday morning Carole decided to take her books back to the library but first she sat down at the piano and played a bit of the Fauré. She made a resolution to practise a bit every day so she would really be a useful member of the choir. Then she went upstairs to get her coat and took a long look at herself in that mirror. It was a cheap brown-framed mirror on legs. She noticed for the first time that it had hinges on either side so you could move it to the most convenient position for viewing yourself. She swivelled in and it creaked with indignation. How long was it since she had really looked at herself? The years had flown by and she had been too busy to care.

She looked calmly at the person staring back at her. It was like meeting someone for the first time. What had happened to the young and beautiful person she had once been, the girl that Michael had found so attractive. She had been beautiful once upon a time like the fairy tales. But in fairy tales the princess is timeless and always marries the prince whereas old hags are always menacing and locked in ugliness. She felt she was between categories. She would never be a fairy-tale princess but she wasn't the old hag reaping revenge on her enemies either. A mental picture of Magda crossed her mind briefly.

She quickly turned her attention to the image in front of her. Her hair was naturally curly but looked as though she had had a perm a long time ago. The curls were hanging from her head all over her collar and turning up at the ends like a bedraggled hanging basket. She had kept her body in reasonable shape although it was difficult to tell from the baggy jumper she was wearing. Her face had very few wrinkles perhaps thanks to a good diet, no alcohol or sunburn and a reasonably calm existence, perhaps too calm when she thought about it. She didn't exactly like herself but the person she was getting to know didn't look too bad as human beings go!

She started walking to the library. Exercise was good for you. Perhaps she would even think about selling the car. Maybe later. It was too early to be making big decisions. She came to the bus stop and it reminded her of something – *oh, yes*. It was where the Cancer Research charity shop was. It was in fact directly opposite the bus stop. She stopped outside the window and stared at the display. There was a lot of junk but also some rather nice jewellery. There were several people wandering round the shop so she was able to go in without feeling as though she was being watched. She hated the 'Can I help you?' sort of shop assistant who made you feel as though you must have come in with a purpose and would helpfully get you so confused you ended up buying something you didn't really want.

Inside, the shop was like a cavern full of treasure. There were shelves of books and DVDs, masses of toys, lots of shoes and racks and racks of clothes. There was even a surfboard. In the middle of Liverpool! It was another world! Nobody bothered her. She was dying to buy something just for the experience. She felt like laughing as she thought of Magda. No, she wasn't a Magda. She was more like Valerie. And what on earth would Paula have said about a place like this? Then she reminded herself that she and Paula had never bought any clothes other than the occasional items of underwear. In Paula's world clothes generally didn't

33

wear out and if they actually let you down in that way they were viewed with astonished disappointment and resentment. Well, Paula wasn't here to criticise and she was going to buy something!

A book would be an easy thing to get but she always used the library so there wasn't much point. Most of the shoes had pointed toes and huge heels. She could almost feel people desperately squashing their feet into the trendy shoes and she felt their tension as she wriggled her own toes in the sensible beige lace-ups. Empathy was one of her virtues. She could well imagine their agony and disappointment when they found they couldn't wear them. Well, she would wear someone else's shoes without worrying, but not that sort! She went towards the clothes, idly pushing the hangers apart to get a better look. She looked over her shoulder. Would the assistant be laughing at an old woman looking at teenage clothes? Nobody was looking at her. The assistant was far too busy with an irate customer who had brought something back in a large bag and didn't have a receipt. Carole thought they were about the same age but under the makeup and hair-sprayed messy dyed curls she was much younger.

She felt sorry for the polite lady who was explaining that the customer would have to take something else as she couldn't give her her money back without the receipt. The situation was getting quite unpleasant. The customer obviously thought that shouting was the best method of getting her £5 back. Something drove Carole towards the situation where normally she would have retreated. She felt so sorry for the little lady who wasn't much bigger than a child and who wasn't getting paid for this hassle.

'Excuse me,' she broke into the conversation. 'Here's the £5. I'll take it, whatever it is. It's money for cancer research. How can you be so rude to this lady? She's not getting paid for this. She's working to help people like you and me.'

The woman stopped dead in her tracks and rounded on her. Carole caught her breath. She had heard of situations like this on the news. People had actually been killed for getting involved. She braced herself, her heart thumping so much she felt as though people would hear it. The woman stopped suddenly as though turned into stone then came back to life and stared at Carole, unsure what to do. Obviously she wasn't used to being attacked by kindness! She must have had a hard time. Perhaps nobody had ever done her a favour. Speechless, she passed over a black bin bag containing something bulky then grabbed the money from Carole, dropping a £1 coin onto the floor. It momentarily shone in a ray of sunlight then rolled into a dark crevice. She turned her back and slunk out of the door, her shoulders stooped. Carole felt a moment of triumph which was perhaps not totally justified as she had just lost £5 and now had a mystery item of some sort in a plastic bin bag.

The little lady kept thanking her until it was almost embarrassing.

'Let's look for the coin,' she suggested, getting down on her knees. The old lady didn't look as if she could do that. Carole scrabbled around in the dust and saw the coin. She gave it to the assistant, who shook her head.

'No, it's yours. Keep it for good luck.'

Carole laughed. 'Thanks,' she said, not wanting to keep arguing about a £1 coin. 'I wonder what's in the bag. I'll tell you what. I'll take it home and open it later. It'll be a bit of fun. Meanwhile, now that I'm here I'll have a look at the clothes. I could do with smartening myself up.'

'Have a good rummage.' The old lady chuckled. 'Some nice things came in this morning. There haven't been many people in today so you might find something good. Some people have got more money than sense. They buy stuff then don't wear it. Well, it's money for the charity so I suppose that's OK.'

Carole went back to the clothes. It was amazing how cheap they were and furthermore there was no guilt involved in buying them. Each item was a contribution to cancer research. She went through one whole rack then on to another one, noticing that many of them were well worn and well washed. She might not find anything. She kept looking with more discrimination, chuckling mentally at the idea of learning a rather unusual new skill – charity shopping. Many of the clothes had famous labels

– Next, Per Una, Gap, Wallis and many more. She had heard of these shops although she had never visited them.

Suddenly her efforts were rewarded. She came across an embroidered top very like the one she had loved when she was a teenager but updated and a good make. The red embroidered poppies looked almost real with their black centres shining against the white material. Someone had bought it and then for some reason not worn it. Snobbish people had sometimes sneered about buying things belonging to dead people. Well, Carole was a practical person and rationalised that if the person was dead they didn't need it and if they were alive they wouldn't miss it as they'd got rid of it! Almost immediately she found a pair of beige cotton trousers that were casual but not jeans. She asked the little lady whose head barely came above the counter if she could try them on. She nodded, pointing to the changing room.

Making sure the curtain was well closed, she quickly got undressed and hastily put on the new clothes, trying in vain to remember when she had bought her last clothes. They had never indulged in anything that wasn't essential. Carole began to wonder if Paula had been economising to pay the mysterious standing order. Were things falling into place or was she just making it up because she needed an explanation? Ambiguity wasn't something she felt able to cope with very easily. She stared at herself in the long mirror. Her blond hair was tinged with white but what could you expect at sixty-one? She was quite slim. She had never had more than the odd alcoholic drink and didn't smoke. She realised with some satisfaction that she was in good shape and hopefully healthy. The changing room was rather small so she drew the curtain and backed out to give herself a longer view. There was a gasp from the little lady. 'You look lovely like that! Who would have thought it? You look like a different person.'

'That's really nice of you.' Carole smiled, blushing with pleasure. 'I can't get over how lovely these clothes are. I'm surprised someone wanted to get rid of them.'

'Oh, there are all kinds of reasons. People put on weight and eventually give up trying to lose it. Then some people have got more money than sense. "Waste not, want not" seems to have gone out of the window. They get fed up with things and buy new ones. It's all crazy but the charity wins. Mind you it's good fun shopping here. You can buy things cheap and try them out; you know change your style. If it doesn't work at least you haven't spent a fortune.'

Carole stood in her new clothes, amazed at what she had just heard. There was no sign of this little lady doing what she had just mentioned but maybe she had changed! Perhaps she had been a different individual a few months ago. She took a deep breath, amazed at the potential of a charity shop. The afternoon's routine visit to the library had turned into an adventure quite as exciting as anything that had happened for a long time. She retreated into the changing room, quickly reverted to her previous state then approached the counter.

'I'll take these, please,' she said resolutely getting out her purse.

The little lady nodded and wrapped them up. 'There's a nice necklace in the cabinet. It would go well with the poppies on that top.'

She could see the little lady took her unpaid job seriously. The necklace was beautiful and she was right. The crimson ceramic beads and the red poppies complemented each other marvellously. She almost felt Paula's breath over her shoulder. Wherever she had gone her mouth was set in a straight line. She was trying to warn her about being extravagant. She had just forked out £10 plus the £4 spent in behaviour management with the stroppy girl. In their world it was an unheard of thing to do! She firmly put Paula in her place wherever she was and resolved to visit the shop again soon. Then she picked up her three parcels, the clothes, necklace and the bulky mystery package, and went back into the normal world of traffic and hurrying people.

Walking to the library gave her her exercise for the day and made her feel virtuous. The media never stopped warning people that their lives would be cut short if they didn't move about. There were threats of diabetes, cancer, memory loss and lots more. It was enough to make you sell the car! Well, she wasn't going to do that. It was too useful but she would continue to make an effort to stay alive. Her life was getting interesting. The assistant in the library had been once again too busy to talk to her but it didn't seem to matter so much.

When she got home with several new library books, she put the kettle on and then dumped the two packages onto the bed. She looked at the bulky carrier bag and laughed out loud. What a good job nobody could hear her! They would think she had gone senile! She would have her tea and some lunch and wait until later to open the bag. It was as much fun as Christmas used to be when she was a child. Father Christmas was coming early!

She slowly drank the hot strong tea and ate a sandwich, all the time musing on what could be in the carrier bag. It was big so it might be some old coat that the girl had had second thoughts about. Then again it might be a jumper or an exotic sequinned top that she would only wear in secret or if she decided to change her personality as the little lady had suggested might be possible. Of course she could do that. She had no job and no ties. She could turn into…what? At least she had a future and she was lucky to have it. She would do something with it, not just waste it.

It wasn't Christmas but it was nevertheless time to open the mystery parcel. The two bags were still on the bed where she had thrown them. She opened the first one and after a quick look at her new clothes she put them into the laundry basket. They looked new but she would wash them anyway then wear them for the next rehearsal. The second bulky bag was waiting patiently. She picked it up, took a deep breath and emptied the contents onto the floor rather over-impulsively. It might have been something breakable but fortunately there was no sickening smash. A large hairy yellow object fell softly onto the carpet. As she picked it up two soft brown eyes stared gratefully at her. It was an extremely large dirty teddy bear. His fur was matted with chocolate and what looked like a mixture of house dust and dried baby food. She stared at him in horror. A rescue operation was required. She couldn't take him back to the shop and she couldn't keep him in his present state.

It seemed like a productive way to spend the afternoon or at least part of it. She gave the bear the nearest thing she could to a bath. She sponged all the dirt away, leaving him looking bedraggled as though he'd been for an unseasonal swim. She towelled him all over as you would do with a baby then left him in front of the kitchen radiator to dry. She couldn't help thinking that her impulsive intervention at the charity shop had cost her money she might have spent on a few luxury cups of coffee at a café in town. What on earth could she do with the tatty bear that now looked more like a large drowned rat?

When she woke up on Saturday, she realised she didn't have any plans for the weekend. In the past she and Paula would probably have been going out to the cinema or a concert. Now she would have to face loneliness. She would need to find something to do to pass the time. She put on her dressing gown and made her way downstairs. The heating had been on for a while. She had decided to use it a bit or the house would get damp. She had forgotten about the new occupant of the house. He was lying on his back stretched out next to the radiator as though he was sunbathing on an exotic beach. She picked him up and her mouth dropped open. It was a complete transformation. She stroked his fur. He was soft, clean and dry, his yellow coat shining like a brand-new bear. He looked as though his self-esteem had been restored. She hugged him and her loneliness evaporated. She looked him in the eye.

'We're going to be friends, you and me. You can be my mascot.'

She carried him upstairs, his head flopping on her shoulder, his brown eyes looking thoughtfully backwards down the stairs at the way they had come. He was so big and yet so soft and light to carry. She gently placed him on the bed like a baby then stepped back to savour the effect. He looked so comfortable leaning on the pillows. He seemed to brighten the room. She was happy with her hard work yesterday. Perhaps the money had been well spent after all.

She had managed to get a CD of the Fauré Requiem out of the library so she resolved to spend Saturday night listening to it and singing along with the soprano parts. She put the CD on as the November night drew in and sat down in front of the coal fire. She felt warm. Life was not so bad even if she was spending Saturday night on her own. She felt half sorry that she hadn't gone back to Pippa's Pizzas on Friday instead of washing a teddy bear but life suddenly seemed rather busy. She would go next Friday and meet up with Jenny and the children.

The CD had lots of tracks so you could easily choose. She flicked from one to the other rather idly, not really concentrating, staring at the flames licking round the coal, her eyelids threatening to close. Finally she let it play right through from the beginning. As the end approached her head became heavier and heavier against the ancient cushion. *'Libera me domine.'* It was a male voice singing the solo. 'Free me oh God from...' She couldn't remember the translation but the words echoed round her head. Suddenly the whole room was red and a sensation like water escaping rippled through her from head to toe. She had experienced it before many times, had almost learnt to live with it but it never got any easier. The colour and the rippling made her think of the ten plagues where the river was turned to blood. Why didn't God free her from this if he was up there? Then again, why had he given her this terrible burden? She loved the Fauré Requiem but it was more than a piece of choral music, it was a Mass for the dead. Waves of grief rolled over her. She felt as though she was drowning.

Chapter 5

Monday 19th November
A Questionable Performance

AROLE HAD BEEN to the coffee morning and paid her subscription. She had gone in on her own and was feeling quite proud of herself. Valerie was sitting on her own, pushing a biscuit round a plate. She looked far from happy and didn't react very much at all to the news that her friend had paid her subscription and was now a valid member of the U3A and the choir. Carole was a bit taken aback. She had thought of Valerie as one of the people in the world who had got things right – house, car, husband, independent children. She supposed that sounded a bit superficial but that was how she had seemed up to now.

'Are you OK?' She couldn't think of anything more appropriate to say!

Valerie looked up and shook her head. 'Not really. I know you've got your problems but life isn't easy for us either.'

'You don't need to tell me about it,' Carole replied, quickly. 'Only if you think it would help. I'm not the nosy type, you know.'

Valerie smiled. 'I know. I didn't think you were! I usually keep things to myself, especially when there's no obvious solution.'

'Well, you can try me if you want. Whatever you tell me won't go any further, you know!'

'OK,' she began, taking a deep breath and pushing a lock of unwashed hair out of her eyes. 'You know I told you that when we moved here our children were settled with their own lives. Well, it wasn't exactly true. You see, we have three children. We had the first two when we were in our twenties then Mark came along when I was nearly forty. It was a bit of a shock, to tell you the truth, but he was a lovely baby and we thought the world of him.'

Carole looked quite envious but just listened, not knowing what to say. She ate her chocolate biscuit without even thinking about it.

'I couldn't afford to stay at home. We had a big mortgage – the usual story. I found a good child minder and he seemed happy, probably happier then he would have been at home with me. I'm not exactly an earth mother! Anyway, he turned out cleverer than Helen or Jonathon. Neither of them got to university although they're both in good jobs. He went to Manchester to do Law.'

'Wow! That's quite something.'

'We were ever so proud to see him training for a real profession but then things started to go wrong. He never talked about the course. I thought, well, it's his business and if he wants to keep it to himself then that's OK. Kids don't like parents interfering so we kept out of it. When the first year results came out he'd failed. We couldn't believe it. He was so clever! He went back for half a year then came home.'

'So what did he do then?'

'You wouldn't believe it. He bought a great big keyboard with the rest of his student loan and shut himself in his bedroom with it. I've never heard him play. He plays with headphones. He had piano lessons so I suppose he knows how to play but he's just a mystery. Then he started smoking. I felt really annoyed about that. He had a student loan and we'd also been funding him. It nearly drove me mad seeing our money going up in smoke not to mention the smell and the health risks. The keyboard must have cost a fortune as well.'

Carole nodded sympathetically. She'd always assumed people out there had uncomplicated lives. How wrong can you be?

'Then he grew his hair long. At first I thought he just hadn't had time to go to the barber's but it just got longer and longer. I kept thinking about The Beatles and their eastern mysticism and their drugs and I panicked. But I don't think he's on drugs. I think he just didn't cope with university life. You know what it's like when you go away from home. You need more than brains, don't you? You need coping skills.'

'Did he enjoy the course?' Carole asked, thoughtfully.

'I don't know. He didn't know what course to do at university. One day he mentioned law and I thought it was such a good choice. It's a profession and you earn a lot of money as well but I don't think he did any work. Since he came back here he's had a few jobs. He had to sign on, you see, but they never last. I think he thinks they're beneath him.'

A good choice maybe, but whose choice? Carole wondered. 'Perhaps he didn't like it. People make mistakes, don't they? If he wasn't interested in the course he wouldn't learn. I hated anything boring; you know, things I thought were boring. My dad once gave me an encyclopaedia to read. Well, you don't read an encyclopaedia, do you? You consult it sometimes. I was into Enid Blyton adventures so I never read it.'

Valerie managed a small smile. Carole had intended to be a good listener but she kept on talking instead. 'I remember there were a few parents who bought work books for their children and were always competing with their friends. They knew which reading book all the children were on and they were desperate for their child to beat the others! It was a kind of status symbol.' Carole chuckled.

She enjoyed reminiscing about teaching. She could still see the faces of the parents and children as she talked. She'd been so absorbed in her memories she hadn't looked at Valerie for several minutes. When she did she got a shock. Her friend's face was red and she looked as though she was about to burst into tears or flames.

'A status symbol! Is that what you think of me?' she blustered. 'I don't need a status symbol. I really regret leaving him with a childminder and now I'm being accused of using him as a status symbol. I don't need a law student to boast about. I just want him to be happy.' She got up, nearly knocking her chair over and stalked out, leaving half a cup of cold coffee on the table.

Carole was transfixed with horror. She should have kept her mouth shut and listened but it was too late. The damage was done. She pushed her coffee away. She couldn't drink any more. She wasn't up to this new life. She just didn't have the social skills she needed. She'd grown up with a mum who didn't have any friends. Her parents wouldn't have known anything about social skills. Her dad had been too busy working all day and some nights sorting and delivering mail while her mum struggled to make ends meet. What a pity they hadn't had more children. She would probably have learnt how to cope better with other people if she had had brothers and sisters.

She heaved a sigh. She should count her blessings. After all she had had some form of higher education unlike her parents. They had been proud of her and they had made sacrifices to keep her at the teacher training college. She knew she should be grateful but she felt almost sorry in a way that she had got into a sort of halfway house. She was a bit like a lottery winner, trying to get into a world she had not been born into. She didn't have the money either! She could see that some of the people in the U3A were pretty well off. She'd only been there twice and she had heard snatches of conversation about restaurants and holidays to Venice and Rome. How could she possibly fit in? She would go back to the life she had had with Paula. It had been a barren existence with meagre pickings but with none of the trauma she was now experiencing. Then with alarm she realised that she couldn't go back. She was in the middle of a bridge. At one end there was desert and at the other the angry, threatening faces of the future.

She went home, wishing she hadn't paid her subscription but it was too late. She could hardly say she had changed her mind and ask for a refund. She couldn't face the rehearsal now. Valerie would be there and she wouldn't be able to face her. She felt as though everybody must have been staring at the two of them having a row. She would come across as a trouble maker. Nothing could be further from the truth but it was too late. She should have mixed more when she was young but there was no going back. Suddenly she wondered if perhaps she could go back and relive her past. Maybe she could remember parts that had gone wrong then bring them into the present and reshape them for the future. The possibility of making some use of past mistakes changed her mood a little and gave her some hope that something good might come out of the past.

The days that followed were full of conflict. She was still practising the Fauré and playing the CD. Her love of it hadn't diminished in spite of the awful scene with Valerie. As the hours and days passed between the coffee morning and the rehearsal the pain paled a little and she was able to get things into proportion. Valerie was obviously not as together as she'd thought or she wouldn't have reacted the way she did. She was obviously suffering from a kind of guilt complex that had nothing to do with Carole. She realised she should have listened more and been more careful what she said but she wasn't a counsellor after all! On Wednesday, she finally came to a decision. She would face up to the rehearsal and apologise to Valerie for offending her.

On Thursday afternoon, she put on the new clothes and the necklace. Her sensible shoes looked completely out of place with the casual outfit. She put on her winter boots which looked better and were quite appropriate in the November cold. Time was passing and in the back of her mind she still had the problem of the standing order although she had shelved it, given all the distractions she had had. She added a touch of lipstick and contemplated the overall effect with a certain amount of pleasure. The scarlet poppies on her new top contrasted so beautifully with the white cotton, their vibrant red lighting up the grey November twilight outside. She wasn't dead yet and she intended to make the most of her trip out to the rehearsal later on that evening.

She arrived early. Ruth and Ted were already there chatting to Robert. Fashion-wise they still looked like two book ends that didn't match. Of course it didn't matter. The nice thing about the choir was that people were interested in the music, not the impression they were making. Magda might be the exception but there were always exceptions like the wretched French irregular verbs they had learnt at school. You learnt how to form them only to be given a long list of all the ones that didn't keep to the rules. It had been annoying then and it was still annoying! But then again the verbs had been there before the rules, evolving as people evolved. After all human beings were not machines and this made them interesting!

She took up her position next to Maureen. People didn't seem to have noticed the change in her appearance. She was quite glad about that. She was new to most of the choir so she could start from zero without anybody making comments. In any case clothes were superficial. You could change the outside of yourself but changing the inside was a bit more difficult. Still, the clothes made her look different and feel different too. Also, she had pushed herself into coming to the rehearsal and that was a triumph.

There was no sign of Valerie. In spite of her new clothes Carole had a disturbing feeling of unease. She knew from her experience with parents that some people lived near the edge of a cliff. Valerie might be one of these and could have been pushed over by her ill- judged remarks. She imagined a high cliff with a person right on the edge, falling over as it crumbled. She saw a body on the rocks, one minute visible and the next washed over by white foam. Everything started to turn red and she waited for the familiar rippling sensation. If only she could stop it happening. Going to the doctor's was out of the question. She wouldn't know where to begin or how to explain.

'Page one, everybody. We'll start from the beginning like last time but we'll do some correcting tonight. It's time to start polishing!'

Robert had broken into her nightmare. The colour faded and they spent the next hour singing and repeating the difficult bits.

There was a short break during which Maureen complimented her again on her singing. Life had been so difficult in the past few days it was rather comforting to be told something pleasant. She began to feel much more cheerful and resolved that in the second half there would be no more fantasising about cliffs and bodies.

'Magda. I'd like to hear your solo now. We didn't have time last week. Are you ready?'

Magda nodded. She stood up and looked around at the audience to make sure everyone was paying attention. Carole was glad of the opportunity to just sit and listen. She was feeling quite exhausted after an hour of gruelling work and her clifftop fantasies. She was also curious to hear Magda sing. She thought again of the small blond boy soprano with a voice like an angel who had sung the 'Pie Jesu' so long ago. The silver sound had soared up into the roof of the church, swirling round the rafters and touching the stone baby angels high up on the pillars so they seemed to smile. She had felt as though he should have had wings sprouting from his shoulder blades like the little stone angels. He would be grown up now.

Magda started to sing. Her voice was wavery and when she came to the high notes she screeched like the string section of the school orchestra used to do. It was so bad Carole could hardly believe it. When she came to an end there was a deadly silence as though people were holding their breath. There was no way Magda was going to improve with practice or lessons. She thought that Robert was almost certainly thinking the same thing along with the rest of the choir.

'There's some work to be done there, Magda. Keep practising and we'll have another go next week.'

She sat down, looking a little uncertain, like a somewhat deflated balloon. Had she been expecting applause? She obviously hadn't been prepared for an ambiguous reaction.

Carole sighed, knowing full well that Magda wouldn't improve much in a week. Robert would have to find another soloist, possibly a boy soprano or was she trying to repeat history? At least it was nothing to do with her. She had had enough traumas for now. She resolved that she would phone Valerie and risk being rejected. She couldn't spend the whole week wondering what had happened to her. Her clifftop fantasies were not doing her any good. Her friend probably just had a cold. What was the point of wasting emotional energy imagining dramas when there might not be one at all! This thought left her feeling quite pleased with herself. She was coping better.

She was getting ready to pack up her music when Robert started to take a whole lot of sheets out of his bag. He called the choir to attention. 'It's nearly Christmas. Could you have a look at these carols during the week? I'd like us to do our usual carol singing in the town centre before Christmas – just the popular ones, nothing ambitious. We did very well last year and made around £200 for the NSPCC. Of course you don't have to come. Just have a practice at home and let me know who's coming. We'll have a quick go at them each week. They're not very difficult so it shouldn't be a lot of work.'

Carole packed the extra sheets into her bag. She had only sung carols at school. It would be quite exciting singing in the town centre. She phoned Valerie on Friday morning. The longer she left it the more difficult it would be. She needed to get it over with. She dreaded hearing the coldness in her voice when she realised who it was. Her hands were shaking as she held the phone. This new lifestyle was so exciting but it came with worries too. She was waiting for a cool reception, difficult to endure as she was sensitive. A toneless voice said 'hello' without giving the number. It could have been anybody anywhere in the world or out in space, it sounded so unconnected to anything.

'Valerie! Is that you?' she stammered, then thought maybe it was a silly question.

'Yes. It's me. Who's that?'

'It's Carole,' she said bravely after a slight hesitation. 'Val, I'm sorry if I upset you. I really didn't mean to. I just got carried away and I didn't think how it might be affecting you.'

'It's OK, Carole. You just touched a nerve. It's given me something to think about. How was the rehearsal? Look, why don't you come round and have a coffee. We can catch up. You can tell me about it then. I didn't come because I had a bad cold. I didn't want to pass it around. Anyway I couldn't sing. My throat felt like sandpaper.'

Carole heaved a silent sigh of relief. The coffee morning drama had had nothing to do with her after all. She realised she had a lot to learn about human relations. 'OK. I'll come now. I could just do with a cup of coffee.'

In fact, Carole hadn't done anything that morning to earn her coffee. Her only activity had been pacing around the house trying to pluck up the courage to phone and perhaps face a hurtful rebuff. She had learnt another lesson. People were not as easily hurt as she herself would be and mixing socially, with all its risks, was a happier and healthier way to live. She put her coat on and went straight out to the car.

She knew where Valerie lived. It was the other side of town in the older Victorian area. As she drove, she felt safe enough to talk to herself. She told herself firmly that friendships would not take place in the vacuum of her house, that she had to make decisions and act. Then she turned on the CD and started singing the Fauré as loudly as she could. When it came to the soprano solo, she was at the traffic lights in the inside lane. The lights were red. She stopped and sang even louder, imagining she was the soloist at a concert.

She felt so happy until she turned her head and noticed a Vauxhall Corsa right next to her. The driver was a young man of about thirty. He had the passenger window down and was grinning. As she turned, he started to clap. Of course she should have laughed but her whole face went on fire. She stared obsessively ahead of her, fixing her gaze desperately on the lights. If only they would change! They took what seemed like an eternity. As they went green and the cars ahead of her set off, he waved. She couldn't help noticing and ventured a very small smile as her hot face cooled down and returned to normal. She suddenly waved back but it was too late. He had gone.

Valerie lived in a rather upmarket neighbourhood of detached Victorian houses with long drives. The tree-lined road was wide and quiet. Number 15 had a red door which made it easy to spot. It was perhaps a little more unkempt than many of the other houses but that put Carole at her ease. Life wasn't perfect for other people either. She rang the bell, noticing the green showing through the red in places where the paint was peeling off, like new green flowers emerging from bright-red soil. Her friend opened the door immediately as though she had been just behind it, waiting.

The hall was dark as there were no windows but the lounge was cosy and beautifully furnished with antique furniture. A fire roared in the cast iron grate. At first Valerie thought it was real then realised the coals were too regularly placed, too clean and tidy. It was a gas fire masquerading as a coal fire. It looked quite good and would be no trouble. Perhaps she should get one and save herself some work. She instantly dismissed the idea. She loved her real fire, the spluttering coals, the sparks and the deep red glow. She was always grateful for the sheer pleasure it gave her. She felt a sense of liberation as she realised it had nothing to do with Paula and her endless economising.

She sat down by the fire and Valerie went off into the kitchen. She came back immediately with a steaming pot of coffee and a plate of biscuits. She had obviously had it all ready. Her friend was keen to hear about the rehearsal and Carole was very willing to update her. It was a neutral area of conversation that avoided having to discuss what had upset Valerie. She told her all about Magda and the solo. They both laughed without real malice but nevertheless rather enjoying the situation.

'I wonder if she will get any better by Thursday.'

'I doubt it,' Carole ventured thoughtfully. 'I've heard it sung before. It's very high and not that easy. I don't think she's going to be able to get up to the top notes.'

'There's going to be trouble,' chuckled Valerie. 'She's got a big opinion of herself and she won't take humiliation that easily.'

'I don't know. I wonder if she's not as sure of herself as she seems. Anyway, I'm glad I'm not in Robert's shoes. It'll be interesting to see how he handles it. He seems really nice. I'm sure he wouldn't want to hurt anybody but he'll want to be proud of the performance, won't he?'

'Well, he'll have to find someone else if she doesn't get up to the notes. He won't want a soloist sounding like a cat on a wall! I expect he's got all kinds of contacts.'

There was a silence. Carole chewed on her biscuit and stared into the fire, wishing it was real, a fire with personality. It was Valerie who broke the silence.

'I'm sorry I flew off the handle. It was stupid. I did want Mark to do law and if I'm honest it was probably because I always feel guilty about him. If he had been a great intellectual success I would have felt good about it. As it is I just feel I've let him down somehow. I don't know what to do for the best.'

'How about your husband? What does he think?'

'Jim tends to be philosophical. He prefers to leave things to sort themselves out.'

Carole thought about the state of the front door. That wasn't going to sort itself out!

'It doesn't always work of course! He thinks Mark will come to his senses and decide what he wants in time. I can't wait for that. It's all wasted time, isn't it? Jim doesn't want to fall out with him either. Well, neither of us do. It's just he's prepared to wait. I think he could be waiting forever!'

'Where is he now? Is he upstairs?'

'No, he's gone out with his keyboard. I don't know how he carries it. It weighs a ton! He's got an old banger that he had at university. He can afford it because he doesn't pay us much for living here,' she retorted resentfully, turning red.

Carole nodded sympathetically. She was glad she had no children and no pets, just herself to worry about. It was a very difficult situation. She would have found it hard to cope with it. At that moment, there was a click and the door opened. A tall long-haired young man came in then stopped, dumping a large case on the floor.

'Oh, I'm sorry to interrupt. Mum, I didn't know you had a visitor,' he muttered apologetically, dragging the case backwards with one hand and brushing his red hair out of his eyes with the other. 'I could do with a coffee.'

'You don't need to apologise to me,' Carole intervened quickly. 'Why don't you come and join us? Is that a keyboard?'

Mark looked as though he was having difficulty dealing with two questions at once. He looked stressed then suddenly smiled, his deep-brown eyes brightening as though a light had been switched on. He seemed to have forgotten about the coffee.

'Yes. Are you interested in music?'

Carole nodded. 'I can play the piano but I'm not exactly Chopin. What do you play on the keyboard?'

'All sorts of music – jazz, pop, classical.'

'It must be fun. You can do so much more with a keyboard. All those sounds and accompaniments! I wish I had one but I've got a good piano. I suppose I could buy a keyboard as well.'

'Would you like to hear it? I could give you a demonstration,' he ventured enthusiastically. 'It's a full-sized piano but it's also a keyboard. I can play piano style or with an accompaniment. It's a really good machine. I usually play with headphones so I don't disturb the neighbours.'

'But it's a detached house,' Carole exclaimed, puzzled. 'You won't disturb the neighbours!'

Mark looked across at his mother. 'Well, I just don't like to disturb people,' he explained. 'If I'm using the headphones I don't have to worry.'

'It's nice to play for people sometimes. It's a different experience sharing music with other people like we do in the choir. Don't you ever do that?' Carole persisted.

Mark nodded. 'Yes, I play with my friends.'

Valerie looked nonplussed at how well Carole seemed to be getting on with Mark. She kept looking from one to the other as though she was at a tennis match. 'You can set it up here if you want. Then you can give us both a recital,' Valerie suggested, not wanting to be left out. 'It'll sound better in a big room.'

The room wasn't that big but Mark started setting up the instrument on the stand while Valerie got him a mug of coffee.

'I'll play you a bit of Elgar. I've been practising this piece for a bit. It's really beautiful with the organ sound. He started playing and suddenly they were transported to a cathedral. The sound was amazing. Carole caught her breath. She had struggled enough with music to know that he was good, more than good. He followed the Elgar up with some jazz and then finished with 'The Entertainer' by Scott Joplin. They were all smiling. The music filled the house and they were transported not only to the cathedral but also to a jazz club then a pub with a honky-tonk piano. Mark's anxious face was suddenly filled with sunshine.

'Where did you learn to play like that?' Valerie quizzed him, finding her voice at last. 'I thought you were just messing around up there. You must have really practised a lot to play like that.'

He nodded. 'I had some lessons at university.' A cloud crossed his face. 'I suppose I spent too much time playing and not enough time studying. I just couldn't get interested. Now I play with my friends and we muck in and help each other. I did have piano lessons. Remember? Old Mr White with the big feet and baggy trousers!'

Valerie looked puzzled. 'I remember the piano lessons but you didn't seem to make much progress. Where did you meet these people? All your school friends have left here.'

Mark grinned. 'Haven't you heard of the internet? I typed it into Facebook and that's how we got together.'

Valerie seemed exhausted. It was all too much at once but Carole sensed a different atmosphere. There were positive vibes coming from Valerie's son.

'I ought to be going.' Carole gasped, looking at her watch and realising how long she had been there. 'I didn't realise it was so late.'

'Don't worry about that.' Valerie smiled and said to Mark, 'Carole and I were very good friends when we were young.' She turned back to Carole. 'I'm so glad you came.'

'Me too,' mumbled Mark from behind the couch where he was busy unplugging the keyboard. 'Nice to meet you.'

'And you, Mark. I wish I could play that well.'

Valerie got up to see her out. 'I'll be back at the rehearsal on Thursday, and thanks, Carole.'

The relief on her face left Carole in no doubt that the 'thanks' was more than just good manners. She got into her car with a tremendous feeling of satisfaction bordering on euphoria. She had not only saved her relationship with Valerie. She had strengthened it. She had also been useful to an unhappy young man who was stuck in a vacuum, not knowing which way to turn. It had been a good morning's work. She turned on the Fauré and sang with it all the way home, not caring who might be listening. If anyone waved she would wave back.

It was two weeks since her meeting with Jenny. She decided to go at the same time as last time and hoped to meet them. She walked through the door as though she had turned back the clock and was reliving two weeks ago except that Jenny wasn't coming through the door so it wasn't a replay. She went in and ordered her pizza, feeling a bit dispirited. There was no sign of Jenny. She sighed. You couldn't relive things, only in science fiction books. She sat down, a solitary figure at an over-large table with three empty seats. She was just starting to eat rather unenthusiastically when a child's voice shouted plaintively down her ear.

'Carole! I brought Poppy last week and you didn't come.' The little girl sat down right next to her without being asked.

'Oh, I'm so sorry, Eva. I had a lot to do but I'm here now. I'll meet her another time, I promise.'

James and Jenny soon arrived and the table didn't look too big any more. Jenny seemed really pleased to see her.

'I missed you last week. I suppose I assumed you'd come. I hope you don't mind us sitting here. Eva doesn't ask, she just does things! She's only little so she doesn't think about whether you want to sit with her. Of course, you know all about little children. I'd forgotten.'

'Not all,' smiled Carole, 'but to tell you the truth I'm really glad you've come. The table was too big for me. I was feeling quite lonely. I was hoping to see you.'

Jenny suddenly looked puzzled. She leaned forward, her hand under her chin and stared at Carole. 'You look different. Is it me or have you done something to yourself? You look really nice. Have you bought some new clothes? I like your necklace too. The red suits you. Where did you get it?'

Carole smiled with pleasure, chuckling inside. Should she say that she'd been to Next or Marks and Spencer and bought a new wardrobe? It wouldn't be exactly a lie but she was too honest. It just wasn't in her nature to try to impress people by name-dropping so she told the truth. Jenny was fascinated.

'Really? I didn't know that shop existed and I've passed it a few times. I just never noticed. I'll go in next time and see if I can get a bargain. Aren't you clever to find a way of looking nice without spending a fortune?'

'Oh, it wasn't my idea. It was my friend Valerie who told me about the shop. Its fame is spreading! It'll soon be full of people. Perhaps we'd better keep quiet about it!'

They both laughed then suddenly Carole noticed that James was much quieter than usual and looked a bit subdued. It wasn't like him at all.

'What's the matter James? You look a bit out of sorts. Have you had a bad day?' Carole had a sixth sense about children and their problems.

Jenny answered for him. 'He's been in trouble at school. There's a nasty bully in his class. He doesn't like James so he kicks him when they're outside. He kicked back today and they both got into trouble. Apparently a lot of other kids joined in the fight. It sounded just like a cartoon! It isn't funny though. I don't want James kicking people. He'll get a bad reputation.'

'If you don't kick back he just does it more,' James protested, rocking his chair in frustration. 'His dad should've kept him at home when he fell out of the tree.'

'What tree was that?' Carole asked them, intrigued.

'Oh, it was at lunchtime,' Jenny explained. 'He climbed a tree when nobody was looking then fell out and bumped his head. His dad was going to sue the school. He kept him off until he couldn't stand him any longer. I happened to overhear him telling the teacher!'

They couldn't help laughing but Jenny's face soon returned to an anxious look. 'It's difficult. The school says you mustn't hit back but you have to. Bullies need a bit of their own medicine, don't they?'

Carole nodded. 'Yes, I'm afraid so. I've seen this so many times. If you kick him hard enough he'll stop.' She put her hand over her mouth. 'I shouldn't have said that. Sorry. James, do as your mum says, not what I say.'

Jenny protested immediately. 'No, you're right. James, you must defend yourself but don't start a fight. That's what my mum used to say and she was right.'

James looked happier. Jenny explained that James was bright and popular. This other boy struggled with school and was jealous so he lashed out whenever he could. Carole sighed. It was a familiar situation.

They had all finished. It was time to go. Darkness was gathering outside. The streetlights were on and the November night was drawing in. Carole got up and promised to come next Friday, reminding the children to bring the glamorous Poppy and Lego robot for her to see.

Outside, the soaking withered leaves were hurtling round, blown by a bitter wind. The pavement was treacherous. Carole walked carefully, wondering what she would do if she slipped over and broke her leg. She rapidly dismissed this fear, turning her thoughts instead to her successful day. She felt as though she had been living in a world of cardboard cutouts. Everything had been flat and colourless. Now, suddenly people had come to life as though someone had pulled a switch and suddenly the world was bright and three-dimensional. She almost danced through the wet leaves and opened her front door with a sense of joy. Something had happened to her. She felt real.

It was startling how quickly Thursday came around. She had gone into Liverpool to the art gallery on Saturday. It was full of children making models and painting pictures in a large room. Carole thought it would be good for James and Eva. They would enjoy that. She made a mental note to mention it to Jenny. During her weeks at the bed-and-breakfast place, she had been forced into Southport most days. She had wandered through the shopping centre and down to the beach feeling invisible. Nobody seemed to see her. She had drifted about as if in a dream, thinking that if people couldn't see her maybe she wasn't real. People in Liverpool hadn't seemed to see her either. They were busy shopping or having fun or worrying about their own problems. Now things were different. People even looked different to her. She made eye contact with them, realising that in the past she had not done this. Some people looked back and even smiled as their eyes met.

On Sunday, she had sat down and practised the Fauré. When she came to the eternal rest part she again experienced the red flush and that same feeling like blood or water gushing somewhere. She wondered how she would cope in a performance if it happened. It didn't seem to be at all consistent. She had put up with it for a long time so she was used to it but it remained a mystery. It just happened for no particular reason but the Fauré did seem to spark it off. To distract herself, she picked up the U3A newsletter and decided to join some more groups. Reading her library books was all very well but she needed other activities now.

PATRICIA MORTON

As she read through the pages her eyes grew wider and wider. She could be out of the house every minute of the day if she joined all these groups. In fact she wouldn't need a house! She marked the ones that interested her, realising that there were at least a dozen. She would have to make some hard choices. She considered what she had been good at in the past. It seemed sensible to start with something familiar then maybe branch out later. The French group would be a start. She had been good at French at school and she'd always longed to go to Paris. Perhaps it wasn't too late but she would need to brush up her French. The list of possibilities was endless.

She was hoping something would jump out of the page and solve the problem for her. It didn't so she went back to playing the piano. She'd had enough of the Fauré for the moment so she played some jazz and then, thinking about Mark, she rifled through her music stool and found The Entertainer. As she struggled she realised it was difficult. Suddenly, like a thunderbolt, something occurred to her. She could buy a keyboard or maybe borrow one and join the group. It would be like French, something that wouldn't make her feel too threatened. It would be new but not too new!

There was a music shop in the town centre. She could hardly wait for Monday to go on a visit. How exciting life had suddenly become! She had got up on Monday, ignored the traditional washing activity and gone straight into town to the music shop. The assistant had been very helpful, playing a range of keyboards and telling her a hundred pieces of information until her head started spinning. He was a really good player and made them all sound magnificent. He told her she could have a whole orchestra to accompany her. Did she want this? She didn't know. She supposed he must have sold lots of keyboards to people who thought they would be able to go home and play like him. She knew enough about music to know they would be disappointed. She realised that from her struggles to play the piano. She decided to go to the keyboard group and see what it was like and ask for advice. She was amazed. She didn't feel at all scared at the prospect. Why couldn't she have been like this when she was younger? Life would have been so different.

It was Thursday evening and time for the rehearsal. Everybody was there including Valerie. Her nose still looked a bit red but otherwise she was in good spirits. Maureen was snuffling. There was obviously something going round. Carole felt so elated, almost high as though she had had several glasses of sherry. She simply knew she would be protected from all bacteria. Her immune system felt impenetrable. The rehearsal started and she sang as loudly as she had in the car, secretly grinning at the thought of the man clapping. It was a nice warm feeling, even if she didn't deserve his applause! She tried to concentrate. She didn't want to lose the page again. Robert would begin to think she was dizzy if she didn't pay attention.

After several reruns of the difficult bits it was time for the 'Pie Jesu' solo. Magda stood up, looking very nervous compared with the previous week. She started then stumbled at a difficult bit. Robert patiently asked her to start again. There were a lot more mistakes. Every time she made a mistake the next part was even worse. The rest of the choir began to move around on their chairs and walk their feet around their particular part of the floor. It was an enormously embarrassing situation.

'Stop,' Robert said out of the blue. 'It's not going to work, is it?'

Magda shook her head wordlessly then slumped down in her chair, staring down at the music. She looked as though she was trying to disappear. Carole felt sorry for her even though she had been so rude that first evening.

'It's quite a difficult piece,' Robert told her kindly. 'There's no point in trying to over-achieve. You'll just make yourself miserable. We need you in the main choir to keep everybody together.'

Magda didn't look at all convinced that he meant what he was saying.

'We'll just have to find someone else to do the solo. Is there anybody here who would like to give it a try?'

There was a deadly silence from the sopranos. Carole heaved a sigh of relief. There was no way she was going to push herself forward. Life had been difficult enough lately. All she wanted to do was to fade into the background and have some painless fun. Robert looked somewhat concerned.

'Look. It's nearly December and the concert is on 16th March. There will be no time to practise over Christmas and we'll miss two rehearsals in the New Year. Time will fly by and we can't perform without a soloist.'

'Why don't you have a go?' a voice whispered rather too loudly.

Carole started as though she had been shot. Her heart missed a beat. It wasn't only Maureen's whisper but the date. The end of the month was coming and she would have to confront the business of the standing order. How could she have forgotten? She stood transfixed. The time had rolled by without her noticing it. She had been so busy but now she would have to face up to whoever or whatever it was. Someone else was calling her name and she turned in the direction of the voice. It was another one of the sopranos.

'Go on, Carole. Have a go.'

'Oh, I couldn't do it. I've only just joined. It's too soon,' she stammered.

Robert turned towards her. 'I'll tell you what. If you want you could stay back after the rehearsal and just sing it for me. If you still feel the same or if you're not up to it I'll try and find someone else. You're under no obligation. Just have a go.'

Carole didn't know how to say no. Out of the blue she had suddenly become keen to make the most of life. She had an invitation and it would be unfriendly to refuse. She nodded, trying not to look in Magda's direction. She knew very well how she would be feeling. In fact she felt a hot ray of anger coming towards her. It was almost burning her. She shrugged her shoulders and moved slightly to get rid of the sensation.

Logic told her that she must be imagining it. Such things only happened in science fiction films.

The rehearsal came to an end. Everybody disappeared out of the door one by one while Carole hovered, not quite knowing what to do with herself. Most of her contact with Robert had been at a distance. She was nervous but still had the composure to chuckle inwardly. It was a bit like a one-to-one audience with your favourite pop singer. The crowd had gone and there she was alone with him. She made her way towards the ancient piano. The keyboard player had gone home with the rest of the choir.

Robert was packing his music into a battered case then he turned. 'Right Carole. Let's see what you can do. You seem to have quite a few fans in the sopranos. Just sing and enjoy it. Don't worry about making an impression. That's fatal.' He sat down on the shabby piano stool and played the opening bars.

She noticed how tall he was and yet graceful somehow, and gentle. She forced herself to concentrate on the music. He played the piano with so much feeling she was truly inspired. She started to sing as though she was in the car. She forgot everything except the music, remembering to sing some parts softly and others loudly. She remembered the last time when the conductor had told them all to note the signs on the music, to follow the dynamics and not to sing like robots. It wasn't hard for her as she loved it so much. She came to the end and took a deep breath as though she had forgotten to breathe. Of course she hadn't. She'd just been entranced by the magic of the music.

She looked over at Robert for the first time since she started singing. She had kept her eyes well focused on the score. He was looking at her in such a way that she almost felt as though he was flirting but he couldn't be. She was too old for that, surely. Could it be that he was pleased with her solo? She stood waiting for his response, not knowing whether to move or stay where she was. She kept moving from one foot to the other as the minutes passed.

Suddenly he stood up. 'Carole, that was really good. You've passed your audition.' He smiled, looking like someone just relieved of a heavy burden. 'It needs polishing a bit but you're better than I could have hoped. You must have sung it before.'

'I've never sung a solo before but I've been listening to the CD and I've practised quite a lot.' She felt her face glowing. 'I hope I can pull it off. I'm quite nervous.'

'You'll be fine. I know you will. You have to know it back to front then when you sing in public you can put some feeling into it. It's a fine balance though. If it becomes too familiar it can lose spontaneity but I'm sure it won't happen to you. You'll be wonderful. I can tell. '

'Oh, I hope you're right.' She sighed then looked anxiously at her watch. 'I must go now. It's getting late.'

Robert seemed about to say something else then stopped, wished her a good weekend and said he was looking forward to the next rehearsal. She got into the car and drove home. As she opened the door, her heart missed a beat. She half expected the company or person who had been receiving the money to be waiting for her but the house was eerily empty. There was nobody waiting and no post. It was the end of November. She had a strange feeling that whoever had been getting the money was going to turn up sooner or later.

CHAPTER 6

More New Horizons

IT WAS 30ᵀᴴ November, nearly Christmas. Carole dreaded the thought of Christmas on her own. She had been so busy she hadn't really had time to think about the looming season of goodwill. She wished she could go away but she had spent enough in Southport. She couldn't afford another holiday, especially at Christmas when everything was top price. She didn't really want to go to Pippa's Pizzas either but she had promised the children and wouldn't let them down.

They were all there when she got to the restaurant. The children were jumping up and down with excitement. Some of it rubbed off on her. Children were such good medicine when you were feeling down. You couldn't feel sad for long with them. She wished they were her family as she looked around at all the paper chains, stars and lights. It was such a lovely time for families and such a terrible time for lonely people. An icy shudder rippled through her. She resolved to spend Christmas Day with a homeless charity then felt almost ashamed at using the less fortunate to quell her misery. Thank goodness the children were there. She could use them instead of the homeless at least today!

Jenny looked up at the decorations, a tiny frown forming unexpectedly on her normally smooth forehead. 'It's almost Christmas,' she remarked nervously. 'Everything's so expensive.'

'But Santa will bring us our toys,' Eva bubbled. 'He's bringing me a computer. All my friends have got them – and some new dolls and some books.'

James nodded quietly but didn't say anything. He looked from his mum to Carole then back again, a little questioning frown on his face. Jenny ruffled Eva's hair. 'Don't worry. Santa will bring you some nice things, I'm sure.'

Carole examined Eva's Poppy and the Lego figure that James had brought. She threw herself into taking an interest in the children and their toys in an attempt to get things into proportion. She realised she had a lot to be thankful for but nevertheless, Christmas was a threat, not a pleasure for her. She didn't like to admit that she was scared, scared of the loneliness and still waiting to resolve the problem of the cancelled standing order.

Jenny looked as though she was preparing to make a speech. Her face seemed drawn and anxious. Her lips were slightly parted as though she was about to say something significant. 'Carole. Can I ask you something?' She didn't wait for an answer, just continued. 'We don't have any family and I wondered, if you're not doing anything on Christmas Day, if you would come and be with us. But perhaps you've got other plans?'

A tidal wave of relief flooded over Carole. It was almost as though a bright new star had settled above her head and was following her about. Suddenly the world was full of pleasant people and it was strange the way some invisible force seemed to be taking away all her worries one by one.

'I don't have any plans for Christmas,' she admitted, as her finger idly meandered along a crack in the plastic table. 'To tell you the truth I was feeling quite depressed about it. I was thinking of going to volunteer to work for a homeless charity but I'd much rather come to you. Thank you so much for inviting me.' Her gaze moved away from the crack in the table. Her eyes were shining.

Jenny blushed. 'Perhaps I'm being selfish. I shouldn't stop you helping the homeless.'

'I'll have time later to do something like that,' Carole assured her. 'I shouldn't be rushing off to do good works because I can't face up to Christmas. It seems wrong somehow.'

The children were getting restless. They decided to go home and meet the following Friday to make arrangements for Christmas Day.

Carole had become more and more nervous during the week, thinking about going to the keyboard group. She was so preoccupied she had completely forgotten about the end of the month. In fact it was 5th December. Now that she was feeling so much happier about Christmas the arrival of December had lost its significance. As time went by and interesting things kept her busy the business of the standing order had faded into the background, at least for the present.

She had been quite confident about going to learn the keyboard but it suddenly seemed a bit difficult. She was late joining the group. Would she fit in? When it got to Wednesday morning, she was wandering around, wondering if she should go or not when the doorbell rang. She jumped because normally it was only the postman who rang and he'd already been. She opened the door. Outside there was a blond girl rather like Jenny, probably in her mid thirties. She had a little girl with her, her straggly fair hair in need of a good wash.

'I'm Paula's daughter,' she announced abruptly.

Carole stopped as though she had been shot. 'What? You must have the wrong address.'

The woman shook her head. 'No. This is where she lived. This is where I found her.'

'You'd better come in,' Carole replied, pointing towards the lounge where the grey ashes of yesterday's fire offered no warmth. As their footsteps resounded on the wooden floorboards in the lounge, she wondered what on earth she was going to say. The little girl started wandering around, looking for something interesting to do. She didn't appear to have any toys or colouring books with her.

'Charlotte, come here. Sit down,' her mother commanded, tensing her head and shoulders in a way that made Carole doubly uncomfortable. The child did as she was told, sitting close to her mother so that their arms touched. The woman began to wriggle around as though an invisible insect was crawling on her. 'Move up, Charlotte. You've got the whole couch. What are you sitting on top of me for?' she snapped irritably. The child moved to the other end of the couch, her lip trembling. She looked very small and lonely sitting on the big seat cushion.

Carole scanned her memory, trying to think of something a small child would like to play with. There had never been any children in the house so there were no toys anywhere. She suddenly remembered the new occupant of her bedroom. Of course! The little girl would love to play with him.

'I've got something upstairs that you might like to play with. I'll be back in a minute.'

She tore up the dusty stairs and emerged carrying the large bear, his head resting comfortably on her shoulder on the reverse journey down the stairs. The girl was busy texting or surfing the internet on a shiny red mobile phone. She didn't look up. Charlotte's blue eyes opened wide. She jumped off the couch and flung her arms round the bear that was almost as big as her. Her mother's eyes flashed, her mouth locked in a straight line. Who'd told her to move? Charlotte was too busy making friends with the teddy to notice.

'Ted, ted,' she sang, sitting across his tummy and jumping up and down.

'Stop jumping, Charlotte.' A bad-tempered voice jarred the air. 'Why don't you play nicely? You're just too rough.'

The little girl's face changed from happiness to sadness. Carole felt she had to come to the rescue before she started crying. 'It's OK, Charlotte. He won't break. His name's, er, Samson. He was a very strong man. The teddy is just as strong so don't worry. You can ride him or lie on him or feed him something pretend.'

Charlotte's little face brightened again but she didn't say anything. Carole began to wonder if she could talk. She looked about three and should be talking by now. Her mother looked bored by the whole business, her impatience broken from time to time by sulky scowls at the child.

'I think you had better tell me the whole story but would you like some tea or a cold drink?'

The woman nodded, and Carole came back with tea for the two of them and some orange juice for Charlotte. She still didn't know the woman's name. 'I'm sorry. I should've asked your name. I'm Carole. What's you name?'

'Samantha,' she replied, and suddenly some of the mystery fell into place. SAM 73. That was the reference for the standing order. Of course! 'I was adopted. My mother said she couldn't keep me. My adoptive parents didn't want me to know I wasn't theirs. I didn't get to know for a long time. They didn't like me much either.'

Carole sat stiffly in the armchair opposite, feeling as though she had been flung into another world. She imagined what it must be like to be a counsellor but it wasn't the kind of conversation you had with a stranger. 'Too much information' was the current phrase for this type of situation but she had to say something.

'Why not?' She instantly felt as though she was being nosy.

'I wasn't clever, you see. They thought they were posh. I didn't, like, fit the bill. They wanted a child to boast about with their friends. When I drew things they never, like, looked at my pictures. Well, my mother always said they were nice but she didn't care. She said everything was nice without looking, even rubbish I picked up to put in the bin.'

Carole sighed. She'd seen enough miserable children when she was teaching to know what rejection did. 'I'm sorry. That was wrong. You don't have children to boast about. It's like buying a posh car to impress the neighbours.'

'I won't be doing that with Charlotte. She's thick like me. She doesn't even talk.' The words flew out of her mouth like bullets from a gun.

Carole winced, her eyes turning anxiously in the child's direction. She seemed too busy to have heard her mother but she couldn't help but absorb the atmosphere and tone of voice. She knew children had secret antennae for picking up adults' hidden thoughts. Samantha's thoughts were not even hidden.

'I got married to get away from them. Ken left me before Charlotte was born. He soon got fed up with me too. I don't know where he is and I don't care.' Her eyes flashed with a mixture of hatred and despair. 'He wasn't any good.'

Carole thought she probably did care. She had been hurt by all the people who were supposed to love her. It looked as though she was doing the same to Charlotte, history repeating itself.

'When I had Charlotte I didn't have anyone to help. My parents went to live in Scotland. I've got their address. They did at least give me that but I'll never go there. They don't want me or Charlotte. I was a single parent, you see. They were ashamed of what the neighbours would say. Having a wedding ring didn't make any difference. I was pushing a pram and there was no man around.'

'But didn't they want to see their granddaughter? I'd love to have had a grandchild. I don't have any family,' Carole told her, wondering why she was bothering to tell her anything. There was absolutely no response. It was as though she was deaf to everyone and everything. It was a dramatic monologue without the theatre and the stage.

'I did what people do now. I found my mother. She told me nobody knew I existed and she didn't want anyone to know. It had all happened a long time ago and she had her life all set out. She didn't want it upset by me. She was a teacher and kind of respectable. She hadn't had time to love me. They took me away as soon as I was born. I think she wanted Charlotte to have a good life. She didn't want to feel guilty. That's why she set up the standing order. It meant I could work part-time and, like, spend time with Charlotte.' Samantha closed her mouth as though it was the longest speech of her life then she drank her tea, looking past Carole, over her shoulder at the wall.

Carole couldn't help wondering what she did with the child. Had Paula given her the money to keep her quiet? After all she would have been at the beginning of her teaching career. An illegitimate child arriving out of the blue would have been a disaster. *How did she get away with it*, Carole wondered. She must have taken time off during her pregnancy. There was no one to ask so that would remain a mystery. Paula had never been the maternal type. She had been more into people management than children. She wouldn't have known what to do with a grandchild either.

Carole felt out of her depth, bewildered by the whole situation. Paula had always been a good friend through thick and thin but their friendship had been more of a business arrangement, a 'you and me against the world' alliance. She had never allowed anyone to get close to her. Carole felt angry and hurt. Why hadn't she told her? Their money had been in a joint account. It seemed she had taken advantage of her lack of interest when it came to money. She gave Charlotte a biscuit to feed to Samson then slumped down in the armchair and turned her gaze towards the grey ashes, wishing she had lit the fire. At least that would have added a bit of warmth to the situation.

'I cancelled the standing order because I have less money now that Paula isn't sharing the bills any more and I didn't know what it was. It was the bank clerk who advised me to do it.' She felt awkward. It sounded as if she was blaming the bank when of course it was her decision. 'I don't know yet how I'm going to manage.'

'Well, she left you the house,' Samantha flashed, the words like an arrow aiming at a target.

Carole rebounded as though she had been hit. She felt a tide of anger rise up from her stomach. A waterfall of words spewed out. 'We lived together for thirty years. We were family to each other. We shared the bills. I don't know why I'm telling you this. I'm not Paula. I don't owe you anything.'

'You've taken my mother's house and I bet you've taken her money as well.'

Carole couldn't believe what she was hearing. She wasn't used to this kind of scene and she was quite near to tears. 'I'm sorry but I think you'd better go. It's too soon for me to have to cope with something like this.' She was literally shaking with fear and anger.

Samantha got up and took Charlotte firmly by the hand. 'Come on. We're not wanted here.' She glared at Carole, roughly tore the little girl away from the teddy and dragged her towards the front door.

'You'd better leave your name and address,' Carole gasped, before she could stop herself. She would be so glad to see the back of both of them. It was only a few hours since she had felt so elated, having a meal with Jenny and now the tide had turned. The mystery of the money was solved but not resolved. The whole nasty situation seemed somehow open ended when she wanted it closed. The front door banged and Samantha and Charlotte disappeared into the dark evening, leaving no address.

She carried the cups into the kitchen, aware that Paula's flowery china cups were vibrating dangerously on the tray. SAM 73? That must have been the year she was born. Carole couldn't help wishing strongly that she had never met the woman. It had spoilt her morning and life was precious. She put it behind her, grabbed a quick snack then went off to the U3A keyboard session. It started at one-thirty. As she went in she heaved a sigh of relief. Meeting people was the best medicine for her worries. She was so glad to be away from Samantha she had quite lost her fear of this new venture.

***

The room was full of keyboards of all shapes and sizes and the people seemed to match their instruments like owners sometimes looked like their dogs. Carole looked around, trying to establish who was in charge of this impressive display but it wasn't obvious. Most of them were drinking cups of tea or coffee and exchanging musical experiences. The ones who weren't drinking were playing bits of music to each other or practising with headphones. One chap was sitting behind a box full of money. He seemed to be the right person to ask. She went up to him and explained who she was and asked to speak to whoever was in charge. He smiled a welcoming smile and introduced himself.

'Nice to meet you, Carole. We're always pleased to have new members. I'm Sam by the way.'

Carole froze. What a coincidence! She quickly regained her composure but not before Sam had noticed her reaction. She quickly explained that she had just had a very bad encounter with someone called Samantha and it was all a bit of a coincidence.

'No offence, I hope.' She laughed.

'Of course not,' he replied, pointing out the keyboard teacher. 'Go and have a word with Samantha, no I mean Barbara.' He chuckled.

Carole burst out laughing. Good for Sam. He had a sense of humour. That's what she needed.

'If you can get near her that is! She's got an impossible job trying to sort out all these people but she still likes to see new faces so don't worry.'

Carole approached a woman of about sixty. She was tall and slim with big dark expressive eyes and hair that must have been black but was now a salt-and-pepper mixture of white and grey. She had the high cheekbones of a model and she was still beautiful. As Carole approached she was playing a piece of Chopin, her long fingers rippling over the keys producing a sound like a fast-flowing stream. She waited until she had finished then explained that she thought of joining the group but didn't have a keyboard. Barbara looked really pleased to see her and asked her to stay for the session then they could discuss what she might do.

She collapsed onto one of the plastic chairs that were surprisingly comfortable and surveyed the proceedings, glad to just watch and do nothing. She needed to calm down. Barbara taught the group for half an hour then gave out a piece of music for them to practise. While they all had a go she came over and chatted to Carole.

'You can have a play with my keyboard while the others are practising if you like.'

Carole nodded. It all looked really interesting. She sat down and Barbara gave her a copy of the music. She started playing piano style, amazed at how good the keyboard sounded. Barbara meanwhile watched with interest because Carole could play already. 'You are doing OK with that.' She smiled. 'Of course there's a lot of technical stuff to learn with a keyboard and you need to learn the chords that go with the accompaniment but if you can play the piano you have a head start.'

'Yes, I can play but I'm not a pianist,' Carole admitted, not wanting to appear too clever. The choir was enough fame. She didn't want any more!

'I think Sam's got an old keyboard you could borrow. People start with a cheap one then want something better,' Barbara explained. 'It takes time to know what you really want so you don't want to fork out a lot of money and then find you've bought the wrong one. I know a few people who've done that. Some people buy an expensive keyboard because they think it'll make them a better player but it doesn't work like that.' Her dark eyes twinkled and Carole warmed to her immediately.

She nodded in agreement, thinking about the music shop with its multitude of magnificent instruments and the wonderful demonstration she had been given. She needed to start in a small way. Sam's keyboard sounded like the best idea.

Barbara had a word with him and he agreed to bring his old keyboard the following week. Carole felt really excited at this new challenge. Christmas was coming early! She did let a sigh escape, however. She just couldn't seem to get away from people called Sam. It was such a coincidence. She didn't have much time to dwell on the prevalence of people called Sam because the play around was starting. It was then that she began to realise that playing the keyboard was going to be quite a challenge. It was amazing how good some of the players were. Even the beginners could produce a good tune.

By the end of the session she was hooked. She laughed to herself. Was she aspiring to being an opera star and a belated pop idol at the same time? She couldn't wait to get her hands on Sam's keyboard. She couldn't help asking herself why she was so ambitious all of a sudden. It didn't make a lot of sense at her age and yet it made her feel good. She thanked Sam and Barbara and made her way home, suddenly remembering all the unpleasant details associated with the first Sam.

As she lay in bed in the dark, she found she couldn't sleep. She could still see Charlotte sitting on the teddy and the delight on her little face as she played. Samantha had seemed so angry and turned in on herself, and so uninterested in the child. She shuddered as she thought what life must be like for the two of them. She wasn't yet three and without the standing order she would have to go to nursery all week while her mum worked. Well, maybe that would be a good thing. If her mum wasn't interested in her she would be better off out of the house. This thought made her feel better until she suddenly got a mental picture of Paula. They had been friends for thirty years and Samantha was her daughter and in need of help. She realised that that was why she had been so rude. She was frightened.

Thursday evening was the choir rehearsal. It was the highlight of her week but she had the whole day to wait. It was raining so she went shopping in the car then parked near the charity shop. She hoped she would find something nice to wear for the evening. She didn't feel the need to impress people. She simply wanted to please herself. She had been there several times and always seemed to find something interesting. Of course it wasn't like a proper shop. You had to take what you could find but to Carole that was part of the fun.

She was now on first name terms with the assistant, Joyce, who seemed to spend half her life in the shop. It made Carole feel a bit selfish. She was doing exactly what she wanted now, taking everything she could out of life. She couldn't decide if that was good or not. It certainly felt good! Joyce looked really pleased to see her and had some good suggestions that might suit Carole. They didn't seem quite right but she was grateful nonetheless and touched by the other woman's thoughtfulness. She was struggling to pick something up and Carole rushed to help. 'Thank you,' she almost whispered. 'I've got rheumatoid arthritis. It comes and goes. It's bad at the moment. The medication sometimes works. It's not working today.'

Carole looked at her hands. It was the first time she had noticed. They were twisted and swollen. She was obviously in pain.

'I'm better out of the house,' she explained. 'What's the point of sitting at home feeling miserable? It makes the pain a lot worse or that's how it seems.'

Carole nodded. 'Yes, I suppose it's better to have things to do. I'd be the same if I was you. I've joined the U3A. It keeps me out of mischief and I'm really enjoying it.'

Joyce shook her head. 'I've heard of it but it wouldn't suit me. I like the shop and I've got a big family. The grandchildren keep me busy when I'm not here. I've got five children and nine grandchildren. They all live round here so I'm not short of company.'

Carole felt a surge of envy. That was how life used to be but looking round she didn't see many big families living close together. Most people's children seemed to be miles away, even in different countries. In her case they just didn't exist. She didn't let herself dwell on this fact for more than a minute. There was no point. She couldn't manufacture a family at her age. It was better to get on and make the most of what could be done. In response to her conclusions she bought an elegant plum-coloured calf-length dress that fitted her perfectly. It was an uncanny coincidence that pair of black knee length boots were just her size as though they had been waiting for her. She chuckled inwardly at the notion of personalising the boots. Next thing she'd been talking to herself! Joyce wrapped up the dress and the boots, assuring her that she would look really good in them. Carole didn't need to be told. She was getting good at choosing clothes. She'd begun to form an idea of what suited her and it was working.

She parked the car outside the house, relieved to find a space. It was still pouring with rain. She dashed up to the front door with the parcels, opened it then dumped them down while she went back for the food. She dragged half a dozen carrier bags full of food into the kitchen then went back into the hall for her clothes. It was at this point that she noticed the envelope. It was small, white and unexpected. The postman had come before she had gone out that morning. She left it on the sideboard while she sorted out the food then sat down with a belated cup of coffee. She took the envelope and opened it. Inside was a small card with an equally small message. 'I'm sorry. Here is my address and phone number. Regards, Samantha.'

Carole heaved a sigh as she sipped the remains of her coffee. She wondered what it meant. She had lived long enough to be a bit cynical about people. Was she still hoping to get the standing order reversed? Was she saying sorry because of that or was she genuinely ashamed of her behaviour? Or was she simply apologising for not leaving her address? It was confusing but strangely it was a bit like finding the boots. Was someone or something guiding her towards a renewal of her opportunity to help Paula's daughter in some way? She had no extended family like Joyce. And little Charlotte needed a loving person. It was quite uncanny the way things were happening!

She couldn't seem to get the whole situation out of her mind. The much overdue round of housework didn't help although she was pleased with the result. As she didn't usually have visitors there was little incentive to become a domestic goddess. After a quick meal in the now fairly immaculate dining room, she had a shower then put on her new dress. It was brand-new. Hopefully the owner hadn't died as it had never been worn but she was alive and making use of it. She put on the boots and looked at herself in the mirror. She suddenly realised what a transformation had taken place in the past weeks. She added a little make up and a scarf that matched the dress. If only she could live backwards! How different things would be. But she couldn't so she shrugged her shoulders and went out into the darkness.

When she arrived at the rehearsal, everyone seemed to be staring at her. Did they think she looked different? She wasn't sure. Maybe it was because she was now a soloist and more noticeable than before. The Fauré was really taking shape now and when it was her turn to sing she wasn't really nervous. She knew it very well and felt confident. Robert smiled as she sang and as their eyes met he nodded. She took the gesture to mean he was satisfied. Much to her discomfort he told her there were one or two bits he would like to discuss. Could she stay after the rehearsal for a few minutes? His opinion had become very important to her and she was disconcerted by his reaction. She couldn't imagine which parts needed discussion.

Valerie came up to talk to her in the break and asked her round for coffee the following week. She said she had some news but there wasn't time to tell her then. Carole resolved to talk to Valerie about Samantha and see what she would suggest. It was time to offload some of her worries and she needed an objective opinion. Perhaps Val could help. After the break, they sang the last parts of the mass. Carole was looking forward to the last part, 'In Paradisum'. 'May the angels lead you into Paradise' she sang. It was in Latin but she knew the translation. It was so beautiful she often felt like crying and today was no exception. As she finished singing a surge of grief invaded her and the awful redness started again. This time it was worse and the cold rippling made her shiver. She remembered when it had all started and deep down she knew why, but she had never told anyone about it and never would. All she wanted to do was escape from the horrible sensation and the memories that couldn't be wiped out.

As they finished, she leaned towards Maureen. She felt dizzy. Maureen looked concerned and took her arm. 'Are you OK?' she whispered. 'I thought you were going to faint!'

Carole nodded. 'Thanks, Maureen. I'm OK. I'm just a bit under the weather.'

Robert wanted to have a quick practice of the carols. Everyone was tired and ready to go home but they did their best. Compared with the Fauré, the carols were easy and a fun way to end the evening. The performance in the town centre would be fun and festive, not stressful. The old favourites never lost their appeal and distracted Carole from her worries as she remembered her childhood and also the shining eyes of the children in her class as they made decorations and performed Christmas plays. The carols came to an end perhaps too soon leaving her wondering what Robert was going to object to.

Everyone made their way towards the door. Carole approached the ancient piano once again. The keyboard player had packed up and gone. She still felt dizzy and emotionally drained so she sat down on the piano stool to wait for him. He was putting his music away. Finally everyone had gone and the hall seemed to echo as the wind whistled round the old building. She gripped the music so tightly it left finger marks down the margins. Undoubtedly she wasn't up to scratch and he was going to be critical. Perhaps he regretted his choice of soloist. She wanted his respect so much the thought of being criticised hurt more than it should. What did it matter anyway? The trouble was it did.

Robert finished putting his music away and came over to the piano. She braced herself, staring down at his feet. His shoes were muddy. Then she looked up and saw that he was smiling.

'That solo was beautiful,' he remarked. 'You must have practised really hard. It was pretty perfect.'

Carole's fast-beating heart settled back to a normal pace but she responded to his smile with an uncomprehending frown.

'I'm sorry if I gave you the wrong impression,' he continued. He'd noticed her bemused expression. 'It's just that I wanted to speak to you on your own and I didn't know quite how to go about it. Sorry. You see I wanted to ask you if you would come to a concert with me on Saturday – unless you have other plans of course.'

Carole's heart lurched as though she had just gone down a massive roller coaster at the local fair. She must have misheard. She looked at him in astonishment. The confident and super-organised conductor with the beautiful hair was looking bashful like a teenager. The situation was like the old woman, young woman picture where the drawing changed as you moved your eyes. He was her revered conductor, a tall cultured man she had admired from a distance and now, as she shifted her view of him, he was something different. She really needed time to adjust but there wasn't any time. It was another bizarre opportunity that she had never expected. She had learnt in the past few weeks not to pass up such opportunities as they might never come again. She smiled at the person who had now become a warm, living human being rather than a remote revered figure. She nodded. 'I'd love to come. Thank you for asking me. I'm not doing anything special. What sort of concert is it?'

'The Mendelssohn Violin Concerto and several other pieces. It's at the Phil. They've got lots of seats left so I'll get the tickets tomorrow. We could have an early meal before the concert if you would like.'

'What a lovely idea!' Carole blushed like a teenager. She had wondered if he had been let down by someone and she was just a stand-in but it didn't look like that. As she adjusted her long scarf that matched the dress so perfectly she could hardly believe what was happening. Had she really gone back in time? She had been thinking about it not long ago and it was almost happening. How bizarre!

'If you give me your address I'll pick you up at six o'clock. We'll have plenty of time to get something to eat. I know a good parking place quite near the Phil so we won't have far to walk.'

Carole laughed. 'You make me sound like some sort of invalid. I can walk, you know!'

'I'm sure you can. I was just thinking about the weather. If it's raining we don't want to go into the concert looking like two drowned rats!'

'No, of course not,' Carole agreed, laughing in an effort to release her tension. She instantly felt more relaxed.

She didn't tell anyone. She didn't have anyone to tell. She felt more like a teenager than she had ever felt in her life, even when she was a teenager. She really liked Robert but couldn't decide if it was simply hero worship. He was so knowledgeable and had a certain quiet charisma. Everyone took notice when he was talking and nobody ever argued. He made everyone feel safe somehow because music was his life and he knew his subject inside out. The person underneath still remained unknown. A quiet meal would be a good opportunity to get to know him better.

When Carole woke up, the sun was shining through the curtains. It was Saturday and it looked as though it was going to be a nice day. She hoped that her meeting with Robert would be a similarly sunny experience. She lay there thinking about the past and realising that today could be a new era for her, the first day of the rest of her life. It was a cliché but it could happen. Clichés were clichés for a reason. She knew she shouldn't be too hopeful but suddenly her failed relationship with Michael was reduced from vibrant to more muted colours. She showered and dressed, determined not to make an exaggerated effort that evening. She would wear the first top and trousers she had bought. She had a special sentimental attachment to them. They had been the beginning of her transformation into a new person. There would be no new clothes or hair appointments. It wasn't necessary. He would have to accept her for what she was. She wouldn't be able to maintain some sort of charade.

She had met Jenny as usual on Friday evening and they had exchanged phone numbers so they could make arrangements for Christmas. It had seemed a good idea. It meant she could contact her if she wasn't going to be at Pippa's. Otherwise she would feel uncomfortable. It had become a Friday routine and she enjoyed it. She had got to know her a bit better now. She knew she was a nurse at the local hospital working in the A&E department. The hospital had understood her situation and she didn't have to work nights. James was at school then after-school club, Eva at nursery full time. It was a long day for them all. She was longing for Eva to be in school as the nursery was expensive. Carole was sorry for her but envious as well. The two of them were so lovely. It was a pity Jenny didn't have more time to enjoy them.

At four o'clock she started to get ready. She had vacuumed and tidied up just in case he came back for a drink. She felt just as good in the clothes as she had the first time she had worn them. The red necklace recommended by Joyce really set the outfit off. She had no need to feel under or over dressed. She just felt comfortable although she wished she had bought some decent shoes. She would have to wear the boots. She was ready by five o'clock and wondering what to do for an hour. She tried to read but couldn't concentrate so she played the piano for a bit then watched the television. The news was typically awful, a mixture of murders, forest fires, storms and terrorism. Surely there was something good happening in the world! Of course bad news was more interesting. As she listened to an account of a local arson attack, the doorbell rang. The TV dramas had passed the time. She grabbed her coat and made for the door.

The restaurant was very near the Philharmonic Hall. It was quiet and unpretentious. Robert took her coat then pulled out her chair in a gesture of old-fashioned courtesy. The waiter arrived and took their order and then brought some drinks. They had both ordered fruit juice. Robert was driving and Carole wasn't used to drinking. There was an awkward five minutes as they both struggled to start a conversation. All around them people were talking easily to each other. Robert took a sip of his drink then looked directly at her, his face clouded by unhappy memories in the midst of the animated conversations going on around them. 'My wife died five years ago. I've spent all that time on my own. I've never really wanted any company. We were very happy. Well, we had the odd argument but apart from that we had everything in common – books, gardens, holidays and music. We were always doing things together. It left a big gap that was difficult to fill.' He frowned. 'We shouldn't have lived in each other's pockets. It all seems so obvious looking back! Sorry,' he added, 'I'm being too serious.'

'That's OK,' Carole assured him. 'It's better than talking about the weather or the news. It's obviously important to you.'

Robert nodded, staring across the menu as if it was a wall to be scaled. He laid it down, leaving a free space between them. 'And what about you? I suppose you don't get to our age without having a few skeletons in the cupboard! Although you give the impression of being uncomplicated.'

Carole nearly swallowed her glass. How wrong people could be, she thought, as she recalled the mess over Samantha and her life with Paula, not to mention other things she didn't want to even think about. She shook her head. 'My life isn't that straightforward. In fact there are all kinds of complications but I do enjoy it just the same. I love singing the Fauré and I've joined the keyboard group although I haven't got a keyboard. Someone's lending me one next week.'

Robert looked intrigued. 'Can you play the piano then?'

She nodded, for once not saying she wasn't a pianist. It was time to stop running herself down.

'A keyboard isn't quite like a piano, you know.'

'No, but it might be fun to do something different. And it'll get me out of the house.'

'Do you need to get out then?' he remarked, in between spoonfuls of the lentil soup he had ordered.

He certainly wasn't into small talk but she was glad. They were two-of-a-kind serious people. Carole briefly explained what had happened to her without mentioning Samantha. His gaze softened as he realised they were both in similar situations. She suddenly looked down at her plate. She hadn't started eating her pâté as she had been so absorbed by the conversation. She stopped talking and started eating.

The main courses arrived and soon they were both eating salmon with a delicious spinach sauce and an attractive range of boiled and roast vegetables. They talked so much about films, gardens, music, poetry and literature they took a long time to eat. Robert looked at his watch, realising that they would have to hurry or they would be late for the concert. Robert insisted on paying the bill then they left the now crowded restaurant and made their way to the concert hall. People were still pouring in when they got there. They were in time. They wouldn't have been allowed to go in if the performance had started. They found their seats and sank down, glad to have time to catch their breath.

The violin concerto was played by a young girl in a magnificent red silk dress. Of course the music was more important than the dress but nevertheless Carole couldn't help envying her her almost teenage figure, glossy long black hair and the way the dress flowed flawlessly over her lower body. She would never look like that or play like that. She stared around at the audience. They were all shapes and sizes. How dared she compare herself to this one person with a great talent! She was getting too big for her charity shop boots! Carole Peters, sixty-one, was lucky to be at a concert with a man she really liked and she was still alive.

The violin concerto came to a part that always made her stomach turn over like the roller coaster at the fair. She heaved a great sigh of contentment.

Robert noticed and turned a rather anxious face towards her. 'Are you OK?' he whispered.

She nodded. 'It's wonderful,' she replied. 'I love that bit. I'm really enjoying the whole thing.'

He gently touched her arm. The pressure was so light it was hardly noticeable but as he withdrew his hand she felt as though he had left a deep mark on her sleeve.

They listened to the rest and then there was an interval. They got up to stretch their legs, along with everybody else. Robert asked her if she would like an ice cream. She shook her head, looking at the queue. She had had far more to eat than normal for her so she didn't need anything. They wandered off towards the bar and bought the coffee that they hadn't had time to drink in the restaurant. There was nowhere to sit so they stood against a wall resting their coffee cups on a high table. Suddenly Carole noticed two people with their backs turned towards them, a familiar corduroy coat and a smart camel coat – Ruth and Ted. They turned round almost as though Carole had called out to them.

Robert smiled sheepishly. 'It wouldn't do to have any guilty secrets here, would it?' he observed, looking a little embarrassed.

Ted and Ruth came up and looked knowingly at Carole who felt rather hot. 'Well, nice to see you. Are you enjoying the concert?'

Carole answered as Robert seemed slow to reply. 'Yes. She's a wonderful violinist, isn't she? And she's so pretty.'

Ruth agreed. 'Yes. That dress was beautiful.'

Ted raised his eyes to heaven, grinning at Robert. 'You'd think it was a fashion show rather than a concert,' he joked.

Robert laughed, relaxing a little. 'She's a fantastic violinist but it's a bonus if you're pretty as well I suppose.'

They knew the concerto very well and talked more seriously about the interpretation until the bell went, informing them that it was time to return to their seats. There was a sensation of relief all round, a certain awkwardness that had been covered up by joking about the girl then discussing the performance. Ted and Ruth were downstairs so they parted company but not before Ruth had whispered to Carole 'Well, you're a dark horse!'

She blushed almost as though she had been caught doing something illegal or immoral. The second half of the concert was a symphony: *The New World*. Carole wasn't that keen on symphonies as there was no instrument to focus on like there was in a concerto. It was harder to concentrate although she didn't really want to admit this to Robert. She sat comfortably in her seat, thinking about all sorts of things. Would he come back to her house? Would he ask her out again? Was it just a one-off outing? She felt young again. Perhaps you could go back in time after all. She looked down at her hands and realised you couldn't. They were all wrinkled with decades of sun, cleaning and washing. She would value the evening with him even if it was the only one. Life was a gift and she would savour every minute from now on. She was healthy. She felt she might live for at least another twenty years if she looked after her body. Every minute was precious.

The concert finished and after many minutes of applause people put on coats and picked up their bags and umbrellas. Reality was rearing its ugly head. It was probably raining outside. They struggled back to the car, buffeted by an angry December wind interspersed with blustery showers of rain and drifting dead leaves. She threw herself into the car, luxuriating in the warmth of the velvety seat covers and the escape from the wind howling round the outside of the car. She shivered more from an awareness of the sound outside rather than actual cold.

Robert turned on the engine and the heater. It didn't take long to get back. They were soon parked outside her house. She was in a quandary. Should she invite him in or not? He turned towards her, his hand still on the wheel.

'I'll have to get home. I've got someone coming for a piano lesson tomorrow at nine o'clock.' He sighed.

Carole wasn't sure whether to be pleased or disappointed. 'Well, have fun. I loved working with children. They keep you young, don't you think?'

'It helps pay the bills,' he retorted practically. 'It's OK most of the time. I like to inspire people but some of the kids don't really want to do it. That's when it's deadly! It's the parents who send them. They should be the ones coming for the lessons, not the kids!'

Carole remembered the pushy parents at her school and nodded. 'I know what you mean.'

'I'll see you to the door,' he offered.

She didn't really think it was necessary but it was kind of him. She was learning to look after herself, and not before time, but she thanked him as she turned the key in the lock.

'Can we do this again?' he ventured. 'I've really enjoyed your company.'

'Yes, of course. I've really enjoyed the evening. Thank you,' she replied, wondering if he was just being polite.

'Could I phone you? I haven't got your number.'

She wrote it down for him. Perhaps he wasn't just being polite. Then she said goodnight, wondering if Ruth and Ted would spread their meeting around the choir. She would have to wait and see.

CHAPTER 7

More New Beginnings

IT WAS NEARLY Christmas. Carole had been so busy and preoccupied with her new life she had hardly noticed the Christmas decorations in all the shops. Suddenly she noticed the Christmas trees in all the windows except hers. They glittered in the dark and did something to lighten the cheerless darkness of December. She would have to buy presents for Jenny and the children. Valerie was a question mark. Then there was Robert. She didn't really know where she stood with him at the moment. It certainly wouldn't be appropriate to buy him anything yet. The whole thing might fizzle out. She felt a bit like Scrooge. It was over-commercialised and complicated. You got cards from people then you had to send one back. Of course they knew you had forgotten or left them out so what was the point?

'Don't be such a misery guts,' she told herself. 'Get out there and buy some cards and decorations for Christmas.' It was Sunday but there were plenty of shops open. She drove to the main shopping centre and joined the crowds. She bought cards, some new decorations and a modern set of tiny coloured lights for the tree which was still in the loft. She resolved to make an effort to decorate the house even if she wasn't going to be there on Christmas Day. She would drag the ancient Christmas tree out of the loft and give it a new look if it was still in one piece and not just a heap of branches waiting to go to the tip. It wasn't of course real so the old plastic tree would probably last yet another year.

While she was filling her basket with the decorations, she noticed a white snowman with a hollow body. She bought that too. She would fill it with something nice for Eva and James. She added another one, remembering what children were like. Sharing a snowman wouldn't be a good idea. She turned round and came face-to-face with a lighted Christmas pudding with teeth. It gave her quite a shock then she thought of James and Eva. They would both love that. It was funny and scary. She grabbed a boxed pudding and made for the checkout.

There was a music shop next door. She went in and bought a CD of children's songs. There were Christmas carols, action songs and plenty of others that would be fun to sing and dance to. She certainly wouldn't go empty-handed to Jenny's. As she drove home she passed the local supermarket. She needed something to eat so she drove into the car park and went into the shop. She didn't feel like cooking. There was a busy café selling food. It was jam packed with people who also didn't want to cook either. She joined the queue and ordered fish and chips, feeling rather guilty. What would it do to her cholesterol? *Too bad!* This was a treat.

That evening Valerie rang and asked her round for coffee the following day. She obviously wanted to tell her something important. It would also be Carole's opportunity to discuss the problem of Samantha and Charlotte. She really did need some advice.

She arrived at Valerie's house about eleven o'clock. She already had the coffee brewing and she seemed much happier than last time. Carole was desperate to talk about her own problems but that would have to wait. Valerie looked as though she couldn't wait to begin. 'I'm so grateful to you, Carole. Things are different since you came last time. Mark and I actually sat down and talked instead of sidling round each other like a pair of angry wrestlers. It was nobody's fault really. I suppose I wanted him to get on with his life. I was impatient for him to get on a conveyor belt going somewhere. The trouble was it was the wrong conveyor belt.'

'It's easily done, Val. He's only young. He can change direction, do some thing else. It's when you get to our age you realise you're too fat to become a ballet dancer or a model and too slow to run a marathon!' She stopped, her face expressionless. There was a silence then they both burst out laughing.

'Don't be so sure about the ballet dancing. They've started classes for pensioners. The sky's the limit!'

'Well maybe but I don't see myself as a ballet dancer somehow. I eat too much,' Carole admitted, taking another chocolate biscuit. 'But what about Mark? How's he doing?'

Valerie took a deep breath. 'Well, he's actually got a job. It's only part-time but it's something. It's a foot in the door, isn't it?'

Carole found it hard to believe that anybody could change radically in just over a fortnight when she'd taken sixty years! 'What's he doing? I thought jobs were hard to get nowadays.'

Valerie looked so different, as though a great weight had been lifted from her. 'He's working in the music shop in town. You know, Bradley's. Apparently one of his friends works there and put a good word in for him. They gave him a kind of audition. You see they want someone to demonstrate the keyboards so that they sound really good. Then they'll sell more. That's the idea.'

Carole nodded rather wryly. 'Yes. I went in there the other day. They had this fellow demonstrating the keyboards. He sounded fantastic. Perhaps that was Mark's friend. The trouble is I'll never play like that in a million years but I bet it's a fun job if you're a good player.'

'Oh, he loves it. He's doing what he's good at. Lucky him!'

'Do you mind, Val?' she asked, cautiously, not wanting to say what she was really thinking. It was like tiptoeing over glass.

'I know what you mean. He's a shopkeeper, not a lawyer. Of course I don't mind. I was suffering from an attack of self-pity and guilt. It sends you in the wrong direction. I can't turn the clock back and do things differently. The childminder probably did a better job than I would have done.'

Carole nodded, thinking that Valerie sounded very positive. It was a healthy attitude but she was a bit bemused, racking her brains to think of a similar situation that she had experienced. It was difficult. 'I'm glad you're feeling better, Val. I've never been completely in charge of a human being so it's difficult for me to imagine. It must be a huge responsibility.' She was thinking of Jenny and Samantha. *How inadequate you must feel when you have a child...and how powerful!* She shivered at the thought. After all, the children at school had all gone home at the end of the day. They became somebody else's problem, not hers. 'What does Jim think about it? Is he pleased?'

Val shrugged. 'I told you he was happy to let him freewheel until he made his own mind up. He's so laid-back. I wish I was like that. I wasn't sure Mark would have done anything at all. Jim just said, "I told you it would be OK." He doesn't let things get to him.'

'I'm glad things have turned out OK.' She hesitated. 'Can I ask you something?' It was difficult changing the subject to her own dilemma. 'Val,' she said directly, 'I wonder if you could give me some advice.'

Valerie had obviously thought that Carole was an uncomplicated free-floater – no annoying family, no stressful job and only herself to think about. She seemed quite surprised as Carole filled her in with the details, leaving nothing out. A puzzled frown appeared above her friend's eyebrows as the story unfolded, then her eyes widened with astonishment at Samantha's accusations. She swallowed hard.

'What are you thinking of doing, Carole? You've met the woman so you must have some idea. To be honest, she sounds like a gold digger, playing with people's guilt! I'm tempted to tell you to get the hell out of there!' There was a rapid intake of breath as Val must have realised she'd gone over the top.

'I know, but she's got a little girl. I don't think the child has much of a life.'

'There are lots of children like that everywhere. It's on the television nearly every night and the papers are full of it. It's not your problem really, is it?'

Carole blew her nose with an embroidered handkerchief that had been Paula's. Unlike Valerie she kept seeing Charlotte's little face as she cuddled Samson. She'd been so happy then her mum had dragged her away before she could even say goodbye. Valerie didn't really understand. 'You're probably not wrong about her except she's like a big needy child. It looks as though nobody's really cared for her. How can you give love if nobody's ever given you any?'

Valerie reddened with frustration. 'Carole, there are loads of people like that. I know. I've worked with them and even socialised with them. You'll get hurt. She might even be dangerous.'

Carole began to realise that she would have to make her own decision. Her friend couldn't understand that after a lifetime of childlessness she had the opportunity to do something to make Charlotte's life better, if only she could decide how and what to do. 'I know you've been around a bit more than me, Val, but I won't take risks, I promise. I just want to make a difference in a small way.'

There was a silence as they racked their brains. Valerie was the first to speak. 'Carole, I presume you can't afford to pay her the money and I don't think you should.'

'No, I can't afford it and the way she behaved I wouldn't be happy to do it anyway. She was kind of bullying me.'

Valerie took a deep breath then spoke rather slowly as though she was thinking as she went along. 'I don't know how you'll feel about this but suppose you offered to look after Charlotte one day a week. The mother could do some extra work if she does work. If she doesn't you could at least do something nice with the child. It might be fun and you've got time, haven't you? You wouldn't be giving your pension away to money-grabbing people! What do you think?'

Carole didn't say anything for quite some time. She was thinking hard, staring into the blue-red flames of the gas fire. Was her life getting exciting or out of hand? She wasn't sure. She wondered if she was packing too much into too short a time yet Valerie's idea seemed like a really good compromise. The mother wouldn't get the money but the child would get the attention. She had all the experience to lavish on her, experience that was now being wasted.

She looked up at last, and nodded. 'That's a really good idea! Yes, that's what I'll do, Val. Clever you to think of it. I'll give my time rather than money. I've got more time than money anyway so I might as well use it. That way I won't be exploited by Samantha and I can help Charlotte – that is if she's willing to leave her with me.'

'Oh, she will be,' Valerie replied, smirking cynically.

'I can get her books out of the library. I'll buy some paints and pencils…and jigsaws from the charity shop. It'll be fun.'

Valerie smiled happily. She looked rather pleased with herself and Carole supposed they were now even. They'd done each other a favour.

Carole drove home feeling positive about the situation. For the past few days she had started to feel soiled by the sordidness of it all. She had never met anybody like her. All the accusations and talk about gold diggers made her feel dirty. She didn't like not understanding the woman's motivation and bad thoughts were poisoning her mind. Suddenly she felt better. She would help the child into a different world and maybe also help Samantha if she got the chance.

The phone was ringing as she opened the door. She ran into the kitchen to pick up the receiver but it stopped just as she got there. She took her coat off then checked the voicemail. There was no message. She dialled the number to check who had rung. The number wasn't familiar. It was probably one of those people selling things. Even they were quite welcome at times when she felt lonely.

She made a quick sandwich and sat down in front of the television. She and Paula had always eaten in the kitchen. Now she would do as she pleased. She smiled as she turned on an episode of *Shaun the Sheep*, aimed at the under fives. She and Paula hadn't had that much of interest to discuss over the shiny plastic cloth. It had just been a matter of principle. *Shaun the Sheep* was much more interesting.

The phone started ringing in the kitchen. She jumped. She had no close friends except Valerie and the cold-calling companies. It must be one of them. She felt almost pleased to be interrupted. 'Hello.' She waited in suspense for the reply. They were often foreign and sometimes she didn't understand what they were saying. The last one had told her she had won a Caribbean cruise. All she had to do was… She didn't wait to find out.

'Carole?' Robert's voice sounded a little bit gravelly as though he was doing something that he wasn't quite sure about.

'Robert! I thought it was one of those Indians trying to sell me something!'

'Oh. Do I sound like an Indian?'

She laughed. 'No. I just don't get a lot of phone calls.'

'Well, you're lucky there.'

'How was your piano lesson?'

'Not bad. In fact that little boy was quite good. He likes playing the piano. That helps a lot. His mum plays too which makes a difference. Some of the parents shut the child in the front room with the piano and hope for the best.' There was a silence. 'Sorry, I'm getting on my orange box. I didn't phone you for that. There's a film on at the Odeon. I'd like to see it. I wonder if you'd come with me.'

'When were you thinking of?' she asked then realised she should have asked what the film was.

'Well, I thought tomorrow afternoon or later in the week if you want. I often go in the afternoon if there's something interesting on. It's called *An Education*. Maybe you've seen it. I thought you might like it. It's set in the sixties.'

Carole winced but the pain wasn't physical. The sixties seemed like a lifetime ago. She wondered if he'd chosen it specially for her. She knew it was a film about a girl who had been seduced by an older man. It sounded like a woman's film and it would bring back memories in more ways than one but she'd risk it. 'Would tomorrow be OK? I've got the keyboard group on Wednesday. I'm getting my keyboard tomorrow. How long's the film on for?'

'Probably not that long. Tomorrow then. I'll pick you up at one. We could have a pub lunch. Then you'll have the rest of the week to play with the keyboard, no sorry, play the keyboard.'

'Both.' She laughed. 'I'm dying to get it. I feel like a kid waiting for Christmas. I can't believe how good they sound! Anyway, yes, I'll see you tomorrow.'

As she put the phone down she decided to ring Samantha and ask her round. She realised it would be awkward. Perhaps she ought to tell her what she proposed then let her think about it. She dialled the number and listened to the distant ringing. It was a mobile and it rang and rang then went onto answer phone. She would have to ring in the evening as she didn't want to leave a message. She read for a while then walked down to the charity shop feeling a bit guilty. She hoped it wasn't becoming an obsession. She had seen programmes on the television about people who had a house stuffed full of clothes and bric-a-brac. She hoped to get something nice to go out with Robert. She felt the spectre of Paula over her shoulder and quickly brushed it aside. But she was still hovering somewhere close by as she pushed open the door. There were several people inside and this distracted her from any unwanted thoughts. An old lady with a face like crumpled parchment was loudly airing her medical history.

'I've had two heart attacks, a gall bladder operation and a new hip made of some kind of new metal that doesn't wear out.'

'It's a wonder you're still here!' her friend chuckled, raising her eyes to heaven and making use of the mirror to adjust a summery hat suitable for a wedding.

Carole couldn't help wondering how the health service could cope with all these old people then realised she was well on her way to being one of them. Well, not just yet. She had some living to do with all her body parts still in place. She approached the clothes and found a green cashmere top that lit up her face and made her look quite young. She was finding out how clothes could really enhance your appearance if you chose the right style and colour. She looked at the shoes but there was nothing that would fit. She wondered whether to buy some new ones for Christmas. Looking good had suddenly started to matter.

She rang Samantha again. Frustratingly she got the answer phone. Carole wondered why on earth she didn't have a land line. It was most odd. She was invited to leave a message. She hesitated, wondering what to do. She felt quite relieved in a way that she didn't have to speak directly to her. She left her a message asking her to phone and offering to look after Charlotte. The details could be worked out later. It would give Samantha time to think about it.

She sat down to do some piano practice, not expecting to be disturbed. Far from being lonely she was quite glad to have some free time. After all that's what retirement was supposed to be about. It just seemed to be a bit difficult to get the right balance. She kept thinking about Barbara playing the Chopin so effortlessly with her long, elegant fingers. It made her want to keep practising. She knew very well that Barbara was only that good because of hard work and probably a lifetime of professional training and practice. She gritted her teeth, determined to do at least half an hour which wasn't really that much compared with concert pianists who practised six or even eight hours a day. Then, just as she was getting going the phone rang. She was tempted to leave it. The tone sounded almost aggressive as though it was determined to interrupt her. It went on and on. She gave in.

'Hello.' The voice on the other end of the phone sounded a bit wary. It was Samantha.

'Hello, Samantha. I've been trying to get through to you. I had to send you a message.'

'Oh. I, er, don't always answer. I get bothered by people calling me.'

Carole wondered what she meant by that. After all that's what phones were for, weren't they? She didn't know what to say to that so she launched into her offer to look after Charlotte, explaining that she couldn't afford to pay her money but would give her time so she could work a bit more or have a break. She offered to do Tuesday or Thursday but she explained that she couldn't do Tuesday that week as she was going out. Samantha immediately agreed to bring her on Thursday. Carole could hear crying in the background and wondered if the woman couldn't wait even a week. Thursday was the choir rehearsal but Charlotte would have gone home by then so that wouldn't be a problem.

She put some coal on the fire then set it alight with a firelighter and some paper. Soon it was blazing, filling the room with a warm glow. In fact the warmth seemed to be coming equally from inside Carole and from the fire. She put her feet up on the couch and settled down to read her latest library book. Valerie's idea had turned out to be such a perfect solution. She was really looking forward to Thursday when she would get to know Charlotte. She would show her that life could be so interesting. She breathed in the comforting warmth, unaware that somewhere on the horizon a small cloud was taking shape and growing.

CHAPTER 8

An Education

ROBERT ARRIVED VERY promptly at one o'clock. The film didn't start until two so they went to a pub near the cinema for a quick lunch. Carole felt a lot more relaxed than the previous time. Her new green jumper complemented her blue-green eyes and made her skin glow. She looked and felt much younger than she really was. Her whole week was filling up with wonderful new activities and people who made her happy, apart from Samantha who remained a somewhat disturbing enigma.

She settled for soup and half a sandwich. It was more than she usually ate at lunchtime but she felt it was better to have something to do. The tomato soup was very good. She had hardly ever eaten in pubs. She was surprised at the quality although she assumed it had come in containers. It would hardly be homemade but it didn't matter. She was enjoying herself.

Robert was working his way through a toasted sandwich. She left him to eat. He finally looked up. 'I'm sorry I'm not being very sociable. I'm just hungry.'

'That's OK. People don't have to talk all the time, do they?'

He looked a bit apologetic. 'Well, we don't know each other very well so I wanted to be on my best behaviour, you know, making polite conversation.'

Carole laughed. 'You mean like they do in costume dramas, Jane Austen style.'

'Not exactly. I don't think I'm quite up to that! Is your soup OK?'

Carole nodded, wondering if he thought she was very boring. She couldn't think of anything to say. They finished their lunch then went across to the cinema. The film turned out to be very enjoyable even though it was about vulnerability and exploitation. Still, Carole had an uneasy feeling that the subject matter was a bit too close for comfort. It was dark when they came out of the cinema. The one thing that made her feel old was the drawing in of the evenings so that by four o'clock it was night. She always felt as though she should be in the house once it got dark like in science fiction films where nasty creatures came out to attack you once the sun went down. She shivered and suggested they go straight back to her house.

She had taken some homemade lasagne out of the freezer. It wasn't glamorous but she'd thought maybe he would like to stay for dinner. He seemed really pleased when she suggested it so she offered him a glass of sherry and they sat down in front of the unlit fire.

'I'm sorry. I've only got sweet sherry. I hope you don't mind.'

'It's fine. I'm very pleased to have anything. I don't drink much nowadays. I used to when Jane was ill. I drank rather too much to keep me going. It isn't a solution but it gets you over a bad patch – as long as you don't get addicted.'

Carole had never had reason to drink much at all and had no experience of people who drank a lot. She was quite surprised. 'You always seem so quiet and contented. I can't imagine you drinking a lot.'

He hesitated then his face crumpled with pain. 'I changed, we both changed when Jane got ill. You see, she was so frustrated because she couldn't do anything. She'd always been very sociable and loved her work. When she retired she made new friends and got involved with voluntary work and oh, all kinds of things. She'd been an English lecturer and she kept this interest up. She used to write articles for magazines.'

'What happened to her?'

'She got stomach cancer. It was ages before it was diagnosed and by then it had spread. We went through all the treatment: radiotherapy, chemotherapy, special diets, homeopathy and lots more. It was an everlasting merry-go-round. I'm sorry. I sound unsympathetic. We both changed into people we didn't recognise.'

Carole got some inkling of the person he must have become. He sounded really cynical and angry.

'Nothing I did was right. She would shout at me then I would shout back.' He laughed cynically. 'I was never violent but I came close at times. I decided I didn't have much talent when it came to caring. We became very isolated and that made things worse. I suppose I'm more sympathetic to carers now. I felt as though I didn't know myself any more. It's taken me five years to get back to normal. When she died I felt only relief and that makes me feel guilty too.'

There was a silence. Carole was going to light the fire but she was transfixed, not knowing what on earth to say. She seemed to be surrounded by guilt of one sort or another. The grey ashes reflected the mood of the conversation. Everything she thought of saying sounded like a cliché.

Suddenly his face softened. 'I suppose we don't know each other very well yet but you've helped me to return to the person I was. Of course music has always been there for me but people are important too. You've never seen that bad side of me. I'm back to the person I was, or nearly. I'm still a bit frightened of myself though.'

'I only see the person you are today. Yesterday is over and done with,' Carole said, getting up to light the fire. It seemed like the best thing to do. 'I'm different too. I'm trying to find out who I am. Maybe we can do it together.'

They went into the kitchen to eat the lasagne which had been in the oven for rather longer than it should have been.

'I'm sorry about the plastic cloth,' Carole apologised, looking with her usual distaste at the yellow shiny thing under the plates.

She would have liked to throw it in the bin but she didn't have anything else. 'I've had it for so long I don't really see it, well not until now. It looks worse with that candle stuck in the middle.'

She knew she had a lot to learn about dinner parties but it didn't seem to matter. Robert started to laugh. It was very infectious and Carole found herself doing the same. They laughed so much it relieved the tension.

'It's the food that counts and it's very nice. I like Italian food and I wasn't expecting to be invited to dinner. I'll tell you what. I'll buy you a cloth for Christmas but you can choose it. Will you play the piano for me?'

Carole felt her teeth grinding together. 'I'm not a pianist,' she admitted, then wished she could stop saying that to people. But how could she play for someone who was an expert? It would be so embarrassing.

'Why don't you play for me?' Carole suggested.

'I'm always playing the piano. I'd like to relax and hear you play. But only if you want to.'

She didn't want to but didn't know quite how to say no. Paula's piano stood majestically against the wall topped by two wooden elephants and a vase of plastic flowers. It was a good piano and didn't deserve the flowers. Carole found it curious how she was seeing the world through the eyes of the people she had met in the past few weeks. In all the time she had lived there with Paula she had never noticed the flowers or the elephants. She also looked in dismay at the characterless prints on the walls. They told you nothing about the people who lived in the house. There were no paintings, family photos or souvenirs of happy holidays. She approached the piano as though she was at the foot of a mountain. She took a deep breath and started to play the piece she had been practising. As she played she gained confidence and the old piano sang out its congratulations. The house seemed to come alive as the music rang down the corridors and round the rooms.

'You shouldn't run yourself down,' Robert told her firmly, relaxing comfortably against the red velvet cushions on the couch. They were one of Paula's few recent purchases and they looked almost new. 'You played that really well. Do you do a lot of practice?'

She nodded. 'Yes, I play most days now and it's made a difference. I used to play for assembly when I was teaching but I had a limited repertoire.' She laughed. 'What I mean is I played half a dozen things all the time and nobody seemed to notice.'

'Well, I have my party pieces. If I don't play them for a bit I start making mistakes.'

'I don't believe you! I can't imagine you making mistakes. Play me one of your party pieces then, Robert. I've had my turn. It's your go.'

'OK.' He dragged himself off the couch and they swapped places.

He played a piece of Chopin which sounded rather like the music Barbara had played on the keyboard except that she knew the piece. It was the 'Raindrop Prelude'. As Robert played that same insistent note that represented the drip-drip-drip of the water she pictured the rain dripping off the roof just as Chopin had watched it in Majorca all those years ago. She stared into the fire then up at the elephants who seemed to be listening too. The piano was heavy so they didn't move to the music but she felt her lips curling up with amusement at the situation. It was like an old fashioned musical evening but the only participants were the two of them and the two elephants. She envied him. He played faultlessly and it was the original score, not an easy arrangement. She wondered how on earth he could play the whole thing without the music. It was quite amazing. 'Wow! I wish I could play like that.'

'Don't forget it's part of my job so I should be able to play reasonably well, don't you think?'

'I suppose so. You know I love that piece. In fact I love all Chopin's music. You chose the right music for me.'

'It's my favourite too,' he said softly.

The evening flew by. They discussed the film. It was about a schoolgirl who was seduced by a charming older man, left school to marry him and ended up shocked and disillusioned. They had both found it interesting and funny in places but for Carole it was a bit too close to her own experience. She still remembered Michael. Some memories would always remain. She looked across at Robert and wondered how it would all pan out with them. It could never be the same. She was supposed to be old now although she felt younger than she had for a long time. Was the Michael experience a thing of the past or could it happen again? She came to the conclusion that it could happen but it would be different. No matter how young she felt she had to face the truth. She wasn't young any more and love, if it arrived, would be different.

There seemed to be so much to talk about and as they talked they learnt a lot about each other. He had two grown-up children, one in Manchester and one in London. They were both married with children of their own. Carole talked about her career and her life with Paula but didn't mention Samantha and Charlotte. She kept the conversation impersonal. She couldn't open up to him the way he had to her. She wondered if she could ever tell him the things that had remained shameful secrets for so long. She knew she would have to if their relationship became permanent.

He looked at his watch. 'I ought to go now. It's getting late.' He got up. 'Thank you for coming and the meal of course. Will you be at the rehearsal on Thursday?'

She nodded. 'Of course! I wouldn't miss it for the world.'

'Great. I'll see you there. Will you come out again with me?'

'Yes. I've really enjoyed it. Let's keep having fun. I think it'll do us both good.'

He nodded. 'Yes, let's enjoy the present. We can arrange something on Thursday.'

She followed him down the hall and was about to open the door when he turned towards her. 'Thank you.' He smiled. He put his arms round her and his cheek against hers. She felt the male roughness of his skin and a scent of either aftershave or was it just his body. Something surged within her and she pressed herself against him. Maybe it wasn't too late after all.

***

Samantha had arranged to bring Charlotte at ten o'clock. Carole had been to the keyboard group the previous day then she had shopped for something that she hoped the little girl would enjoy eating. She'd settled for finger foods as she imagined Charlotte would be used to that sort of food. She had filled her bag with cheese, crackers, tiny tomatoes and some healthy crisps. She added red and green grapes and some chocolate biscuits. She bought a cake mix with icing and a lot of funny faces to decorate the little cakes. It would be a practical way of getting to know Charlotte. She had also bought an arsenal of activities to keep her happy: jigsaws, felt tips, paper, a book of nursery rhymes and a set of wooden linking letters. Joyce's charity shop had once again come up trumps. A surge of happiness rippled through her as she looked at the toys. It was a bit like going back to work. She suddenly realised how much she missed her job.

She had picked up the keyboard from Sam and he had given her a quick demonstration on how to use it but she couldn't remember what to do. There was so much to learn and she began to wonder if it was going to be too difficult. The appeal of the piano with the two ever-present elephants increased in dimensions but she was determined to have a go. She got the manual out and started reading it while she waited for Charlotte, only to realise that you needed an interpreter to understand the instructions. She banged it shut just as the doorbell rang.

They were early. Carole offered Samantha some coffee. The woman seemed anxious to go but she did reluctantly agree to stay for a coffee. Carole wanted to find out if there was anything she ought to know about the child who would be with her all day. She gave Charlotte some paper and crayons while they had a talk. She was just about to open her mouth to ask a few questions when the crayons fell off the table and bounced all over the floor and under the armchair. Charlotte gave them a challenging look or did Carole imagine it?

Samantha shrugged and raised her eyes to heaven. 'She's always the same. She makes messes all the time. She never plays, just goes round causing chaos. I've bought her loads of things. They just get piled up in a heap. It's not worth bothering.' She narrowed her eyes while her cheeks flushed with temper. 'Pick those up now or you'll be sorry.'

Charlotte appeared to ignore her. She was busy tearing up the paper and making it into balls. She dropped them on the floor one by one, her eyes moving thoughtfully from her mum to the paper balls then back again. She still had a challenging look on her face. She was waiting for trouble.

'Pick all that up now,' Samantha growled, rather like a tiger about to pounce on its victim.

Charlotte did her best to hide behind the armchair but couldn't escape. Her mother viciously slapped her on her arm, leaving a big red mark. She started to scream. Samantha looked as though she was ready to follow up the slap with a few more. Carole stared, transfixed. She didn't want to interfere but she felt so sorry for the child. After all, all she had done was spill the crayons.

'You're a naughty girl and Carole won't want you to stay. Tell her you're sorry.'

'Don't worry about it. It's OK. She's only little. It was just an accident.'

Samantha shook her head. 'Oh no, it wasn't. She did it on purpose. She does it all the time to annoy me. Just you wait and see,' she warned, biting her nails. They were bitten right down. Her fingers were suspiciously yellow. 'I'd better go,' she snapped, tossing back her hair which needed cutting. I'll pick her up round six if that's OK.'

She made for the door without looking back or saying anything to Charlotte. When the child saw that she was about to be left she ran after her mum and grabbed her skirt, screaming with panic. Samantha raised her foot in an attempt to disentangle her from the skirt. She looked as though she was about to kick her out of the way. Carole was forced to pull Charlotte away and hold her while her mother banged the front door and disappeared. She was literally shaking. Her opportunity to do something good for the little girl was turning into a nightmare. She sat down on the couch holding the child forcibly against her. She squirmed and yelled to be put down. Finally Carole gave way and let her go.

She went straight to the front door and tried to open it, yelling for her mum. She seemed to have very little feeling for her but she was at least the person who looked after her to some extent. Carole knew she couldn't open the door so she let her cry until she was finally exhausted and came back into the lounge. She went behind the armchair and lay down, still sobbing quietly. Carole left her, knowing that she couldn't do anything for now. She sat leaning against one of Paula's velvet cushions on the couch wondering what would happen next. She knew how to deal with five- and six-year-olds but Charlotte was hardly more than a baby. She knew nothing about babies and toddlers and the child was undoubtedly still at a baby stage. Her new life was getting very complicated.

She sipped her coffee and thought about a stray cat that Paula had befriended at one time. It was a black cat with white paws. It had been thrown out by someone and was scrawny and mangy. It had stared warily at Paula with big green eyes filled with fear. She remembered Paula moving towards it with a bowl of milk and how the cat had retreated. Paula had said that the cat needed to be in charge of the situation so she put the bowl down and moved back. The cat then had to make a decision. It was hungry. Nobody was menacing it. It made the move and came for the milk. That's what she would have to do with Charlotte but how?

She thought for a while. A saucer of milk wouldn't work but something similar might. They were, after all, animals as well as humans. She got up and went over to the piano. She had some children's songs in the piano stool. She got the faded, rather tatty book out, thinking back to afternoons when she had sung some of the songs with the Reception children. She started with 'The Wheels on the Bus'. It had always been popular with the smallest children. She started to sing.

When she got to the part where the dogs barked all day long she began to feel a bit silly, shouting 'woof, woof' into thin air. Grown-ups didn't sing songs like that to themselves, only if they were going back to second childhood. The neighbours might be listening too. They had always thought the two old women next door were unfriendly and eccentric. This would just add to their suspicions. She stopped abruptly, bending over the keys in a semi-foetal position when she heard a dog, no it wasn't a dog. She turned round. Charlotte was standing behind her saying 'woof, woof' over and over again.

The child's blue eyes looked warily at Carole just like the cat's. Her face was black with the tears that she had wiped away with a dirty hand. Carole didn't attempt to touch her. She kept thinking about the cat. 'I'm going to make some cakes. You can come and help if you want,' she told her, walking towards the kitchen with a show of confidence she didn't really have.

Charlotte didn't say anything. In fact Carole hadn't heard her speak much at all. She marched towards the kitchen without turning round to see if the child was following. She instinctively felt it was better not to seem to be hassling her, and just like the cat Charlotte followed her into the kitchen. She got the cake mix out and poured the powder into a bowl. 'We have to add an egg and some milk.' She didn't want to risk a drama with the egg so she cracked it. As it went into the bowl Charlotte's eyes opened wide with astonishment. 'Would you like to pour the milk?'

Charlotte took the jug and with some help she poured the milk onto the sponge mix and the two of them mixed it with two forks.

Charlotte's hands were not exactly clean but Carole decided to ignore this. She didn't want any kind of conflict with the child at that moment. Charlotte held the cake cases while Carole spooned the mixture into each one. She seemed mesmerised by the mixture and the pleated paper cases. They both arranged them on the baking tray and Carole put them in the oven.

'Look. You can see them through the window. They'll start to rise in a few minutes. Let's go and wash our hands then we'll have a look through the window to see how they're getting on. We need clean hands to put the funny faces on.' She ran some hot water into the yellow washing-up bowl then added some washing-up liquid. They both splashed their hands in the soapy water. Charlotte laughed for the first time. The sound seemed almost creepy to Carole it was so unexpected. She noticed that the child's nails were still black but didn't try to clean them up. She'd be pushing her luck a bit too much. They went to look at the cakes which had now risen above the cases. Charlotte stared fixedly at them, seemingly unable to grasp what was happening.

'They'll soon be ready then we can put the icing on and the funny faces.'

She continued to stare silently into the oven through the window. At least she wasn't crying. Carole heaved a sigh of relief and mentally thanked the cakes. It had turned out to be the right thing. She took them out of the oven taking care to keep Charlotte away from the hot baking tray. 'We'll have to leave them to cool now. Let's have a look at the faces while we wait.'

There were glasses, noses, eyes and smiling mouths with lots of teeth, moustaches, different coloured hair and lots of eyelashes. There were also several pairs of earrings. The cakes soon cooled. They mixed the icing, spooned it on to the cakes then started to put the faces together. Charlotte seemed to have little idea how to create a face. She also still hadn't said anything other than 'woof, woof'. It was all very curious. She passed the eyes to Charlotte and showed her where to put them then did the same with the nose and mouth. Carole kept repeating the words. There was no response but she was enjoying the activity.

Finally they came to the end. All the cakes were complete.

'Would you like a cake? Which one would you like?'

Charlotte seemed at a loss to know what to do. Carole picked up the cake with the glasses and offered it to her. 'How about this one?'

She shook her head and pushed it away. She then selected the face with blond hair, red lips and white teeth. The cake looked a bit like Eva's Poppy.

With an inner sigh and an external grin Carole took the one with the glasses. The cakes both reflected the appearance of their owners. They both took a bite and then came the breakthrough. Charlotte spoke across a mouthful of sponge. 'Cake,' she muttered, beaming through the crumbs. Carole almost jumped.

'You can eat the hair now. I'll eat the glasses.'

There was no more talk but at least it was something. She wasn't deaf.

Carole went over to the sink with the mixing bowl, feeling quite triumphant. She hadn't lost her touch after all. As she ran the hot tap and watched the water rising in the plastic basin there was a sickening smash. She wheeled round as though she had been shot. The cakes were all over the floor pierced and sprinkled with shards of glass. Unfortunately the plate had been a French glass one. Charlotte was standing at the table with that same challenging look on her face, her lips curling up ready to break into a smug grin at any moment. This time there was no doubt in Carole's mind. She had done it deliberately and she was waiting to see what Carole would do.

They stared at each other like two duellists. Carole reacted quickly, but at the same time wondering precisely what she was dealing with. 'Well, Charlotte. I'm afraid that's the end of the cakes. What a shame! We could have had the others later. Now they'll have to go in the bin. Will you help me to brush them up but don't touch them. You might cut yourself on the glass.'

She got the brush and started clearing up. She felt quite near to tears then mentally shook herself. She was sixty-one, not six. All her years of teaching reminded her that it was important not to show she was upset. Children needed above all to feel safe. Charlotte watched but didn't help. Her blue eyes had hidden depths unreadable by Carole. She did however have her theory about what was going on. She knew that in Old English the eyes were described as the windows of the soul. She didn't know precisely what was happening but she had some idea. She felt she needed to be very grown up to deal with a child like this. At sixty-one she was probably ready!

She knew she had to make a stand. She couldn't ignore what had happened but she didn't want to punish her. She sensed it wouldn't work. She suddenly had an idea and dashed upstairs to get the teddy. She brought him down and put him on the floor.

'I've brought Samson down,' she told the child. 'He's lonely upstairs. He would have liked a cake too but now he can't have one. He's sad and so am I.'

Charlotte's eyes changed expression. She hugged Samson and looked as though she was going to cry but she wasn't going to say sorry. Carole didn't expect that. Perhaps many times she'd been cajoled into saying the words with threats and slaps.

She finished the washing-up then took Charlotte and the teddy into the lounge and started making the fire. She had invested in a second hand fire guard to keep Charlotte safe. She struck a match and lit the firelighter, taking care to put the matches back on the top shelf of the massive book case in one of the alcoves. She was taking no chances. She put the fireguard round the now crackling fire, sat down on the couch and asked Charlotte if she would like a story. She looked puzzled but bit by bit she climbed on to the couch and Carole started the story 'The Three Little Pigs'. She found that little children usually liked this story but after a few minutes Charlotte got restless. Carole suspected that she had so few words in her little head she would need something for younger children. She tried a picture dictionary and this kept her attention a bit longer.

Lunch filled another piece of the day. Carole put Radio 3 on and there was some noisy music with lots of drums and trumpets. Charlotte responded well to the different sounds and this gave Carole some more ideas of things to do in the future. She didn't want to take her out at the moment. She was just too unpredictable! The ancient Christmas tree was out in the hall. Carole was sure she would enjoy decorating it. She dragged it into the lounge then they put it in a pot. She draped the new lights over the branches then they covered the tree with baubles and various old decorations going back years. At the bottom of the bin bag there was a small teddy with a red bow. Charlotte clutched him jealously. She didn't want to put him on the tree.

'You look after him.' Carole smiled. 'He doesn't need to hang on the tree.'

They finished it off by throwing on handfuls of silver foil and paper decorations like two little children having fun. It wasn't exactly tasteful but Charlotte was thrilled. Carole switched the lights on. The gaudy silver foil flashed with a multitude of colours in the darkness. Charlotte's eyes were shining as she held on tightly to the tiny teddy. They sat down and had a snack. Soon after that the doorbell rang. Samantha had come to collect her.

Carole opened the door. The girl walked in staring down at her phone without even making eye contact. Carole felt a hot flush rise from her neck. It might have been the end of the menopause but in fact it was resentment.

'Is she ready? I've got to go shopping and it's getting late.'

Carole felt a bit like a Victorian servant but at least servants got some pay and maybe some respect if they were lucky. She put Charlotte's coat on and fixed the woolly hat over her blond hair.

'Thanks. I'll bring her next week.' She grabbed Charlotte by the hand and nearly pulled her off her feet as she dragged her towards the front door. She disappeared into the night like a spectre without allowing Charlotte to even say goodbye or asking her if she'd had a nice day.

Carole felt herself wrestling with her emotions. Samantha wasn't grateful. She was resentful. In her eyes Carole had stolen half the house and her mother's money. And she was stuck with a child when she was only a child herself. Carole tried to be rational. After all she had offered to have Charlotte. Had it been for selfish reasons underneath? Had she wanted to relive her youth and be the mother she had never been? Samantha was hardly more than a child even if she was over thirty. Some people never grew up. Carole started to get ready for the choir rehearsal, glad to be going out even though it was dark. She needed something to distract her from her conflict. She grabbed her music, threw on her coat and went out into the December darkness.

When she arrived she noticed that Magda was back. She was talking to Ruth and Ted. Carole felt a surge of anxiety. She wasn't going to be easy to get on with after what had happened over the solo. She sat down next to Maureen and asked her how her week had been. She embarked on a drawn-out story of how her shower had leaked into the lounge doing massive damage to the ceiling. Carole listened patiently and gratefully. Maureen was filling up the time until they got started, avoiding any kind of confrontation with Magda.

The rehearsal started with the 'Introit' and 'Kyrie'. *Requiem aeternam* – Grant them eternal rest. Carole found her eyes filling with tears and the world started to turn red. Could she control it? The men were singing the first part. Fortunately she didn't have to come in immediately. This gave her the opportunity to take herself in hand. A familiar shiver ran down her spine. She thought of Charlotte. She would help the child. She would give her the affection she wasn't getting from her mother. She would do something good to make up for the past. Everything she did for Charlotte would be a step towards reparation and forgiveness. That's what the Requiem was all about. The whole choir came in. '*Exaudi orationem meam* – Hear my prayer'. As she sang she thought about Charlotte. The unpleasant sensation retreated. A warm feeling of relaxation took its place.

It was soon time for the solo. She wasn't at her best but she had to get on with it. The combination of the past creeping up on her and the hostility of Magda in the present made it difficult for Carole to concentrate and sing well. She was aware of anger being directed towards her as she sang. She knew the 'Pie Jesu' so well by this time that she didn't make a mistake but she nevertheless felt that she hadn't sung as well as usual. As she sang Robert was watching her. His eyes were sending her messages telling her not to worry. Everything was going to be fine. This gave her a certain surge of confidence. She sat down feeling that she hadn't let herself down too badly.

At the break he asked her to go into Liverpool with him on Saturday. There was an Impressionist exhibition at the local art gallery and he suggested a meal in the evening. She agreed, glad to have something interesting to do at the weekend. Magda overheard him inviting her. Her face was black with resentment. Carole noticed and wondered why she was getting into these situations. There were now two people who resented what they perceived to be her good fortune. It was like reliving teenage years except that her teenage years had been far from a television soap. As they sang the rest of the Fauré she breathed deeply and raised herself to her full height. Maybe she was going back in time. She felt more like a teenager than she had when she was in her teens. It was a great feeling and all those jealous people would just have to put up with it!

They practised the carols again. The town centre performance was scheduled for Saturday 22nd December, just a few days before Christmas. Most of the choir had agreed to go so there would be a good turnout. They all hoped it wouldn't rain as there was no shelter. They would all get soaked. Carole tried the Teletext forecast. It was too far ahead to be certain but it didn't look too bad.

CHAPTER 9

Saturday 15ᵗʰ December

SATURDAY DAWNED SUNNY and fairly warm for December. Carole had phoned Jenny on Friday to tell her that she wouldn't be going to the restaurant. The weather was really bad and she wanted to stay at home. She invited her and the children round for tea on Sunday as she hadn't seen them for a while. She also felt a bit guilty that she was going to spend Christmas Day with people she didn't meet very often. Jenny and her children were hardly more than strangers but she had invited her so there was really no reason to feel guilty about it. She knew very well that for lots of people Christmas was something to get through, not a reason for celebration and she was one of them.

Robert picked her up and they went off to see the exhibition. The art gallery had a lot of paintings on loan. Many of them were scenes from the south of France. There were several pictures of the *Mont Sainte-Victoire* by Paul Cezanne. Carole liked his landscapes. They looked a bit like mosaics or a patchwork quilt. They were so very different from Monet and Van Gogh. She wasn't an expert when it came to paintings but she was happy to learn. Many of the paintings were familiar as the card shops were full of *Sunflowers* by Vincent Van Gogh and fields of poppies by Claude Monet to mention just a few. She hoped that she could go and visit the south of France one day and see where these artists had painted. She felt so lucky. She had so many interesting things to do and time to learn. She also now seemed to have a companion who knew so much and could help her and share the fun.

Robert preferred to spend time on each painting. Carole got really tired and confused so she chose one or two that she liked and concentrated on those. She had soon been round the whole display and she felt quite light-headed with exhaustion. Walking slowly round art galleries balancing on one foot then the other was as bad as walking up a mountain, worse in fact. Robert seemed to have endless energy when it came to paintings. She decided it was better to be herself and not try to make an impression.

'I'm tired, Robert. I'm going to the café. You take as long as you want. I don't mind.'

'Are you sure?' He seemed slightly anxious.

'Yes, I'm sure. Come and find me when you're ready.'

She went off and was soon sitting at a table with a coffee and a large piece of chocolate cake. She took a bite thinking that she wasn't a teenager after all. When she was young she would probably have followed Robert round until she was ready to drop. They were different people and there had to be a compromise. The piece of chocolate cake fitted the bill perfectly.

Robert finally gave up on the paintings and came to the café. They had lunch then did a bit of Christmas shopping. They went to look at the area where they would be singing the following Saturday. It was right in the town centre where a huge Christmas tree was stretching up into the grey sky. There was a Christmas market and a wonderful festive atmosphere. Hundreds of people were rushing around carrying parcels of all shapes and sizes. There would be no shelter for the choir next week so they both hoped it wouldn't rain. The weather forecast for the following week wasn't too bad but they both knew you couldn't rely on it. Things could change.

They wandered under the twinkling lights above their heads watching the various street singers. They stopped in front of an accordionist. He was singing 'Besame Mucho' while the vibrating notes of the accordion filled the air around him. He had an amazing tenor voice. Robert looked envious. 'We could do with him in the choir.' He chuckled. Then, out of the blue he said, 'Would you like to come and have a meal at my house? I haven't planned anything but we could get a takeaway if you don't mind.'

'Yes. Great! Thank you. I'd rather do that than go to a restaurant tonight. I'm really tired.'

They stopped at the local Indian restaurant and picked up a variety of dishes. Robert lived in a Victorian terraced house not dissimilar to Carole's. She was amazed to see that all the walls were covered in watercolour paintings. He noticed her eyes scanning the walls. 'A lot of the paintings belonged to my mother. She was a good artist. Some of them are mine. I inherited her interest but maybe not her talent.'

'Well, you can't be good at everything. Which ones are yours?'

He pointed out some landscapes that looked really good to Carole. There were also some beach scenes that looked as though they had been painted somewhere exotic. He had obviously been around more than she had. Once again she got the same old feeling of having missed out. She shook her head rather violently as though she was trying to get rid of an annoying fly. It wouldn't do, all this regretting things!

'You said you weren't much good. I think they're lovely, particularly that one.' She pointed out a forest with a path running through it. It was mysterious because you couldn't see where the path was going. It just disappeared into the trees. There were also flashes of sunlight glinting through the foliage. 'I like paintings that are ambiguous,' she remarked. 'Then you can walk into them and make them part of you. If everything is cut and dried and too precise it doesn't allow you in somehow. Do you know what I mean? I'm not explaining very well.'

Robert smiled and nodded. 'Of course I know what you mean. It's very nice of you to be so complimentary and I'm glad I've allowed you into my painting. Shall we eat now? Down to basics.' He grinned.

They spread the food out on the dining room table. Robert got two plates out and they had an informal help-yourself meal.

While they were eating Carole wrestled with the idea of telling him about Samantha and Charlotte. She would wait until the right moment came. It was time to stop making polite conversation and really get to know each other. Robert had started last time. Now it was going to be her turn. She was hungry but she tried to eat slowly. She was hardly concentrating on the food, waiting for an opportunity to talk about Samantha.

'How are you coping since your friend died? You were together so long. I suppose there were a lot of legal formalities, just when you could do without them. I remember it all too clearly!'

'Yes, there were some legal issues to sort out but most of it's over now. There are just one or two problems.' She took a deep breath and launched into the story of the standing order and Samantha and Charlotte.

Robert listened open-mouthed. He looked as though he was listening to a story on the radio but this was only too real. When she finished there was a silence. He was obviously processing the information and wondering what to say. Finally he broke the suspense. 'Just be very careful. You seem such a nice person. People can take advantage. She's obviously had a bad time but don't let her give you a bad time. Help by all means but don't let the situation escalate.'

Carole looked puzzled. 'How do you mean?'

'Well. You're just doing one day but she might try to increase it or ask you for money. Who knows! I'm perhaps a bit more cynical than you are about people. Disturbed people can end up hurting those trying to help them because their needs are endless, like a bottomless pit.'

'Yes. I expect you're right. I know people like that. If you don't get what you need as a child you can stay needy for the rest of your life.'

'Exactly, so be careful. Set the boundaries if you can and don't give her money!'

'OK. I'll be as strong as I can but it's not easy. Charlotte's so little and innocent. We've started to bond. It's a dangerous thing, bonding. Once it's done you can't undo it, can you?'

'No. I suppose not but I don't want anything nasty to happen to you.'

Carole felt warmth spreading inside her. Nobody had cared for her since her parents died and they hadn't cared that much. Paula had been more interested in administration than real friendship.

'Thank you,' she said, gratefully.

Robert had a beautiful baby grand piano which took up half the room. He played a Chopin 'Mazurka' for her then they watched some television. It was Saturday night and *Strictly Come Dancing* was on. The programme was coming from the Tower Ballroom in Blackpool. They both agreed that it was the best thing on offer. Carole was quite surprised. She hadn't imagined that he would like it. He sensed what she was thinking.

'I don't just like classical music,' he explained. 'I used to go dancing a long time ago. It brings back memories. I bet you can dance.'

Carole nodded. 'I used to dance, like you – in the past.'

Two glamorous people were dancing a waltz to 'The Blue Danube'. He took her hand and they started to dance in the rather limited space. It wasn't quite Blackpool but it felt adventurous. Instead of the trousers and jumper she imagined a ball dress made of chiffon with a multitude of sequins glittering in the lights. He swung her round rather too enthusiastically and she banged into the piano. It definitely wasn't the Tower Ballroom but then life was more about bumping into things and people rather than whirling round in a ballgown. That was for princesses in fairy tales. They came to a halt, unreasonably out of breath given the size of the space. They danced cheek to cheek. He held her tight against him. She knew he was going to kiss her and she wanted him to. He sensed her willingness. It was so natural and it raised their relationship onto a different level.

'I hope you didn't mind,' he said, quietly. 'I wouldn't do anything to hurt you.'

Carole put her arms round his neck and looked solemnly into his eyes. He looked a bit anxious, as though he might have somehow spoilt things.

'It's all right. Don't worry. It's a long time since anybody kissed me.' She stood on her tiptoes and kissed him, moving against him in a way she had never done before. His slight stubble brushed against her cheek and warmth flooded her whole body. She felt him responding. Christmas had arrived early.

***

Carole spent Sunday morning making cakes for Jenny and the children. When she bought the cake mix with the faces on, she had gone back and picked up another one. She knew James and Eva would enjoy the cakes too. She also made a jelly in a rabbit mould she found in the cupboard. The mould was made of metal and looked as though it had been there for a hundred years. She had to wash it first as it had never been used, as far as she remembered. She didn't know where it had come from but it was very welcome. She made a pile of sandwiches and put them on the kitchen table with the cakes, a fruit cake she had bought and a packet of sausage rolls that would need to go in the oven. She added cubes of cheese and the baby tomatoes she had bought for Charlotte. There were plenty left.

Jenny arrived promptly at three o'clock, flushed, her blond hair tangled by the wind. Carole had got out a collection of the toys that might interest the children but she didn't need to worry. They had a carrier bag each with lots of things to do. They rushed over to hug Carole. It made her feel warm inside like when Robert had kissed her but different. How much she wished they were her real grandchildren. They settled down to play, leaving the grown-ups time to talk.

They discussed Christmas Day and Carole offered to bring a cake and anything else Jenny wanted. It was all quietly arranged with the children playing happily at the table. It all looked so idyllic. Carole couldn't help comparing them with Charlotte. They were so different. Of course Eva was a year older than Charlotte and that was a long time in a child's life. James was six so there was no comparison. She told Jenny a bit about Charlotte without revealing any of the problems. What should she tell and what shouldn't she tell? She instinctively felt that there was a question of confidentiality so she kept quiet about the money and the drama with the cakes.

Eva started to get restless. Carole felt quite relieved. They weren't angels either, just children. She hadn't put the faces on the cakes. She knew James and Eva would love doing that. She took them into the kitchen and reopened the packet. All the parts fell out and the two of them started to make the faces. Jenny looked impressed. 'I can see you've been a teacher,' she laughed. 'They're really enjoying that.'

'Don't be too impressed, Jenny. I've got to get the rabbit out of the mould yet. I'm not sure how to do it.'

'Rabbit? Which rabbit?'

Carole pointed to the fridge by way of explanation and Jenny's eyes followed her finger.

'Oh. I see. That'll be interesting!'

'That might be the wrong word!'

The cakes were finished and it was time for the rabbit. The children watched as she took the mould out of the fridge. 'Now we've got to get the jelly out. How can we do that?' Carole asked them.

'Bump it up and down,' Eva suggested.

'Cut it out with a knife,' was James' suggestion.

Jenny laughed. 'That won't work,' she said. 'You need to put it in hot water. The outside'll melt a little bit then it should come out.'

Carole ran some hot water and put the mould into it, being careful not to get any in the jelly. She wanted it to be a perfect rabbit for the children. After a few minutes she reckoned it would

PATRICIA MORTON

have dissolved enough to come out in one piece. With a dramatic gesture she turned the mould over onto the plate. Four small eyes were transfixed, watching the silver-grey rabbit mould sitting on the plate. It looked almost like a real rabbit.

'Now count to five and I'll lift the mould up.'

They counted as though it was a voyage into space. 5, 4, 3, 2, 1. She lifted the mould and the rabbit fell onto the plate with an enormous slurp. It collapsed into a rather flat and sad-looking strawberry rabbit. Instead of being upset the children started laughing then Jenny started. Carole looked dismayed then she started laughing. It was the highlight of the afternoon.

It was close on six o'clock when they went home. They were having such a good time it was hard to go. It was also dark outside and the fire was pulling them in rather than encouraging them to depart. They had ended up playing games and dancing to the CD of children's action songs that Carole had bought. As they danced she was back in the classroom with her pupils. It was so real she almost gasped. Then she blinked and it was over. She was back in the present! It was sad in a way but they were happy memories. The present and the past could be merged into one after all. They hugged each other and said goodbye until Christmas Day.

CHAPTER 10

Thursday 20th December
Adventures in the Park

SAMANTHA RANG THE doorbell at nine-thirty precisely. Carole had only just got dressed. She had ended up with Charlotte on Tuesday as well. It wasn't that she minded but she couldn't help remembering what Robert had said about exploitation. Samantha had told Carole she wasn't well and needed to sleep so could she look after the child as a special favour. She might have negotiated and offered to do Tuesday instead of Thursday but she felt a bit mean. It was nearly Christmas and the season of goodwill. She wanted to put it into practice, not just sing about it.

Charlotte came in quite happily. There was no more screaming. She was already used to the situation. Tuesday had gone well with no more accidents. Carole hoped today would be the same. She had Samantha's mobile number but on Tuesday she had tried to ring her as she hadn't said what time she was coming for Charlotte. The phone was switched off. She had tried several times without success. When she had asked her about the phone she was again very evasive. She said rather furtively that her former boyfriend was hassling her so she left the phone off. She didn't want to speak to him.

She was halfway out of the door when Carole stopped her. 'Will you make sure your phone is switched on? I might need to call you if there is ever a problem. You just never know.'

'OK, I'll do that.' She almost ran out of the door.

Carole couldn't imagine what the real problem was. Surely a boyfriend could be told that she didn't want to see him. She had seen stories on the news about women who had been stalked by men over a long period and sometimes murdered but that was on the news. This was real life and wouldn't surely be like that.

Carole had some last-minute shopping to do. She was caught in a trap. She didn't want to take Charlotte out in case she reacted badly but she did want to get the last-minute shopping. They had spent all Tuesday in the house and the little girl had been quite happy but two days without any fresh air seemed wrong. She decided to take her to the park and run off some energy then go to the shops.

The park was just down the road so they got there quite quickly. She didn't have a pushchair but Charlotte was quite capable of walking. When they got there she seemed puzzled as though it was a new experience. She screamed when Carole tried to put her on a swing. She couldn't use the slide because she wouldn't go up the ladder. There was a metal horse with several seats. Two other children were already rocking backwards and forwards, helped by the parent of one or both of them. Charlotte stroked the horse's head and eventually she was persuaded to sit on a seat, held on by Carole.

She opened the gate of the playground, deciding that enough was enough for one day. She felt quite triumphant. At least she had persuaded Charlotte to go on the horse. Suddenly a duck flew out of the pond nearby. Carole had bent down to fasten her shoelace. It only took what seemed like a second but must have been longer. Charlotte had started to run towards some bushes, screaming with fright. She ran remarkably fast for a small child and before Carole could get to her feet she had disappeared into the bushes. At the other side there was a steep drop into the water. Carole's whole body froze as she ran faster than she had done since her twenties.

She shouted and soon several other people had gathered, wondering what was happening. Tears of terror were running down Carole's face. She was screaming the child's name and the other people started looking too. 'She might fall in the water,' Carole sobbed.

A man in a tracksuit made his way through the bushes. 'I'll stay near the edge,' he said calmly.

Carole thrashed her way through the shrubbery, unaware of the blood running down her face. The thorny bushes were exacting their own punishment. A stray branch knocked her glasses off and she barely had the time to pick them up. It was too late for regrets. In fact she didn't have the emotional energy to regret anything. She must find the child. Suddenly she heard the man's voice. He seemed to be talking to someone. 'Here she is. I've found her just in time. She was right on the edge of the drop.'

Carole followed the voice and emerged from the bushes, her face black with tears. Never, in all her years of teaching, had she ever been in such a dangerous situation. The man handed her over looking a bit concerned. 'I'd keep hold of her hand all the time if I were you,' he ventured kindly. 'Don't worry. You get nothing for nearly. Have a good Christmas.' He patted her gently on the shoulder.

She took hold of the child's hand and bent down to look her directly in the face. 'You must never run away like that again. I'll have to keep hold of your hand all the time now until I feel I can trust you. You might have hurt yourself or fallen in the water.'

Charlotte stared wordlessly at Carole with that same challenging expression that was becoming a familiar feature of their relationship. She tried to pull away but Carole had tight hold of her round her wrist. There was to be no escape. She was so upset by the whole thing she was tempted to go straight home and avoid the shops. However, she did have some things to get for Christmas and she didn't want Charlotte to get the impression that she had somehow won a battle.

They made their way to the nearby shopping centre and into the first café they came to. She gave Charlotte the choice of milk or orange juice. Making a small decision seemed to calm the child down. Carole could see her whole body relaxing. She drank a hot strong coffee and felt a bit better. It was an uphill battle but she would keep going and she decided not to tell Samantha what had happened. If she did she might decide not to leave Charlotte with her again. Robert would probably think that was for the best but she was determined to help the child. Charlotte didn't have the words to explain what had happened. In this case it was just as well. She could relax.

She cut the shopping down to the absolute minimum. Usually she would check prices and shop around to save money. On this occasion she simply threw the money at the nearest store, picked up the shopping and fled. She was so glad to open the front door and lock herself and the child safely inside.

She off took her coat and sat Charlotte on her knee. She didn't struggle like she sometimes did. Carole looked into her unfathomable blue eyes and smoothed her straggly hair down. 'Next time you get scared by one of those ducks don't run away. You might have got hurt. Come and hold my hand instead. Do you hear?'

Charlotte stared at her for a long time as though she was processing the information. 'Duck, duck,' she said anxiously, getting hold of Carole's hand. Suddenly she laid her head on Carole's shoulder.

The day passed quickly. She didn't need to phone Samantha. She was relieved about this because instinctively she felt that there was something odd about the situation. When the doorbell rang at six o' clock she was glad there were not going to be any further complications. She offered Samantha a hot drink, glad that Charlotte's vocabulary wouldn't allow her to explain what had happened in the park. The woman looked depressed and almost as lost as Charlotte had seemed in the playground. Her face was white and the black shadows under her eyes made her look sick and much older than she was.

'What are you doing for Christmas?' Carole asked her. It was a popular subject of conversation at that time of year.

She shrugged her shoulders. 'Nothing really.' She'd always seemed so hard and yet Carole could see the look of desolation that had spread across her face.

'Are you going to be on your own then with Charlotte?'

She nodded. 'My parents don't want us. They don't even send us a card.'

Carole was shocked into silence. She had to do something but what? She couldn't let Jenny down. She couldn't take Charlotte to Jenny's. That would leave Samantha alone on Christmas Day. She couldn't turn up with both of them, or could she? That was the only solution. She would have to ask Jenny if she could bring the two of them. The three children could play together. It might be fun. 'Look, Samantha. I'm going to spend Christmas with a friend and her two children. I could ask her if you could come with Charlotte if you would like. What do you think?'

Samantha looked mystified as though she must have some hidden ulterior motive.

'I'll phone her later and ask then let you know. Or you can ring me at seven o'clock. It has to be early. I'm going out to a choir rehearsal. '

She nodded. 'I'll ring.'

Carole thought this was predictable. Her phone would be switched off to avoid unwanted phone calls. Were they from this boyfriend or somebody else? Instinctively Carole thought it was the latter.

She said goodbye to them then immediately phoned Jenny and explained the situation. Jenny understood completely. She was on her own too and could empathise with Samantha. Of course she didn't know anything about the background to the situation but she didn't question it at all. She had accepted Carole so spontaneously and she trusted her. When Samantha rang at exactly seven o'clock she was able to tell her that she would be welcome at Jenny's but to bring a contribution towards the food. Carole felt she needed to tell her this, suspecting she wouldn't think about it. She didn't know how her mind worked but she knew she was completely self-centred. Life was getting more and more complicated.

She arrived at the rehearsal somewhat out of breath. They were going to have a final practice of the carols before their performance on Saturday. She sank down in her usual place ready to enjoy the carols and relax a bit. Robert was going to spend Christmas with his children. He hadn't invited her. In any case it was a bit too soon and he knew she was going to Jenny's. They were going to spend Saturday together singing in the town centre then doing something in the evening. They hadn't planned anything in particular. Their relationship had become a bit more relaxed lately. They were getting to feel at ease with each other.

At the break Carole found herself next to Magda. She felt awkward. The ex-soloist looked unhappy. She no longer strutted about organising people. She seemed to have retreated into her shell.

'Are you coming to the carol singing on Saturday?' she asked her.

Magda jumped as though she was surprised to be spoken to. 'I don't think so. Nobody's asked me.'

'Well, I don't think anybody's been asked personally. People have just volunteered to go. Do come. The more the merrier and it's a good cause!'

It was as though the tables had been turned. It should have been Magda making a list of who was going but she seemed to have opted out. It wasn't that long since she had been telling Carole that she hadn't paid her subscription in her rather strict teacher manner but Carole didn't bear grudges. Magda seemed so unhappy and it was time for some Christmas spirit. She didn't know where she got the energy from, after her experience in the park, but she gathered her courage together. 'Yes, do come. It won't be the same without you.'

Magda suddenly lit up like a Christmas light bulb. 'OK. I'll come and thank you for asking. You're the first person who's spoken to me for ages.'

Carole was aware that she had been missing for a bit so people hadn't had much chance to talk to her. In any case she wasn't very approachable in general but Magda seemingly hadn't thought of that. She was obviously going to stay hurt for a long time.

CHAPTER 11

Christmas Day

CAROLE LAY LOOKING at the flowered curtains. The sun was shining through them and it gave her the same pleasure as always. The curtains had always been there but they never seemed to lose their colour. The flowers were unfashionable but they looked like a spring meadow. She lay there imagining she was walking somewhere romantic then suddenly realised that life was romantic. It was Christmas Day and she was going to be with friends. They were young as well, which was good. She spent too much time with people her age. They all had the same outdated ideas about life. Things had changed and young people kept you up to date, or at least made you realise you had to upgrade yourself. She chuckled at the thought. She knew nothing about computers or mobile phones but seemed to manage very well without technology. Then again, she knew it was part of the modern world. It was just too hard keeping up to date or in her case getting up to date!

The carol concert in the town centre had gone very well. The rain had stayed off which was a blessing. The town centre was crowded with people. They all appeared to be in a good mood and consequently put lots of money into the box for the NSPCC. They had ended up with £250 and it had been such fun. Ian, the keyboard player had come along with an amplifier, a duffel coat and a Liverpool football scarf and hat. He'd obviously armed himself against the December cold. The accompaniment was really professional. His nose was a bit red but he beamed from under the woolly hat. It had all gone very well. At the end

Magda was talking to Valerie and Ruth and Ted. She seemed quite relaxed.

Valerie was in good spirits too. She had good news about Mark and could hardly wait to tell her friend. 'He's been offered a full time job at the music store. I think he was on probation. He's done so well they are really pleased. I suppose they have to be careful. I don't think you can get rid of people that easily now. Anyway he's thrilled. You'd be amazed at how different he is, Carole. Come round over Christmas and see us. I'll give you a ring.'

As she lay in her warm bed everything seemed so wonderful. The carol singing had finished at four o'clock. Robert had surprised her. She thought they were going to have another evening at home but he had booked a restaurant overlooking the river. She had gone home to get changed then he had picked her up. The restaurant was a Thai restaurant. It was quite exotic. She had been adventurous and chosen prawn spring rolls and fish with rice, decorated with interesting colourful vegetables and a rather hot sauce. They had sat opposite each other watching the candle flickering on their faces and the food. Outside on the river ships were gliding over the black water, their lights making glittering ripples, adding to the festive atmosphere. Carole held her breath, wondering if all this was just a dream. It was only weeks since she had stumbled through the gate, wondering if there was still a reason for living.

Afterwards they had gone back to her house for coffee. The heating was on but the fire was out. It didn't seem to matter. They listened to the radio and talked about the future. The Fauré concert would be there before they could blink and there were some other short pieces to practise. Robert seemed to see their future as a couple. He told her he was sorry they were not going to be together for Christmas. 'I'll miss you. I'd rather be with you but I can't let my children down and I know you've made other arrangements.'

'Don't worry. It'll soon be New Year and we can all get back to normal. Christmas is fun but so is ordinary life. At least it is for me now.'

He'd got up to go, looking as though he didn't want to. He moved slowly then kissed her. She ran her fingers through his beautiful curly hair, wondering how long it would be before he wanted more out of their relationship but she was happy with it as it was. Her brief affair with Michael was so long ago. This was gentle in comparison. It was different, a teenage romance for two pensioners. It was quite a funny concept but perhaps not reality these days. Teenagers were experimenting with sex early now. When she was that age she was just a child. They were probably more innocent than the kids they saw in groups in the street but she didn't mind. Life seemed full of promise but the future held more challenges than just romance. She didn't realise it but her elation would be short-lived. A storm was gathering.

Samantha had phoned and Carole was pleased to tell her she could come to Jenny's. Carole was going to have to drive there early to borrow a car seat. Samantha didn't have a car. She had arranged to take them to Jenny's at eleven-thirty, in time for pre-lunch drinks. She got up, drank a quick cup of tea then went out to the car. It was only just after nine but of course they would have been up for hours. When she got to Jenny's, the children greeted her with such excitement she couldn't rush straight off. She refused a Christmas sherry. She was driving and she hadn't even eaten breakfast. She did, however, spend time looking at the new toys.

'I'll be back for lunch and then I'll have a good look and we can play with them. I came straight out to get the car seat. I haven't had any breakfast yet!'

'You can have breakfast here,' Eva suggested with the straightforward logic of a four-year-old.

'My breakfast is on the table waiting for me so I'd better go. I'm coming back with Charlotte and her mummy. You can all have fun together then. I won't be long.'

'Who's Charlotte?' Eva asked, a bit puzzled.

'She's a friend of mine,' Carole explained. 'I'm bringing her and her mum with me later.'

Eva nodded. Life was so simple for her. Carole sighed and almost wished she was four again except when she thought of Charlotte and how vulnerable you are when you are little. Perhaps it was better to be sixty-one after all.

It wasn't long before she was back having a coffee and the breakfast that she hadn't had time for. Not that she needed much. They would be eating a big lunch, no doubt. She got dressed in a red woollen dress that she had bought quite recently from Joyce. They had become so friendly Joyce often saved things for Carole. It wasn't really allowed but Joyce felt that she gave so much of her time she had the right to do it. Anyway, the clothes could have been for her. Carole was so grateful and admired the older woman's generosity.

'I like to see people smile,' she ventured, her own smile lighting up her wrinkles. 'It's more blessed to give than to receive. Well, that's the Christian message, isn't it?'

Carole nodded. 'Yes, I'm sure you're right.'

Joyce was a bit like Eva. She was so uncomplicated. Carole had been tempted to retort that a lot of people she had met didn't seem to take much notice of Christian principles. They seemed to Carole to have double standards. Wisely she kept her mouth shut. Why try to disillusion someone so high minded? She'd probably never met anyone like Samantha.

The red dress looked really good. The belt was covered in small shiny buttons. It would have emphasised any rolls of fat but Carole was quite trim. The red ceramic necklace and earrings that Robert had bought her for Christmas really set it off. She thought briefly of the evening when she was scrabbling for the front door key in the dark and smiled inwardly. Life had moved on in a big way. She was such a lucky person and it had all begun with her meeting with Valerie. Bless her!

She ran to answer the door. Samantha was on time. She had only her handbag with her and Charlotte of course. The little girl ran straight inside without being asked. There was no sign of food or presents. Not that Carole was expecting anything for herself but she had said categorically to her that she should bring a contribution to the meal. Her exasperation must have shown on her face because Samantha started an explanation.

'I can't come with you. I've got really bad period pains. I…I only just made it to here. I'll have to go to bed instead. Don't worry about me. It sometimes happens. It'll be OK by tomorrow.'

Carole didn't know what to say. In her experience you took two paracetamol and got on with life. She looked more closely at Samantha. She was dressed up rather smartly for someone who was going to bed. She was wearing eye shadow and mascara and a brand-new woollen coat that hadn't been bought from any charity shop. Carole felt her tension draining away. It wasn't her business. She would take Charlotte to Jenny's and perhaps it would be better that way. A day spent with people who didn't know each other might be stressful. Perhaps that was why she was making excuses. Maybe she was scared and this was her way out.

'OK. I'm sorry you're not well. Have a rest but leave your phone on in case there's a problem.'

She felt as though she had switched herself on and was uttering some kind of automated message. She always said the same thing and like automated messages the person at the other end didn't reply.

Samantha disappeared as quickly as she had arrived. Carole assumed she was going home on the bus then she suddenly realised she didn't know where she lived. She resolved to ask her when she came to collect Charlotte. Judging by the expensive coat perhaps she lived in a posh house. Then again, if she was well off she wouldn't have been so resentful over Paula's money and she would have had a car. And why was her phone always switched off? There was something odd about that. It was time she got to the bottom of it. She closed the door and went into the lounge, nearly falling over Samson. Charlotte had gone upstairs and dragged him down step by step. Carole burst out laughing in spite of feeling a sense of anxiety. She could have fallen down the stairs but she hadn't. 'Nothing for nearly,' she said half to herself and half to Charlotte, who didn't hear. She was too busy jumping up and down on Samson's back. She had really started making herself at home and the thought filled Carole with the delicious warmth of a glass of good red wine. She was like the granddaughter she had never had.

At eleven-thirty, she gathered the presents together and put their coats on. She had made a Christmas cake and she got it out of the cupboard, staggering a little under the weight. Cookery wasn't her strong point. Maybe the heaviness was a bad sign. She had also made some small sponge cakes for the children. At least they looked fine! She had iced them and then let Charlotte add lots of sugar stars. The little girl was fascinated by the different colours. Several hadn't made their way onto the cakes, particularly the pink ones, but Carole had ignored that. It was Christmas and it was something to do to keep her happy.

She had a trauma putting Charlotte into the car seat. She looked as though she had never been in anything as terrifying as a car. She screamed when she realised she was going to be strapped into the seat.

'It's to keep you safe. If you fall out you could bump your head.'

It didn't work She squirmed and screamed so much that passers-by started to stop and stare. It was no good trying to reason with her. Carole was desperate. She could feel streams of panic rippling across her chest, turning her face as red as the winter sun that she would normally have admired through the black branches of the trees. She had visions of the police arriving, thinking the child was being abducted. She suddenly thought of the chocolate teddies she had in a carrier bag. Reasoning had failed. She would have to try bribery.

'If you stop crying and let me fasten the strap I'll give you two chocolate teddies to eat on the way to Jenny's.' She took the teddies out of the bag. 'Look, you can choose which ones you want. There's a red one with a hat on. He looks nice. And there's a girl one carrying a star. Which ones would you like?'

As if by magic Charlotte stopped crying and concentrated on choosing the teddies while Carole fastened the seat belt. She felt a bit as if she had dropped down from her high principles by resorting to bribery. She shrugged her shoulders. Of course that's how mothers and others got through the day. It wasn't straightforward managing children. Sometimes you had to take short cuts. Thanks to the teddies, the onlookers had dispersed, probably disappointed that the interesting drama was over. She dumped the stuff onto the front seat, well away from Charlotte, and started the engine.

When she arrived at Jenny's James and Eva were at the window. They started jumping up and down when they saw the car stop. They looked as though they were bouncing on a trampoline. She didn't need to ring the bell. Jenny was at the door with the two excited children just behind her. The smell of roast turkey drifted through the air and made Carole feel hungry. She hadn't eaten much breakfast. The conversation with Samantha had somehow taken her appetite away but now, in happier circumstances, it had come back

'Where's Charlotte's mum?' Jenny asked, looking into the space behind the child as though expecting to conjure her up from out of the frosty air.

'She's not coming. She's not very well,' Carole replied cryptically. 'She's gone back to bed. She's got some sort of bug.'

It was a white lie but Carole didn't believe the truth either. *Period pains!* Surely you didn't let a thing like that spoil Christmas. And Charlotte? How would she feel without her mum on Christmas Day? Strangely she didn't seem bothered. She was too busy touching all the decorations on the tree one by one with a tiny pink varnished fingernail.

Eva came up to Carole and grabbed her by the hand. 'Come and see my new doll,' she insisted, dragging her along like an enormous sack of coal. 'She's got hair you can dye and high heels.'

Carole tried to sound enthusiastic but found it difficult. Girls didn't look like that. Eva's dolls always looked as though they were off to a party. Life was about wearing jeans and getting messy, not living in glittery tee shirts and pink high heels.

'She's lovely,' she gushed half-heartedly. 'But she won't be able to do housework or gardening or walk in those shoes, will she?'

Eva looked at Carole, astonished, as though she had come from another planet. 'She doesn't do things like that.'

'Well, what does she do?' Carole asked, picking up the long-legged doll with the tiny waist and hair nearly down to her ankles.

'You comb her hair and dress her. Look, I've got all these clothes and shoes. She's got three handbags and a horse.'

Carole thought handbags and a horse didn't go together but she didn't say so.

'What does she wear when she rides her horse?'

'Pink trousers and her glittery T-shirt.'

'What about her shoes? She can't ride in high heels, can she?'

'She's got boots. Look!' Eva held up a pair of white cowboy boots with gold bows. She looked quite triumphant as though she had won a round at a verbal boxing match.

Carole laughed, defeated. She was rather pleased that the doll had proper boots and would be able to go riding. 'Come and see what I've got in my carrier bag.'

All three of the children converged on Carole as she opened the bag and got out some presents. She gave them out and soon the floor was covered in paper and ribbon. The three little faces were brimming with excitement. The toys were only small but carefully chosen. Eva had a kitchen set for Poppy and her new friend. Carole was determined to show her that her new doll could be useful as well as glamorous. She suddenly felt guilty for being old-fashioned. Eva really loved her glamour dolls. She had been tempted to buy a doctor's set but she couldn't find one. She knew Eva would be happier with the tiny cakes, vegetables and pots and pans. At least the new addition would be doing something useful. She wasn't quite ready for a medical degree.

James had a Lego set and Charlotte had a cookery set with a variety of pretend food. Carole reckoned it would give her lots of play and vocabulary. She didn't know the names of many vegetables or fruit. She and Jenny exchanged boxes of chocolates with a laugh. They were almost identical. Carole gave her the cakes, hoping the Christmas cake would be acceptable even if it was heavy.

Jenny seemed to have everything ready so Carole wasn't needed. She had volunteered to help but Jenny was ready with glasses of sherry for the grown-ups and soft drinks for the children. They had soon finished and were off playing. Carole and Jenny relaxed and chatted. Carole was curious to see what Charlotte would do. She had only seen her on her own, not with other children. It would be interesting to see how she coped.

James was engrossed in building a large spaceship from a page of instructions. He didn't want to be disturbed. Eva started playing with the dolls' food. She had a big cardboard box which had been turned into a house. Charlotte watched then wandered off after a few minutes. Jenny gave her some paper and crayons. She sat at the table for a few minutes then knocked all the pencils off onto the floor. It was like an action replay on the television. It wasn't an accident although Jenny thought it was and generously picked everything up.

The only thing that Jenny hadn't done was set the table. Carole offered to do it and asked Charlotte to help. The child put the crackers by the plates then disappeared, leaving Carole to do the rest. She had only been gone for two minutes when there was a yell from the lounge. James came running into the dining room howling with tearful rage.

'She's wrecked my spaceship. I'll have to start all over again. Why did she have to come?' he sobbed. 'She's spoilt everything.'

Charlotte was behind him. She should have been upset by what he said but she seemed curiously calm and her blue eyes glittered mysteriously with a look of something verging on triumph. All attention was focused on her. She braced herself for the slap which didn't come. Sometimes she seemed like an alien.

Jenny put her arms round James 'We'll all rebuild it together after lunch. Was it an accident?'

'No, it wasn't,' Eva retorted indignantly, holding her new doll protectively close to her chest. 'She picked it up and threw it on the floor,' she shouted rather too loudly, pointing her finger accusingly at Charlotte who seemed to be enjoying the drama.

Carole took her by the hand and led her through to where the ruined spaceship lay on the carpet. 'Look what you've done. We are all upset for James and you've spoilt his spaceship. Now say sorry to him.'

Charlotte didn't say anything. She was pulling away from Carole but unsuccessfully. Carole had tight hold of her hand. Charlotte screamed and screamed until she was exhausted. Finally she gave in and collapsed on the carpet. Carole sat her on her knee and put her arms round her. The drama was over but in some ways the child had got what she wanted – to be the centre of attention. And she hadn't said sorry.

Jenny looked concerned. 'She's got some growing up to do, hasn't she?'

Carole nodded. 'I'm sorry, Jenny. I didn't expect this. I suppose I should have guessed. She doesn't seem to be used to other children. She doesn't play very well either so it's difficult.'

Carole had explained a bit of Charlotte's background to Jenny but didn't want to elaborate too much. She would have to watch her closely for the rest of the time. She couldn't afford any more bad behaviour or the whole of Jenny's Christmas Day would be spoilt. She was glad, however, that Samantha hadn't come. It might have been even worse if she had. The child would have been smarting with several hard slaps by now. At least Carole was in charge of her. There was no ambiguity. She would keep things positive from now on so that she would have something good to report to Samantha when she picked her up. It would be awful to have to tell her that Charlotte had behaved really badly and the day had been a disaster.

Lunch went down well. Charlotte needed a lot of help but managed. The crackers were pulled and the little toys were shared out without any further problems. Everybody had a paper hat to put on while they ate some trifle. Eva ended up with all the toys as they were so small and only suitable for her doll. There was a minute set of keys for an invisible car, a mini clock, a tiny tool set, glasses, a magnifying glass and a tiny book. Carole was delighted with the tool set and the magnifying glass. Poppy number two or whatever her name was would have a new image. She could be a car mechanic or a modern Sherlock Holmes.

In the afternoon, they all helped with the rebuilding of the space ship. It had been nearly finished so they got it back to where it had been when Charlotte threw it then James did the rest. At least he was happy but he was old enough to have a longer memory than the others. He hadn't forgiven Charlotte and remained wary of her for the rest of the afternoon. Once the space ship was finished and installed on a high shelf out of the way they played Pass the Parcel. Everybody won something, much to Carole's relief. These games were supposed to be fun but could end up causing something resembling the Third World War. In this case everybody was happy, even Charlotte, who was busy munching a Christmas tree decoration, drowned in a sea of newspaper and red Christmas paper. This was followed by Musical Bumps and Statues.

Jenny had done her homework and recorded some fairy tales and several cartoons suitable for all three of them. They all settled down to watch. Carole couldn't leave Charlotte but she seemed happy. Maybe she was used to watching the television as she seemed perfectly at home in front of the screen. At five o'clock, Jenny served sandwiches and Carole's sponge cakes. They cut the Christmas cake and ate a large slice each with mugs of tea. Jenny was very impressed. The cake was a success, not a heavy disaster after all.

Carole and Charlotte helped Jenny to fill the dishwasher. She was determined not to leave her on her own with Eva and James. The child was quite happy doing something practical and it was obviously good for her to feel useful. Carole found it hard to build Charlotte's self-confidence when she was so difficult. She needed to say 'good girl' but often she was a bad girl!

At six o'clock she packed Charlotte into the car and fastened her in. She was tired and didn't make a fuss. She didn't ask for any chocolate teddies thankfully. Carole didn't want to give her

the impression that the teddies were part of the deal. She thanked
Jenny and promised to invite her round for a similar afternoon in
the near future. She couldn't help wondering if Jenny was pleased
to see them go. She wouldn't blame her! Samantha was due at
six-thirty. Carole planned what she was going to do that evening
when Charlotte had gone. She decided that she was so tired and
drained the best thing to do would be to watch a good film on
the television if she could find one. Surely on Christmas night
there would be something interesting to watch. Never mind the
calories, she would open Jenny's chocolates and have some fun.
She deserved it after all the traumas of Christmas Day.

Charlotte helped Carole to make the fire. She screwed up
the paper and then put the kindling on top. They both piled the
pieces of coal on top of the wood. and paper, ignoring the mess
they were getting into. She talked to her all the time about what
she was doing but the child still didn't say much.

'Wood gone,' she said suddenly, her secretive blue eyes
suddenly serious.

'Yes, it's all on the fire. Now I'll put some more coal on then
we can light it.'

Carole struck the match and the flames licked round the coal.
It made such a difference to the room. She put the matchbox
on a high bookshelf then they both went off to wash their coal-
covered hands. Charlotte looked thoughtfully at the water as it
turned from transparent to black. Carole watched it with a new
level of interest, seeing it in a different way.

'Thank you for helping me. It'll soon be nice and warm.' They
went back into the lounge.

Charlotte's unfathomable eyes were filled with firelight.
She stared thoughtfully at the reddening coals as they both sat
together on the red woollen rug. She suddenly lay back using
Samson as a pillow, stretching her short legs out in front of the
fire. They had left him downstairs when they went out. Her eyes
were closing and it made Carole realise that it was getting late.
She had been so busy with the fire the time had flown. It was
seven o'clock. Samantha was half an hour late.

Charlotte was fast asleep on the rug. Her bedraggled blond hair was spread out over the teddy and the two of them looked the picture of contentment. The time was passing more quickly than usual. At half past seven, Carole dialled the mobile number then redialled. Robert's words were echoing through her mind. Her hand was shaking so much she thought she might have made a mistake. The phone was switched off. She paced up and down the room. Part of her couldn't believe what was happening. She couldn't ring the police. If she did Samantha was bound to arrive and she would look silly. The chocolates and the *Radio Times* lay neglected on the sofa. So much for her relaxing evening in front of the TV! She felt her stomach and chest tightening up with anger as the minutes turned into an hour. She saw Robert's face warning her. He had been right.

Paula's ancient clock struck nine, echoing through the house like a warning bell. Carole waited until it had finished striking. As silence returned she sprung into action. She covered Charlotte with a blanket then rang a surprised Jenny and told her what had happened.

'Jenny, what should I do? I'm new to this kind of thing. I don't want to start a melodrama but I can't leave her on the floor all night, can I? If I phone the police they'll probably take her into care then her mum will arrive.'

Jenny sounded bemused. 'I thought she had a bug. She said she was going home to bed, didn't she? She might be really ill.'

Carole nodded then remembered she was talking on the phone! She brushed a hand across her forehead, realising it was wet.

'She was all dressed up. I thought there was something funny about it. You don't get made up and dressed up if you're going straight home to bed do you? Unless you're one of the people who wouldn't ever be seen without make-up. Samantha has never looked that posh. Well, she did this morning. That's what made me think she was going somewhere. I suppose I don't really know her at all.'

'Look, Carole. The best thing to do is put Charlotte to bed and see what tomorrow brings. It's too late to do much else. Have you got a small towel? Make it into a nappy in case she wets the bed. Put a plastic sheet over the mattress if you have one. Undress her and she can sleep in her vest and pants.'

'OK, Jenny. You're right. I'll do that and see what happens tomorrow. I really can't believe this is happening to me!'

'No. It's not fair on you. You did her a favour.'

'I know. You go to bed and don't worry. I'll have to phone the police tomorrow if she doesn't turn up.'

'Well, keep in touch. I'll help if I can.'

Carole started to look for a suitable towel. The enormity of what was happening to her began to sink in. She grabbed the offending plastic tablecloth off the table. It would make a good mattress protector. She hated it anyway so that was one problem solved. She got one of the spare beds ready then woke Charlotte. She was so fast asleep she had to half carry her upstairs. She had no idea how to put a nappy on a child. She had no big safety pins so she wrapped it round her and put her knickers back on to keep it in place. It was hardly a work of art but it would have to do. She tucked her in then decided to sleep in the other bed. The child might wake in the night and be scared.

She usually had a bath or shower at night but she just didn't have the energy so she brushed her teeth and lay down, leaving the landing light on. She lay awake in the semi darkness feeling totally bewildered. Robert wasn't due back until the 27th. She wished he was coming back tomorrow. He would know what to do. Then again he would probably say 'I told you so'. He had warned her about Samantha. Outside car doors slammed, people chatted as they walked along past her house. She pulled the duvet up until it nearly covered her head. She wanted to shut the whole world out but she couldn't. The outside world had clashed with her world like two meteorites colliding in space. The result was asleep in the next bed.

CHAPTER 12

The Clashing of Two Worlds

IT WAS SIX am. Outside there was nothing but a dense blackness. Carole had finally got to sleep at about three o'clock. There was movement in the other bed. The unfamiliar noise woke her from a deep sleep and it all came flooding back like a dam bursting. She let out a silent groan and rubbed her eyes. Three hours' sleep wasn't enough. The movement in the next bed increased, accompanied by little animal noises that rapidly turned into a panicky wail. Carole leapt up to calm the child.

Two wide eyes looked out over the duvet. Her tangled blond hair was spread out over the pillow like a spider's web. Feeling Carole's warm hand in hers stopped the cry but didn't remove the little frown from her forehead.

'Mummy? Where Mummy?'

'I don't know. She'll be back soon. Samson and I will look after you.'

She looked around the room, her eyes searching for the teddy.

'Shall I go and get him for you?'

Charlotte nodded. Carole ran next door and grabbed the big bear. She smiled as she remembered him falling out of the bag. He was a real piece of good luck.

'Do you want the toilet?'

Carole stripped the duvet off. The sheet was soaking wet. Charlotte looked down at the wet mark then calmly took her knickers off with the towel and left the soggy mound on the floor.

'Thank you, you horrible plastic cloth,' Carole muttered to herself. At least it had saved the mattress. Charlotte would have to wear her tights without knickers until Carole managed to get some more.

She dressed Charlotte in the only clothes she had. Her vest was wet too so she added it to the pile of wet clothes and sheets. They had breakfast then Carole let the child watch the television while she had a think. Charlotte was perfectly happy sitting on the couch with Samson. She needed clothes. Jenny would help. She picked up the phone.

Jenny arrived an hour later carrying a large bag full of clothes and other items. She was followed in by an excited Eva and a still wary James.

'I've brought enough clothes for a month.' She laughed. 'Eva's grown out of a lot of things. I don't know why I kept them but it's a good job I did. I've brought some toys as well.'

'Thank heavens you were there. She's got nothing to wear; only what she had on yesterday.'

'What are you going to do?' Jenny's expression had changed from giddy schoolgirl to someone more serious.

Carole shook her head. 'I don't know, Jenny. I'll have to give it another day. What would you do?'

'I'd have gone to the police by now. Mind you, I can't imagine anyone leaving a child just like that. I've never heard of anything like it. Weird!'

'I'll wait till tomorrow. I don't want to do anything too dramatic. Samantha might turn up today. I need to wait a bit. It's fun having a child in the house. It's so different. I just think she might walk in any minute.'

'You're not thinking of keeping her, are you?'

'Of course not! Anyway, I wouldn't be allowed. I just enjoy being with her. It makes me feel useful.'

'Oh, Carole! You should be enjoying yourself. Little kids are hard work. I know all about that I can tell you!'

Jenny had arranged to meet a friend in the town centre so she didn't stay too long but promised to phone in the next few days. Carole and Charlotte had a lovely day doing jigsaws, painting and playing with the toys that she found in Jenny's bag. They went to the park in the afternoon. Strangely, Charlotte seemed totally at home. She kept a sharp eye on the little girl, wary after the way she had behaved at times, but there was no running away and no breakages. The day passed happily for both of them. They were so busy neither of them gave a thought to Samantha.

Jenny had thought of everything. Carole found a pair of pyjamas and even nappies and plastic pants. When Charlotte got into bed, she looked as though she had suddenly remembered who she was.

'Mummy,' she whispered, puzzled. 'Where's Mummy?'

It was the first real sentence that she had put together. With a jolt Carole came back to earth. Her lovely day of role playing suddenly fell flat. She didn't know what to say.

'Mummy will be back soon,' she asserted more confidently than she felt.

The little girl looked as though she was about to burst into tears. Carole gave her the tiny teddy from off the Christmas tree but Charlotte lay rigid in the flowery fluffy pyjamas, her lip trembling. She put out her hand and Carole's heart melted as she grasped the little hand. Charlotte wasn't going to settle easily.

'Look, Charlotte. I'll push the beds together then you can hold my hand if you're scared. Would you like that?'

She nodded so that's what Carole did. The bed was on casters so it wasn't too difficult. Once they were in place next to each other, she lay down on the bed. There was no way Charlotte was going to stay on her own in the dark room. She lay in the semi-darkness stroking her head to calm her. Suddenly a little hand came out of the bed and took hold of hers. A flood of mixed emotion almost drowned her. She would have to imprint this moment on her memory and yet she almost wished it had never happened. You can't go back like Doctor Who. Suddenly the hand started shrinking until it was just a tiny hand gripping her finger. A raw grief filled her head and cold rippled through her. Then the whole room turned red. She tore her hand away from Charlotte as though she had been burnt. Nothing happened. She was fast asleep in the scarlet sunset of Carole's regrets.

It was two days after Christmas, 27ᵗʰ December. The phone rang at nine o'clock. It was Robert. He was back as he had promised and wanted to come round. He arrived at ten-thirty. She hadn't told him about Charlotte. It was too difficult over the phone. He breezed in with a bunch of flowers and a handful of new CDs he had got for Christmas. He walked into the lounge and fell over a pile of wooden blocks and Samson sprawled across the rug. He looked from Charlotte to Carole then back again, wondering if he could possibly be in the right house.

'What's going on?' he asked, bewildered.

'Let's go in the kitchen and I'll tell you what's happened. I couldn't say anything over the phone.'

She told him the whole story over a cup of coffee. He didn't say anything, just listened until finally she stopped. She noticed the sharp contrast between the happily playing child and his bewildered face. A deep frown had formed between his eyes. 'Do you realise how serious this is? You should have contacted the police straight away. Suppose the mother's had an accident in the house. She might have fallen. She might even be dead.'

He had turned the situation on its head. Carole gasped. She hadn't considered any of that. She suddenly visualised Samantha lying injured or dead in her house, waiting for help that never came. The pleasure she had felt at seeing him had turned into anxiety. 'Robert, I didn't think of that. You see, she was so dressed up I thought it was very odd. You don't get dressed up to go to bed. It just seemed strange. I suppose I remembered what you'd said about her exploiting me. It was in the back of my mind. I assumed that was what she was doing, taking advantage.'

'You know you've got to phone the police. I don't know what they'll say when they know you've kept her since Christmas Day.'

'Well, I can't go back. I'll just have to phone now, I suppose.'

Robert's forehead contracted into a puzzled frown. 'You sound as though you don't want to. You can't just keep a child, you know. She'll have family somewhere.'

'She hasn't got anybody but I know I can't keep her.'

'Go and do it then you'll feel better.'

The phone felt like a heavy rock. She didn't want to dial 999. It seemed too urgent, too final. They would come and take Charlotte away in a police car. She'd be crying and the house would be empty again. She tried the local police station, got through and explained what had happened. The lady on the other end took all the details. She could almost see the whole thing going down on paper, reduced to a collection of words. When she went back into the kitchen, Charlotte was sitting on Robert's knee. He looked rather pleased like Father Christmas doing a good job. It was strange that she had attached herself so easily to a stranger.

'Well, how did you get on?'

Carole heated her coffee up in a pan, regretting again that she didn't have a microwave. 'Someone's coming round this afternoon.'

'Oh! I thought we might go out somewhere. Of course I didn't know you had an unexpected visitor. Do you want me to stay? You don't know what they'll do about all this.'

'Would you? I'm not looking forward to it. I'll make us some lunch.'

They seemed like a married couple with their first child. Or were they grandparents? It was as though time was getting confused. Suddenly Charlotte jumped down off Robert's knee.

Carole laughed. 'She's like a little car, filling herself up with attention instead of petrol.'

She went back to play, dragging Samson after her.

'There's a New Year's Day party at the U3A on Tuesday. I've got a ticket. I was hoping you'd come with me. I know they've had a few cancellations. Some people from the keyboard group are playing and there'll be some nice food.'

'What am I going to do with Charlotte?'

'They'll probably have taken her into care by then,' he replied, practically. 'They might even take her this afternoon.'

Carole stopped halfway through cutting a slice of bread. 'Surely they won't do that. They have to think of the child.'

'That's what they'll be doing, thinking about child protection. They don't know who we are, only that you've been left with a child. We could be child traffickers or abusers.'

Suddenly Robert made the whole situation seem different. Why hadn't she thought of these things? Another frightening thought came into her mind. She realised she was very fond of Robert, maybe more than just fond of him. She knew she didn't want to lose him. He wouldn't want the sort of complication she was getting herself into. There was no room in his world for a child. She might have to choose between them. Then again she might not have the choice. The three of them sat down and ate some lunch.

When the doorbell rang Charlotte was having a sleep.

'I'm Police Constable Wood, John Wood,' he informed her, 'and this is Police Constable Annette Baker. Can we come in?'

They both looked around then sat down. They were both young enough to be their son and daughter. The man was older and gave the impression of being in charge. He started the conversation while the woman kept looking around.

'You must have had quite a difficult Christmas,' he started, sympathetically. 'Incidentally, where is the child?'

'She's having a sleep.'

Carole poured out the whole story up to Christmas Day. It was at this point that she got into difficulties. The young policewoman just listened. Constable Wood started probing.

'Why didn't you call the police on Christmas Night when the mother didn't come back?'

It was exactly as Robert had predicted. He made her feel as though she had been irresponsible beyond belief. When she admitted she didn't even know where Samantha lived, Constable John Wood's eyebrows shot up in amazement.

'She might have had an accident, might need an ambulance. Didn't you think of that?'

Carole felt herself blushing with shame. All her good intentions had suddenly been reversed to make her look culpable. She'd come to the conclusion that Samantha was going out on the town in her glamour clothes but maybe it was the wrong conclusion. She looked down at her shoes like she used to do when she was a child in trouble. Then a hot surge of anger hit her like an electric shock. She stared pointedly at the interrogator. 'She was dressed up to go out. She went somewhere and didn't come back for Charlotte. I waited to see if she would turn up. I think she had it all planned. That's what I think so don't start blaming me. Go and look for Samantha.' She felt better for not letting him walk all over her.

'There's no need to get upset. It's a difficult situation all round. I'll have to find out where she lives and contact the social services. Meanwhile, we need to see the child then we'll leave her here until arrangements can be made. There may be a problem finding a foster family at short notice but that's not my department. Could you take Annette to have a look at the child? We need to know she's OK then we'll leave you in peace for now.'

'For now' had a menacing ring about it but the use of the woman's first name made things seem a little less formal. Carole took her upstairs to the spare bedroom. Charlotte was just waking up. She looked very relaxed.

'Don't let John upset you. He's only doing his job. I'm sure it'll all get sorted out in the end. These things usually do. It's a pity we don't know where they live. We could go and check that she's not in the house in need of help.'

Carole nodded miserably. If only she had the address she would be able to sleep that night. She knew very well that she would spend half the night imagining all kinds of terrible things like living a horror film. She'd been having such a lovely time with Charlotte almost like playing games with dolls. She hadn't considered anything else. She was sixty-one and behaving like a child herself. Tension screwed her up until all her nerves were taut. She wanted to run out into the street and find the house, but how? Even if she found it she wouldn't be able to get in.

Charlotte rubbed her eyes and wriggled out of the bed, holding the miniature version of Samson. She stared at the policewoman then put her arms out for Carole to pick her up. They all went downstairs and she sat on Carole's knee, staring from one of the officers to the other and back, pushing her straggly hair away from her face. Annette went up and tried to talk to her but she buried her face in Carole's jumper, clutching the tiny teddy to her as though she thought he was going to be stolen.

'Do you want to stay here with Carole?' she asked.

Charlotte gave a tiny nod.

'Well, she seems happy enough for now,' Annette said, patting the little girl on the head then turning to look at John.

He nodded. 'She's obviously OK so we'll make some enquiries and come back probably tomorrow. You know she'll have to be fostered, don't you?'

'You mean she has to go to strangers?'

'Yes. I'm afraid so. You see you're not a relative. You'll need a CRB check. That's a police check to make sure you haven't got a criminal record. Without that, we couldn't leave her with you for any length of time. We might have to leave her with you for a few days. It'll be up to the social services. That's their job.'

Carole couldn't believe what she was hearing. 'You make me sound like a criminal! All I've done is look after her for two days.'

Police Constable Wood shook his head. 'You can't imagine the things that go on. This is just one case. We're dealing with missing people and children at risk all the time. That's why there are rules. We have to be objective or we couldn't do the job. It's not up to us to make judgements about you as a person. You've got to understand that.'

Carole nodded, suddenly seeing the bigger picture. Her little world was expanding more and more.

After the police had gone, Robert and Carole sat down in the lounge to discuss what could be done. They were both shaken by their journey into unknown territory. Robert was somewhat philosophical about it all but Carole's imagination was working overtime. She kept imagining Samantha lying dead or injured in a house out there with nobody to help. She wondered why on earth she hadn't asked her for her address. She thought of all those little houses as though she was a bird up in the air and looking down. One of them was Samantha's.

Robert took one look at Carole's face and knew what was going on inside her.

'Carole, you'll just have to let the police do their job. You made a mistake not phoning straight away but you had the best of intentions so stop beating yourself up. Look, I've got to go to the bank and get some shopping. I've got nothing to eat in the house. I'll get a takeaway for us and come back round seven. If you'd like, that is.'

'Of course I would. I'm so glad to have you back. All this is too much for one person. It'll be nice to have some fun. I'll get Charlotte into bed then we can have the evening together.'

Robert laughed rather despondently. 'Like a couple of young parents! You know it takes nine months to have a baby. We've got one early. We haven't even known each other that long!'

'I'm glad you can laugh about it. I really want life to get back to normal. But I do enjoy looking after Charlotte.'

'Yes, but not permanently. From time to time, yes. I'll see you at seven with the takeaway.'

When he had gone Carole sat down, anxiety gnawing at every part of her body. How was she going to sleep? Suddenly an idea came into her mind. Samantha had left her a message before all this had started. She hadn't noticed if there was an address. It hadn't seemed important at the time. But where on earth had she put the letter? She had probably put it in the bin. If she had it would be well gone now. Charlotte was happily bouncing on Samson. In fact this was her favourite activity. Carole started going through all the drawers in the sideboard with no success. Her heart sank. She had thrown it out.

She tried to think where she was when she read the letter. She realised she had opened it in the hall. She retraced her steps. There was an ancient glass and wrought iron telephone table in the narrow hall, purchased by Paula when they had first got a telephone. It had a shelf underneath where the directories were lying, covered in dust. She picked them up, wondering if

Samantha's name would be in the phone book then cursed her stupidity. She only had the wretched mobile that was always switched off. She was just about to replace the phone books when she noticed an envelope. It must have been next to the phone and somehow slipped down the back onto the shelf below. It was her letter.

She grabbed it then dropped it in her impatience to get at it. Her fingers were stiff and awkward. She fumbled with the envelope then pulled out the sheet of paper. At the top was a tiny label with Samantha's name and address. Carole's stomach turned over. This is what the police would be looking for but even if she gave it to them they wouldn't go today. Things didn't work that quickly. She dreaded the night. She was upset enough already. She just couldn't go the whole night without knowing that Samantha wasn't somewhere in that house in need of help. She pulled their coats on then strapped Charlotte into the car seat. It was an Anfield address. She knew the area. She and Paula had both taught in a primary school there. It was familiar territory although she didn't know precisely where the road was. She found it on the A to Z map.

She turned into the road with a sense of trepidation. Once again she should have phoned the police but this time it was her self-preservation that was at stake. Her anxiety level was at boiling point. She checked the number on the letter even though she knew it was number 11 and stopped the car outside the house. It was a well- kept council estate although number 11 looked somewhat neglected. The lawn was a tangle of weeds and hadn't been cut for a long time. The hedge bushed out onto the pavement, making it far narrower than elsewhere. She took Charlotte out of the seat and pushed open the rotten gate which was hanging off its hinges. The whole place needed a makeover.

They walked up the moss covered path. Carole looked through the window, feeling like a potential burglar. There were no net curtains. With relief, she saw that the lounge was empty. But what about the rest of the house? She had to know. She prowled round the back, hoping to get a view of the kitchen. As she approached the back door a voice shouted, 'Hi. Can I help you?'

Carole jumped, feeling like a burglar, then looked over the low fence where a girl of about twenty-four was staring at her with curiosity.

'I'm looking for Samantha. She left Charlotte with me and she hasn't come back. The police are going to take her into care if they don't find her mum. Do you know where she is?'

'No. I haven't a clue but I do have a key. I don't suppose she's left an address but why not look. Poor little Charlotte! I hope she turns up soon.'

'Could you bring the key round and come in with me? I don't feel I should be going in on my own.'

'OK. I'll just get the key and the baby. I'll be round in a minute. By the way, I'm Tina.'

'Pleased to meet you. I'm Carole. Thanks. I'm out of my mind worrying about it all.'

Tina came round and opened the door. The house had a dank, airless smell as though it had been locked up for a long time. Carole shuddered. It needed a good clean unless… She stopped herself from thinking the worst. They went into the lounge and she stopped dead in her tracks. There was an enormous flat-screened television that filled almost half the room. Underneath it there was an expensive hi-fi and video recorder. The sofa was brand-new and made of the softest leather. A laptop lay open on the glass topped coffee table. The whole room could have been a picture cut out of a glossy magazine.

They went round the rest of the house. There was no sign of Samantha and no address or message. The main bedroom looked new as well. A wardrobe door hung open as though someone had left in a hurry. Inside it was stuffed with clothes and shoes.

Tina shrugged her shoulders. 'She's probably run away to escape the debt collectors.'

'The what?' Carole was out of her depth.

'Well, look at all this stuff. Where would she get the money to pay for it all? She's not working as far as I know. I don't know her very well but she was always around. She's not been here very long. She only moved in in September. She said something about moving nearer to her mother. I bet she put all this stuff on cards.'

Something clicked inside Carole's head. 'Would the companies try to contact her on her mobile?'

Tina nodded. 'Yeah, they might although usually they send you letters. That's what they did to me when I spent too much on my credit card. But I paid it off. She's probably gone off with some fella.'

Carole didn't touch anything. She'd seen films where people wore gloves to avoid fingerprints. She'd done what she needed to do. She would be able to sleep knowing that at least she wasn't responsible for Samantha's death. Charlotte picked up a big doll. Carole smiled. 'Do you want to take her with you?'

Charlotte nodded. She would be wondering where her mum was. Carole had no answers. She thanked Tina for her help and told her she would have to tell the police that she had found the address. 'Please don't tell them I've been here. I really shouldn't have gone in but I was so worried. They'll be really angry if they know. I'll give them the address and let them get on with it. I expect they'll come to you, thinking you might have a key. Just don't tell them I was here. I'm already in their bad books for not telling them earlier!'

Tina laughed, raising her eyebrows. 'You can trust me. I won't say a word!'

Carole got back into the car with Charlotte feeling better but bemused. Why would anyone buy all those things if they didn't have any money? She remembered the yellow plastic cloth that was now a mattress cover. It had lasted for thirty years and it didn't have a hole in it. Paula would be horrified at its fate. And the plastic flowers! At least they had gone in the bin and she hadn't shed a single tear!

She parked outside the house, determined to buy a new cloth. Robert seemed to have forgotten about buying her one for Christmas. Indignantly she argued with herself that if Samantha could buy all that stuff she could at least afford a new cloth. She didn't need the flowers because Robert had brought some but she thought she would buy some plants. That house needed to change but in small ways. That would be enough. Charlotte was restless from being cooped up for too long. It was too late to go out. They would have to do some exercise in the house but first she would phone the police and give them the address. With a bit of luck, they would never find out that she had been there.

Once she had got that over with she felt liberated. They danced to the music she'd taken to Jenny's. It was such fun they both laughed like a pair of little children although one was much bigger than the other. She gave Charlotte some tea then bathed her and read her a story. She had just finished when the doorbell rang. Robert was on time and maybe they could get back on track now.

He came in with a bag full of Indian food. 'Oh. Where's the cloth? I was going to buy you a new one, wasn't I?' He dumped the food straight onto the bare table. Where the cloth had been there was now a black and yellow speckled surface made of Formica. Bad to worse! It was a very old and ugly table straight out of the sixties.

'I had to use the cloth to cover the mattress!'

'Well I'm glad it came in useful. You didn't like it anyway, did you? It's a good way of getting rid of it.'

'Yes. It was well past its sell-by date and I don't have to look at it any more. I'll probably keep it on the bed though. I don't like throwing things out.'

Robert laughed in a kindly way. 'We were brought up like that, weren't we? Waste not, want not. Make do and mend! We'll go and buy a new cloth when we get the chance. I think you could do with a new table as well.'

'Yes, you're right. Those black and yellow spots are worse than the cloth. It looks as though it's got smallpox.'

'It reminds me of a leopard skin!'

In spite of the table they had quite an exotic meal. There were several dishes – chicken dhansak, vegetable biriani, a spinach and potato side dish, naan bread and mango chutney. It was from the Indian restaurant in the next street. It had an excellent reputation. The food was delicious, especially the naan peshwari bread that was more like a fruit cake. They both ate too much, Robert because he was hungry, Carole because she had used up so much energy worrying about Samantha. Now at least she could relax and do what Robert had advised – let the police sort it out.

Neither of them spoke about the looming problem of Charlotte and Samantha. They didn't agree not to do it. It just happened. There was a good film on the television. They had both seen *As Good as it Gets* before but they both wanted some fun and Jack Nicholson was just what they needed. For two hours they forgot everything and enjoyed being themselves. Robert put his arms round her and kissed her deeply. He was so strong yet gentle and kind. She felt that same desire that she thought belonged to the past run through her. She responded, suddenly feeling truly alive in a way she hadn't been for decades. She knew then that she wanted him very badly and felt almost relieved at the thought that Charlotte would have to be fostered. Then she remembered how she had clutched her hand in the dark.

As she said goodnight to Robert, she felt guilty that she hadn't told him what had happened in the afternoon, after he'd gone off shopping. Her life had become a web of deceit like an old-fashioned melodrama. She hadn't told the police or Robert as much as she should have done. She had gone to Samantha's house and involved Tina in the deception. She hadn't wanted to talk to Robert about it because it would have spoilt the evening. And he had told her to leave it to the police. She would do that from now on.

CHAPTER 13

Friday 28th December
An Unwelcome Visit

CHARLOTTE WOKE UP at six o'clock and by six-thirty they were having breakfast. The little girl seemed to have settled into Carole's life with amazing ease. She remembered that little children adapted more easily to new situations. At the other end of life people found it hard to change. At precisely nine o'clock the phone rang. Carole jumped. It was so early. It could only be the police. Surely they couldn't have been to the house yet. She felt her heart thumping. Had they found out that she'd already been there. Then again how could they?

She picked up the phone. It was a woman's voice but it wasn't Annette Baker.

'Hello. Could I speak to Carole Peters please?'

'Speaking.'

'My name's Jean Parkinson. I'm a social worker. I'd like to come round and see you, today if possible. I've had a message from the police about a child staying with you.'

'Yes. That's right. They were here yesterday. I've been looking after Charlotte. Her mother's disappeared.'

'Would this morning be OK? I won't keep you long.'

'Yes, of course. I'll see you later then.'

She put the phone down with a sense of dread. So it was all going to start happening earlier than she had anticipated. She put the television on for Charlotte with a sigh. She had always disapproved of people who used the TV as a babysitter.

Now she was doing the same thing. She needed to get ready for the visit. She had to clean up the kitchen. The woman might think she was living in a tip. That wouldn't help. But she also needed to calm down and prepare herself. A few cartoons wouldn't hurt the child but she turned them off before the visitor arrived. With a shudder, she thought back to school inspections when people who didn't know you or the children watched and made judgements. The police had already done that, now it was the turn of the social services. She knew she mustn't lose her temper but she was the innocent party, caring for a deserted child and she was being treated like a criminal. Tears of frustration welled up. She swallowed hard and wiped her eyes with the back of her hand, leaving telltale traces on her face.

The doorbell rang at precisely eleven o'clock. Charlotte was playing with the pretend food, feeding her doll from a flowery plastic plate that Carole had found buried in a cupboard. It all looked as idyllic as it could possibly look! She opened the door. The person on the doorstep was a diminutive lady of about forty, dressed very smartly in a leather jacket. Her dark hair was shoulder length and glossy, as though she was in good health. Nevertheless, she looked tired, her face white under a layer of powder.' Carole? I'm Jean Parkinson,' she said quickly, showing a card.

Carole nodded but hardly looked at it. It was fairly obvious who the person was. 'Come in. Would you like some coffee?'

'Yes, please. White, no sugar.'

They went straight into the lounge. 'Do sit down. I'll go and make some coffee. Oh. This is Charlotte. Charlotte, this lady's come to see you. Her name's Jean. Are you going to say hello?'

Charlotte didn't venture a word, just hid her face in Carole's skirt.

Jean smiled. 'Don't worry. You make the coffee. I'll have a play with Charlotte.'

Carole went off with a certain relief. Making the coffee was easy. Dealing with Charlotte and a social worker was not.

When she arrived back with a tray of coffee and biscuits, they were playing together on the floor with the plastic food. Charlotte was feeding Jean who was pretending to eat a rather inedible looking green and white cauliflower. Her little face was solemn. There was not a trace of a smile. She really believed Jean was going to eat it.

To Carole's surprise, Jean suggested they turn on the television for Charlotte a bit later while they had a talk. So social workers made use of the TV as well! Meanwhile they drank their coffee and watched Charlotte playing. She was now trying to feed Carole with a red tomato. She pretended to like it then asked Charlotte if she could have an apple. She came back with one and said 'apple' quite clearly smiling rather proudly.

Jean asked Carole to put the television on while they had a talk. Charlotte seemed happy enough half watching and half playing with the food and her doll. Carole told her what had happened as briefly as possible, avoiding the excursion to Samantha's. She had expected more criticism from the social services but she was surprised to find Jean quite sympathetic. She got the impression she was a really nice person.

'She seems happy enough with you, doesn't she?'

Carole nodded. At least she didn't have to make up a false tale here. It was obvious she was happy and starting to talk more. 'She doesn't say much but she's coming on. I don't think she's had much contact with people and her mum doesn't seem to have talked much either. Of course I don't know for sure. I've hardly ever seen them together.'

'You know she'll have to be fostered, don't you? Did you want her to stay with you?'

Carole looked confused. 'I can't be a parent to her, can I? I'm sixty-one. I'm more of a grandparent, I suppose.'

'Well, it would only be short term at the moment. We can't assume her mum's gone for good. It's only a few days since she disappeared. Charlotte could come back to you once you've got a CRB – a police check.'

'I know. The police told me. How long will it take?'

'We can probably push it through fairly quickly, say a week or two.'

'So she'll have to go to a stranger for two weeks. That's a long time for a little child. Will I be able to see her and take her out?'

'You'll be able to see her but you won't be able to take her out on your own.'

Carole felt her chest tighten with anger. Charlotte was going to suffer because of social services' red tape. 'She's going to be very upset.'

'I know but we can't take chances. We have to stick to the rules.'

Carole winced at the phrase 'take chances'. She felt guilty. They were making her feel like that when she hadn't done anything wrong but it was no use arguing. 'How long will it take to find a family?'

'A few days. Until then she can stay here. I'd like to leave her with you but I can't. I daren't break the rules.'

Carole nodded silently. She wasn't sure what to do. She wanted Robert. He already had grandchildren. He probably wouldn't mind having another grandchild but he didn't want to go back to being a parent. He might decide he just wanted his life back with no complications. She could end up losing both of them. She would be back to that day she had nearly had to smash the window in the back door. She would still have the U3A to fill her time but Robert and Charlotte were more important. They had become almost the family she had never had. Jean was waiting for a response. She would have to say something. What she needed was time to think.

'I don't know what to do about all this. I'll have the police check then at least I'll be able to take her out, even if I don't have her here.'

'OK. I've got a form here. You can fill it in then we'll wait and see what you want to do.'

Carole wasn't convinced that any amount of time was going to solve her dilemma but at least it gave her a bit of leeway to think things out clearly and maybe talk to some friends. All the people from the choir had faded into the background, even Valerie who she had promised to visit. She longed to get back to the choir rehearsals and get going with the keyboard group. The U3A wouldn't start up again until after New Year. She suddenly had another thought. She wouldn't be able to go to the party on New Year's Day if Charlotte was still with her. Robert had bought her ticket. She couldn't let him down.

Jean got up, took the form and put her coat on. There was nothing more to be done so it was time for her to go. 'I'll be in touch soon as I can find a suitable foster home for Charlotte.'

The phone call came the next day, far sooner than Carole had expected. Jean had found a family and wanted Charlotte to visit initially then she would move in on Sunday 30th, the day after the visit. The visit was arranged for two o'clock. Jean agreed to pick them up at one-thirty as the family lived in Crosby, six miles away. Carole had hoped Charlotte would be just round the corner but that was unrealistic. Foster families must be in short supply. She had thought of going to meet Valerie but she hadn't arranged anything. She just didn't have the energy so she played with Charlotte, let her watch some television then gave her an early lunch. Uneasily she realised that they had settled into a routine so quickly and comfortably and now it was going to be shattered. How much could the child cope with? It was all too much for someone so little.

They set off promptly and half an hour later they arrived in a street of Victorian houses a bit like her own. At least the house would be similar. That might help. The house had a long front garden with a curved path. The front door seemed a long walk away from the gate. The door opened as they arrived. Someone had been waiting for them. Laura Butler was a heavy woman with red curly hair. She was standing in the porch with two other children, a small skinny boy of about six and a girl around ten with a painted tattoo on her arm. They both looked wary and yet curious.

They went into a well-worn living room furnished with comfortable couches with floppy cushions and a large coffee table marked with crayons and felt tips that had slipped off the paper leaving indelible memories of past and present foster children. Laura introduced the other two children, Mary and George, and then she went off into the kitchen to make some tea. The two children followed her while Charlotte sat squashing Carole on the couch, burrowing into her jumper like a little animal. Mary came in carrying a tray with cups and saucers. George was carrying a plate of cakes, balancing it on his hand a bit like a juggler. Carole held her breath until it was safely deposited on the table. Laura hadn't asked the children to help. Carole wondered why they had gone instead of getting to know Charlotte.

George helped himself to a cake, swallowed it almost whole then helped himself to another one, wiping his nose on his sleeve. The children had juice while the grown-ups drank their tea. Charlotte ate her cake on the couch next to Carole.

Jean broke the silence. 'Would you like to show Charlotte your toys? I bet you've got some nice ones,' she said to the boy and girl.

'Yes. Go on. Go and play while we have a talk,' Laura exclaimed.

Charlotte was having none of it. She stayed firmly planted on the couch, glued to Carole who was beginning to feel very uneasy.

'She'll be OK tomorrow. They're all like this but they get over it,' Laura said, shaking her head slowly in the direction of Charlotte who disappeared even further into Carole's woollen jumper.

They didn't stay long. 'Perhaps it would be better tomorrow,' Jean suggested hopefully. Carole was frozen with anxiety. She knew very well that it wasn't going to work and she dreaded it. She cursed the system that was going to leave the child traumatised.

When they got back to Carole's house Charlotte was very clingy. Nothing had been said about her going to Laura's but she seemed to know that something was going to happen. Carole was tempted to tell her but didn't dare. It was Jean's job to arrange it all, not hers. They had pizza out of the freezer for tea. It was Charlotte's favourite. It reminded Carole of the times they had been to the pizza place. It seemed a long time ago now. So much had happened. She gave her some fruit and then a little bowl of sweets of different sorts. Carole called it a goody bowl and Charlotte had quickly learnt the words. She knew that spoiling the little girl with sweets wouldn't solve the problem but she couldn't resist.

After tea, she played for a bit then Carole bathed her and read her a story. When she tried to settle her she wouldn't let go of Carole's hand. She had to lie down on the other bed and wait for her to go to sleep. 'Mummy,' she whispered in a sleepy voice, gripping Carole's hand. A warm ripple seemed to flow down her arm and transfer itself to Carole's. She lay there in the dark, her eyes watching the shadows playing on the wall. She knew all this shouldn't be happening. It was out of time and wrong for everybody but still her heart sank at the thought of the next day.

Jean came early. She played with Charlotte for a while then told her that she was going to stay with the lady she had met yesterday. The little girl showed no sign of understanding what was going to happen. Carole had packed her a case with the clothes that Jenny had given her. She gave her the little teddy to keep with her. Jean took them in her car. Charlotte played with the little teddy, making a kind of two-way happy conversation with limited words. Carole kept quiet. She dreaded what was going to happen.

They arrived at the house. It was like rewinding a film. The two children were once again at the door with their foster mum. Laura had her arms round the two of them. Carole felt better when she saw this or was it a put on act? She couldn't tell. They had the same drink and biscuits as yesterday except that it was coffee instead of tea. This time the children played together. Charlotte was a little more relaxed but didn't stray far away from Carole. Then it was time to go.

Jean looked knowingly at Laura who got up and got ready. Jean knelt down so she was on a level with Charlotte.

'We have to go now, Charlotte. Laura will look after you, and Carole will come tomorrow to see you. Is that OK?'

Charlotte looked as though she didn't want to be interrupted. She was busy playing with George's train set. They said goodbye. It was only then that Charlotte began to understand what was going to happen. She dropped the train and made for the door, grabbing Carole's skirt with her little fists. Laura grabbed her and pulled her away from Carole. She started to scream. The woman seemed totally unmoved by this. 'She'll be OK. You can't explain. She's too little but she'll be OK.'

The other two children backed away. George looked scared. Mary looked blankly at the scene, running her fingers over her tattoo. Her face said it all. *This is life. What's the point?* Laura was holding Charlotte and telling them to go. Jean gripped Carole's elbow and guided her towards the door. As they went towards the street the screams vibrated like swirling music along the winding path. They got into the car and Jean started the engine. As they drove, tears ran down Carole's face. She couldn't stop them. The silent tears turned into sobs. It was the same feeling that she always tried so hard to cover up. Loss!

Jean stopped in a lay-by then turned to face her passenger. 'It'll be all right. Don't worry so much. There's no point, is there? You're getting things out of proportion. It's not as though she's your child or even a relative. With a bit of luck the police will find her mum.'

Carole knew she was right but Jean didn't know her. She didn't know what had happened to her in the past. She shuddered. The past never went away, just added itself to traumas in the present. It brought her pain to the surface. Jean didn't know that. 'I know. You're right. But she's so little and she's had so many things to cope with. It isn't fair.'

'No. It isn't but whoever said life is fair? We know it isn't. When you're working in this field all the time you get used to it. I have to sleep at night and be a wife and a mum to my own children so I have to be a bit objective. I do care but only so much. When I go home I leave it behind. I have to. I wouldn't be able to keep doing the job otherwise.'

'It's really hard for me. I'm not a social worker.'

'You seem almost too involved with this child. You need to get on with your own life. Go and see her but let her go at least for now.'

'It'll be just as bad tomorrow.'

'It'll be worse if you show you're upset.'

'I'll try not to get upset. I know it won't help Charlotte.'

'Good. Let's get back.'

Jean dropped her off with a promise to visit sometime in the week. It was only one o'clock as Carole opened the front door but the sky was so grey it looked as though it was going dark. The house was cold and empty. She looked round at the faded, impersonal prints that had no meaning for her. Why were there no photos or paintings, nothing to show she had done more than just exist? It was nothing more than a shabby lodging house. She was hungry but she didn't feel like eating anything. Samson lay neglected on the lounge carpet. The tears started again and this time she couldn't control them. She lay down on the floor with her arms round the teddy and sobbed like the toddler she had been so long ago.

The phone started to ring. She hardly heard it but at last she got up and went to answer it. It was Robert. 'Carole! Where have you been? What's the matter?'

'They've taken Charlotte away. She's gone to a foster family.'

'Well, isn't that a good thing? You can get on with your life now.'

She knew he would react like that. He didn't understand either. His calm, practical attitude was good for her though. It was helpful to get things back into proportion. Of course he was right. She knew she mustn't let the past interfere with the present. It would ruin any chance of a relationship with him and she valued that enough to stop feeling sorry for herself. 'I know. You're right. I shouldn't have got attached.'

'Of course you should! But it'll be hard for a bit. Shall I come and pick you up. We could go for a walk then to that pizza place at the end of your road. It's not exactly The Ritz but you sound as though you need to get out.'

She smiled as she wiped the tears away. She caught sight of herself in the mirror over the telephone table and almost laughed. Her face was streaked with black marks. She looked as though she had fallen flat on her face in some mud. Robert was good for her. He didn't seem to have any baggage to carry around. She suddenly felt lucky. It was time for a wash.

She tidied herself up. He wouldn't want to spend the afternoon with a miserable person. The sky was grey enough without adding to the general feeling of malaise after Christmas. He was soon at the door and she grabbed a coat and a woolly hat and scarf. It was cold outside, not the best weather for walking but better than staying in. He was wearing a similar hat and scarf and they laughed as they looked at their reflection in the mirror. They looked like two kids going out to play.

The park was deserted. They went down to the lake. A single ray of muted sun broke through the cloud and shimmered briefly on the half-frozen water. Several ducks were walking about cautiously in the half-light, slipping on the fragile ice. Carole was half sorry they hadn't brought some bread. The ducks and one or two coots looked rather lonely and hungry. She suddenly felt hungry too. She remembered she hadn't eaten any lunch. As they sloshed through the frozen grass leaving a trail of footsteps, the image of the pizzeria with its warmth and light filled her mind with pleasure and staved off the nagging hunger pains.

They got to Pippa's Pizzas half an hour later. They had forced themselves to walk and the exercise had done Carole some good. It was amazing how a trip out to see some frozen ducks on a pond could cheer you up! They ordered then found a table. It seemed ages since her first visit or even her last one yet the familiarity was a very comfortable feeling. She looked across the table at Robert. His curly hair was slightly longer than usual and she realised that was the first thing she had noticed about him. The curls were nothing short of beautiful and she longed to touch them. They made him look like a little boy. He certainly didn't look a bit like the talented musician that he was, more like an overgrown schoolboy in a football hat. They grinned, knowing that they both looked the same, hardly glamorous but happy.

Carole ate hungrily, remembering her first visit. So much had happened since then. She felt like a different person. She was so at ease with Robert although they had been going out together for such a short time. She wondered if perhaps time contracted as you got older. After all, life seemed to go at a rapid pace, not like when she was a child. She ordered a coffee even though she knew it would stop her sleeping then wished she hadn't. Depressing thoughts were always worse in the middle of the night.

'I've got you a ticket for the New Year's Day party. Are you still coming?'

Carole nodded. Her relationship with Robert was still fragile. She couldn't afford to be a problem. Anyway, she wanted to go to the party.

'I'll go and see Charlotte tomorrow then I'll have New Year's Day free to have some fun.'

Robert looked pleased. Carole could see that he thought she would be better off without the hassle of a little child. But she couldn't get Charlotte's face out of her mind and she felt as though she could hear her crying. She shook herself out of the melodrama. She told herself she was creating something like a soap opera and it was a useless activity. She had to get on with her life. She had a lot to look forward to like the party on New Year's Day. They walked back to Carole's where Robert had parked his car. They were both tired so he went straight home with the promise to pick her up on Tuesday.

She went to bed wondering what she would find when she visited Charlotte. She lay in the darkness wondering if she was being selfish. What if the police didn't find Samantha at all? What if they didn't find her for months? Should she foster her once her CRB check came through? There were so many questions with no answers. She regretted the coffee but eventually she went to sleep thinking about the party. It was better to think happy thoughts last thing at night. She knew the theory but she could still hear Charlotte screaming.

***

She woke up the next morning feeling relaxed. Then she suddenly remembered a dream that she'd had during the night. It was still so clear it could have been real. She was on a beach with Robert and Charlotte. It was a sunny day. She was young with long blond hair blowing in the wind. They were running across the fine sand holding Charlotte's hands, swinging her between them like a doll. Robert was young too and they were happy.

She phoned Laura to make sure it would be all right to visit. She said it would be fine. Carole felt a bit more comfortable. There was no noise in the background. That had to be a good sign. It was New Year's Eve, a new beginning for most people. It was certainly a new beginning for her and Robert. She felt a sense of relief. She could go back to her U3A life without having to worry about Charlotte. She and Robert could concentrate on getting to know each other properly. Jenny had told her how hard it was to meet a possible new partner when you had two children in tow. Carole wasn't in Jenny's position but nevertheless she wouldn't be an independent person with a little child to look after. She suddenly remembered the Fauré Requiem. She had completely forgotten about the choir. The Samantha saga had taken over her life.

Robert phoned, telling her that a few members of the choir were getting together for a quiet evening around nine o'clock. Would she like to come? She said yes with no hesitation. Her life was getting back to normal. She must have sounded happy because Robert seemed quite surprised. She realised she had been giving him a bad impression and she regretted it. She wasn't a depressed person at all. She would have to show him the better side of her. It wouldn't be difficult as she felt so optimistic all of a sudden.

She drove to Laura's after lunch. She was early so she went down to the beach. She parked the car opposite the sea and stared out at the Antony Gormley statues looking rather lonely as they stood up to their waists in the sea. The tide was right in and the seagulls and a crowd of aggressive starlings were fighting over a pile of bread. She noticed the starlings' shiny green feathers and listened to the screeching of the gulls as they circled in the blue sky. Since Samantha's disappearance, she had stopped noticing things. It was only a week but it seemed like months. She had an insane desire to get out of the car and run into the sea. The sun was shining and from the inside of the car it all looked idyllic. When she opened the car door a wave of icy air hit her in the face and she changed her mind. It was freezing!

There was an ice cream van parked quite close by. She wouldn't run into the sea but she joined the queue of optimists buying ice cream. In the end she bought a choc ice and sat in the car watching the braver or crazy people sitting on the wall in the wind. The sky was full of kites. One looked like a grey swimmer. Several others were octopuses and other sea monsters with tentacles blowing around in the wind. How could she have thought of running into the sea? She almost laughed out loud as she ate her choc ice and watched the kites. Life was wonderful. She was so glad to be alive.

She listened to the radio for a while in the comfort of the car then drove off to Laura's. She wasn't sure what she would find or whether she was doing the right thing. She was thinking of herself really. She wanted to know that Charlotte was all right. Was that for Charlotte or to satisfy herself so she could get on with her life? She wasn't sure. She couldn't go back and be a parent. It was too late. She knew she should grasp what was possible with both hands. If Charlotte was happy she could get on and do just that.

She parked outside the house and felt a shiver run through her. Laura opened the door before she could knock and invited her in. Before long she had the kettle on and kept on preparing a pile of vegetables while it boiled. The house was very quiet and Carole wondered where all the children were.

Laura smiled, almost as though she had read Carole's thoughts. 'I'm having a few minutes peace.' She laughed. 'Susan's gone shopping, Mary's gone to her friend's house for the day and George is playing in the garden with the little boy next door.' She poured the tea and emptied some biscuits onto a plate. 'You see, they have a normal life. Just like other kids.'

'Where's Charlotte?' Carole asked, anxiously.

'She's watching television. She didn't want to go out to play.'

'I'll just go and say hello to her.' Carole went into the lounge. Charlotte was sitting on the couch staring at the screen and pulling her hair. She didn't turn her head when Carole walked in. Carole said 'hello' in a friendly voice as though nothing unusual had happened. There was no response. Her heart sank. It was unreasonable to feel guilty but she did and she couldn't disguise it. She retreated into the kitchen, knowing Charlotte was punishing her for betrayal.

'Don't let her upset you. It's not your problem. You should be enjoying yourself, not worrying about somebody else's child.'

'I know,' Carole admitted, 'but she's so alone and now I feel as though I've let her down. She's only three and her whole life's been turned upside down. It isn't fair.'

Laura shrugged. 'Life isn't fair. You learn that very quickly doing this job. I do what I can. That's all I can do.'

The back door opened and George came running in howling. The bump on his head was rapidly turning purple. He ran straight into Laura's arms and she took him on her knee. He buried his head in her jumper and she kissed him better. He stopped crying and started swinging his legs backwards and forwards like the pendulum of a clock, sucking his thumb. He looked younger than his six years. Five minutes later, he was running out into the garden again carrying two biscuits.

'Charlotte doesn't talk, does she?' Laura commented thoughtfully

'I don't think anybody's talked to her very much. She was starting to talk quite a bit to me.'

'I haven't heard her say anything yet but you have to be patient. She's had a lot of upset in the last few weeks. She'll be OK.'

'Are you sure?' Carole asked as much for her own satisfaction as Charlotte's. It was a silly question but she needed an answer.

Laura looked at her curiously. 'It's none of my business really but you seem so attached to the child and yet you're not a relative. If her mum doesn't come back the social worker might find some relatives to take her. What about grandparents?'

Carole shook her head. 'I don't think there's anybody who would take her, from what her mum said about them.'

'Poor kid! Fancy not having any family! She can stay here as long as she needs to. But perhaps you want to look after her when the police check comes through?'

Carole didn't know what to say. She shrugged her shoulders helplessly. 'I don't know what to do. I don't have to decide yet anyway.' One thing that made her feel better was Laura. She hadn't liked her much to start with but she was changing her mind. Laura was doing a good job. Her heart was in the right place. 'It's New Year's Eve. Have you got something planned for tonight?'

'Oh, don't worry about us. Don'll have a drink with his friends then we'll see in the New Year with a couple of glasses of wine. You go and enjoy yourself. Don't worry about Charlotte. She'll come round in a bit.'

She washed her hands and then saw Carole out. She almost ran to the car. It was New Year's Eve and she was free. She could put off making any decision and just live for the moment. She drove home and sorted out a dress for the party later. No. Robert had told her it was a get-together, not a party. She settled for something neutral so that whatever the occasion she wouldn't feel out of place. As she got ready she realised she had no idea where they were going or what they would be doing. She felt as though she was drifting out into a vacuum in outer space but she didn't care. Whatever was going on in the vacuum she was determined to enjoy it.

Robert picked her up in his car at precisely nine o'clock. The old car had seen better days but to her it was as good as any fairy tale carriage. She got in and he started driving. She hadn't had time to worry about the social evening. All she knew was that it was a casual get-together to celebrate the New Year.

'I expect you're wondering where we're going,' he said suddenly, as though he'd read her thoughts. Changing gear he accelerated as he drove onto a main road.

Carole recognised the road. It was the same road she had driven along that morning. 'Yes, I was wondering although I went this way this morning to see Charlotte. Her foster mum lives in Crosby.'

'It's up that way. It's at Barbara's. You know, Barbara Vickers, the keyboard teacher. I got to know David when I was working at Liverpool University. He was in the English Department. I joined his drama group. It was something different to do and it was great fun. We put on all these plays. It stopped me getting too wrapped up in one thing. '

'Don't you have to, to be successful?'

'Well, you can be too obsessed. We actually put on a few musicals together. That was fun too. Then there were parties and well, the sort of thing we're going to now. They live in Waterloo, quite close to the beach. It's a nice house with plenty of space for a party.'

'I thought it was a quiet evening, not a party.'

Robert shrugged. 'I don't know exactly what it is. We'll just have to wait and see.'

Carole couldn't help comparing her past life with Robert's. She visualised all the glamorous events he'd been to, the people he'd mixed with. It made her life seem so drab. She wiped the thought out of her mind. It was her turn and now she was going to be part of his life, to mix with the people he had been talking about. It would be almost like reviving the past and reliving what he had described. It filled her with excitement. She could almost imagine she was young again.

Robert turned into a quiet road. You could just see the River Mersey in the distance. A well-lit ferry drifted lazily past in the darkness, maybe going to Ireland. Halfway down he pulled into a large drive that wound between well-kept lawns up to a large Victorian house. There were already a lot of cars parked nearby. Carole was shaking with nervous excitement. She probably wouldn't know anyone apart from Barbara but she didn't care.

The door was open. They went in and piled their coats on top of lots of others in a small room on the left. They followed the voices through into a large through-room opposite where a table was laid out with drinks. Barbara came up wearing an elegant black dress set off by a white matching necklace and earrings. Her silver hair was drawn back from her face like a ballerina. She might have been about to dance a ballet except that she was wearing high-heeled patent leather shoes that reflected the light.

She threw her arms round Robert and kissed him on the cheek. 'Lovely to see you!' Then she turned to Carole. 'Oh, we've met before, haven't we? At the keyboard group. It's Carole, isn't it?'

Carole smiled. 'You've got a good memory. Yes, I'm coming back to the group after the holiday. Now I've got the keyboard I should be practising but I've been so busy over Christmas.'

'Don't worry. If you can play the piano you'll have a head start. Do come. I'll be waiting for you next week. Help yourselves to a drink.'

They went over to the table where there was a variety of different drinks. Robert looked a bit depressed. 'I'm driving so I'd better just have one drink,' he groaned, running his eyes over the different bottles.

Carole felt sorry for him and didn't really feel like drinking. It was bound to make him feel deprived. However he insisted and she ended up with a large glass of sparkling white wine. She was thirsty and drank it rather quickly as she looked around. There were a lot of people and it looked very much like a party rather than a sedate gathering. She wasn't worried about not knowing anyone. She was quite happy to stand and stare, drinking in the atmosphere. A second glass of white wine made the world look even brighter but she still felt sorry for Robert.

A group of people were gathering in the middle of the room where there was a piano. One man had a guitar and there was also a violinist.

Robert chuckled. 'There's going to be a show. They always have a singing session at these gatherings. It gets everybody mixing. You'll enjoy it. It'll make you feel at home.'

Carole wasn't sure she would ever feel at home but she waited curiously to see what was going to happen. They soon got started and she was quite surprised. She had expected a rather restrained performance but it was far from that. There were blues numbers and country and western, even some pop songs and songs from the musicals. She started to sip her third glass of wine, resolving to drink slowly this time. She knew a lot of the songs and joined in. She had a good voice and she made use of it. Suddenly she didn't feel a stranger any more. She was one of the crowd. Robert had been right.

Barbara came up to see how they were getting on. Robert had gone to talk to David so Carole was quite glad to have someone to talk to. She didn't really like being on her own but she didn't want to force him to stay with her all night. She envied Barbara. She was so at ease in this situation, drifting around talking to different people.

'Are you OK, Carole? I see he's left you on your own!'

'Honestly, it's OK. I love the singing and I'm just glad to be here. It's a lovely way to spend New Year's Eve. I'm not used to this sort of thing though. I'm trying not to drink too much. This wine's really nice so it's tempting.'

Barbara laughed. 'Go ahead and spoil yourself. It's a pity about Robert. He doesn't drink a lot but he could do without a car on New Year's Eve. Incidentally, I'm so glad he's met you. You look very relaxed together. He's been on his own since Jane died. I was beginning to think he would never meet anybody. They were very close, you know.'

Carole nodded. 'I know but it's early days. We're still getting to know each other.'

He came back at this point. The singing was still going on. It was difficult to talk. Barbara shouted rather loudly in his ear. 'Robert. Do you two need to go home? Why don't you stay? The kids' rooms are not being used. They've all left so why not make use of them?'

Robert looked questioningly at Carole. 'What do you think? Do you have to get back?'

She shook her head. 'No, I don't. It would mean you could have a drink without worrying.' At the back of her mind there were certain doubts which she couldn't quite put into words. Her third glass of wine was half finished in spite of her resolution. After all that wine it was easier to say yes than no!

Robert helped himself to another glass of wine and visibly relaxed. People started dancing. He took the two glasses and put them down on a table then caught hold of her and started dancing, holding her very close to him. She stared over his shoulder at the other dancers then thought of the yellow plastic cloth now demoted to a mattress cover and the plastic flowers now in the bin. How things had changed! She wondered if Paula was somewhere watching her. She blushed at the thought. She was free and after three glasses of wine the world was twinkling like a cut-glass bowl filled with light. She moved closer to Robert. He held her tightly and she felt his strong body close to hers. The clock started to strike midnight.

Party poppers exploded and everybody started kissing the people nearest to them and wishing them happy New Year. It was 2013. She felt suddenly frightened at the thought of what it might bring. As they sang 'Auld Lang Syne' she couldn't help yawning. It had been a busy day. They went to finish their drinks.

'Let's go to bed,' Robert said out of the blue. He realised they were both tired and not teenagers any more even if they wanted to be.

Carole looked at the staircase and realised why she had had some misgivings about staying. They were suddenly very clear. Was he expecting to sleep with her? They scarcely knew each other. She looked round the crowded room, at a loss to know what to do. They started up the ornate staircase. It was like climbing Mount Everest. Her feet felt heavy. In spite of the heaviness they would soon be at the top. Her distant life with Paula suddenly seemed comfortable and safe. She gripped the banister so hard she left a wet mark on the wood. They got to the top and started along the landing.

Robert stopped and turned towards her, no trace left of the party atmosphere. His brown eyes were thoughtful. He opened a large panelled door. 'Will this be OK for you? It looks very comfortable. I'll use the one opposite.' He hesitated then said very quietly, 'Can I come and say goodnight?'

'Yes. Of course. Give me ten minutes to get organised.'

She went in, closed the door then flung herself onto the large double bed. He had such dignity and sensitivity. How could she have thought that he would expect to sleep with her so soon? She shivered in spite of the central heating, feeling as though his wife might be watching them from somewhere. Did he feel he was being unfaithful? Surely not after five years. She lay perfectly still, letting her eyes stray round the room, taking in all the details. There was a large window looking out onto the garden. A tree she couldn't identify was right outside, tiny bare branches brushing against the glass. A guitar and a bookshelf full of paperbacks were the only belongings left by the owner of the room.

She dragged herself off the bed and padded across the carpet towards a washbasin. Underneath there was a cupboard full of everything a visitor might need. The only thing she didn't have was anything to wear in bed. The house was warm so she would just have to sleep naked. She washed quickly and leapt into bed. It was very comfortable under the duvet. She had forgotten to draw the curtains so she lay watching the tree gently moving against the window.

There was a knock on the door. Robert was wearing a yellow towelling bathrobe. There was a similar one hanging on the back of the door. Carole had only just noticed it. He sat down on the edge of the bed, his bathrobe gaping enough to reveal to Carole that he was similarly naked. She pulled the duvet up round her neck.

'I expect they all think we're having a passionate affair.' He grinned, his eyes twinkling. He seemed to have the gift of being both serious and amused at the same time.

Carole blushed. She couldn't think of anything to say.

'Goodnight. Sleep well.' He bent down and moved the duvet down a little and put his arms round her neck, caressing her bare shoulders. She shuddered under his touch and they kissed deeply. It was more than a goodnight kiss. They both knew that they only had to move the duvet for things to change radically. It was tempting after the wine they had both drunk but it didn't happen. He got up and went to bed, leaving her remembering her previous experience. They both knew it was only a matter of time.

It was nine o'clock when she woke up. The wind was howling outside and the now familiar tree was tapping on the window. She lay there at first wondering where she was. She stretched in the warmth of the bed, thinking back to the party. If nothing like that ever happened again she would always remember it – a moment of glamour in an otherwise drab existence. She washed and dressed quickly then wondered what to do. She had been too tense to eat very much during the party. Driven by an empty stomach, she cautiously opened the door and stared over the banisters to see if there was any sign of life. She could hear voices coming from the kitchen.

She tiptoed down the stairs feeling like a burglar. Barbara, David and Robert were in the middle of what seemed like a serious debate for New Year's Day. All she wanted was some breakfast and maybe the radio. They stopped the debate, whatever it was.

'I'm sorry if I've interrupted you,' she stammered. 'You were busy discussing something.'

'Nothing serious.' David laughed. 'We were just reminiscing. I'm glad you've come down. We need some new blood. Old people talk about the past all the time. Let's enjoy the present. Would you like some breakfast?'

She was soon sitting down with coffee, orange juice and breakfast cereal. There was an Aga giving out delicious warmth and the smell of bacon but she didn't want anything hot. They both felt the need to go and get organised for the U3A lunch. They thanked Barbara and David for their hospitality and then collected their things ready to go.

'Thanks very much for having us.' Robert smiled. He looked rather eager for them to just go home and relax. 'It wouldn't have been much fun for me if I could only have one drink. Thanks again and see you soon. Happy New Year.'

'And the same to you. Let's get together again soon,' Barbara said. 'And Carole, don't forget the keyboard group. It's a week on Wednesday, the ninth I think it is. See you then.'

'I'll have to have a good go at it.' Carole laughed. 'It's still in the bag!'

'Well, it won't be doing much in there. Get it out and play something. You can play for the group then. You've got just over a week.'

'A week! I'd have to practise six hours a day.'

'Well, why not?' Barbara smiled.

All the trouble over Samantha came back in a split second. Why not indeed? There were plenty of reasons but Barbara didn't know anything about that.

'Are you by any chance going to the U3A lunch?'

Robert nodded. 'Yes, we're both going. That's why we're in a bit of a hurry. We have to get ready.'

'I'll see you there. We're playing after the meal.'

Robert drove back the way they had come the previous day. The roads were almost deserted. 'Are you OK? Did you sleep all right?'

'Yes. I slept really well. The wine probably helped. How about you?'

'I'm a bit tired. I'd rather have had a quiet day but I've got the tickets and you can't let people down. I'm sure we'll enjoy the lunch then we can have a relaxing evening. I'll drop you off at your house then I'll pick you up around midday.'

He stopped outside her house. There was a police car parked next to her car. As she was about to open the gate, John Wood appeared from nowhere. He must have been in the car but she hadn't noticed.

'Happy New Year. I wasn't waiting for you. There was a burglary down the road. I thought I might catch you.' He laughed. 'I don't mean you're a suspect! It's just that I was in the area. It's a coincidence!'

Carole smiled politely. She could have done without John Wood at this time of the morning. 'I've just come back from a party. I'm pretty tired. What can I do for you?'

'I was wondering if you've heard from the child's mum. She was last seen getting into a sports car. The car's been traced to someone who lives in London. I can't tell you any more at the moment. It would be so much easier if she'd contacted you.'

'Her phone's switched off. She hasn't been in touch at all. I think she's run away.'

'That's how it looks. Just let us know if you hear anything. It'll save a lot of time and money.'

'Of course but it doesn't look likely, does it?'

He shook his head. 'Who knows? Sorry to keep you. You look as though you're in a hurry.'

'A bit. I'm going out for lunch. I'm not used to so much social life. It's exhausting!'

He laughed. 'Enjoy it. You'll be dead a long time!'

'Thanks.' She went into the house and straight up to get ready for the next adventure.

CHAPTER 14

Friday 8th February

L IFE HAD GONE back to normal. Carole's police check had come through and she had started to take Charlotte out on a Friday from the middle of January. She had been once or twice to the keyboard group although she found it a bit difficult. The choir had resumed rehearsals and were tackling two new pieces ready for the concert. It was Friday and Carole was getting ready to pick Charlotte up from Laura's. She almost wished she could have the day off. The little girl was getting more and more difficult as time went by. Although she was only three, she seemed to know she was in a three-way tug of war between Carole, Laura and her missing mum.

Carole drove to Laura's and was soon in the kitchen being offered a rather early coffee.

'What are you planning to do today?' Laura asked, as she busied round the kitchen.

'Oh. Something straightforward. We might go to the park. I'll do a bit of cooking with her. She likes that. She's not easy so I don't want to do anything too ambitious.'

'I know what you mean. She doesn't really know who she is at the moment.'

There was a short silence. 'I suppose you think I should just leave her with you.'

'It might be easier in some ways but it's nice for her to have the equivalent of a grandmother. I hope you don't mind me saying that.'

'Of course not. Maybe I'm being selfish. You see, I don't have any family. I suppose I'm enjoying playing at being a parent. I never had the chance. It's a bit like going back in time and changing things. Anyway, it's good to be useful even when she's difficult.'

'Well, she's probably testing you to see what you're made of. That's what children do. She wants to feel safe. Don't we all?'

'Have they found her mum yet?' Carole asked, watching Laura weighing out ingredients for a chocolate cake. 'I haven't heard anything. The social worker mentioned the possibility of adoption.'

'I don't think they've found her. At least they haven't told me anything.'

'Would you adopt her if you got the chance?'

Laura stopped mixing the cake for a moment. 'Maybe. I'll certainly have plenty of time to think about it. These things don't happen quickly.'

'I suppose it's better for you to keep her in that case. She's already had too much upheaval.' Carole felt herself relax a little. There were times when it was a relief to have decisions taken out of your hands. If some god-like person in the social services or the legal system waved a decisive finger at her saying no, she couldn't have the child, it would all be taken out of her hands. Since the police check had come through she had been caught between the prospect of playing temporary parent to Charlotte and enjoying her new life as a single person.

They went into the lounge where Charlotte was playing with a lot of dolls and the fruit and vegetables that Carole had bought. A ripple of pleasure ran through her as she watched.

'Charlotte. Carole's come to take you out. Let's get your coat.'

The child took no notice and continued to feed a rather scraggy teddy with a plastic banana. Carole felt herself blushing uncomfortably. It was awful to be rejected in front of Laura. She pulled herself together quickly.

'Samson likes bananas too. Will you bring one for him? He wants to play with you. He's waiting by the fire. Bring teddy with you.'

A smile lit up her still baby face. She got up and collected the fruit and the teddy. Carole's colour went back to normal. She hadn't lost her touch with little children after all. Laura smiled at Carole with a certain amount of relief, glad that there wasn't going to be a nasty scene.

'I'll take her out to the pizza place tonight. It'll save cooking. We'll be back about seven if that's OK with you.'

Laura nodded unconcerned as she poured the chocolate cake mix into a tin. She was always so laid-back about everything. Carole envied her.

They had a good day. Carole had been expecting trouble but she kept Charlotte busy and the child was happy and well behaved. She let her have a bit of television while she phoned Jenny and made arrangements to meet later. Although they were different generations they had become firm friends. She put the phone down and sat down in the kitchen with a drink. The choir rehearsals were getting more difficult. It was as though something inside her was trying to get out and the Fauré was making it worse all the time. The scary rippling and redness were getting worse, especially during the rehearsals. She hadn't told Robert although he had noticed that there was a problem. Valerie had also noticed and couldn't help but say something during the break.

'Carole. Is anything wrong? You look so tense at times. I thought you would be happy. You seem to be getting on so well with Robert. It must be really nice for you.'

Carole's eyes had filled with tears. She'd been caught off guard. How could she talk to Valerie about something so serious in the middle of a tea break? She brushed the tears away quickly and shook her head impatiently. 'I'm just tired, Val.'

Her friend looked totally unconvinced but they were starting the second half of the rehearsal and nothing further was discussed. As they tackled the Schubert and *Carmina Burana* she felt better. It was the Fauré that caused the trouble. It was almost as though the music was telling her something. A sea of emotion was building up inside her head like a storm threatening on the horizon. She knew she was going to have to tell Robert about it. She had kept it inside all her life. It was time but how?

She met Jenny and they had the usual pizzas. Charlotte was talking a bit better but hadn't really made a lot of progress. James and Eva chatted on. Carole was so glad to have them all as her friends. She felt so lucky and they were a diversion. As they went back to the car in the dark she felt a little hand grip hers. She always avoided forcing her affection on the child as it didn't usually work. She looked down at Charlotte and saw that she was smiling. A thrill of pleasure welled up inside her and warmed her whole body in spite of the winter cold. She put her into the car seat and fastened the straps. The little girl put her arms round Carole and laid her head on her shoulder for a moment.

She took Charlotte back to Laura's. She was very tired and Carole had to carry her into the house. Laura was busy reading a story to George.

'Could you get her into bed for me? She's so tired she'll have to do without a bath. If you could just brush her teeth and wash her face and hands. Just put her to bed. Would you mind?'

Carole took Charlotte upstairs, gave her a quick wash and toothbrush then dressed her in her pyjamas and tucked her into bed.

'Story,' Charlotte muttered sleepily.

'It's a bit late. You'll be asleep in a minute. I know. I'll tell you the story of *The Three Little Pigs*.' Charlotte held her hand and listened but the pigs had only just left home to seek their fortunes when the little hand began to loosen its grip. The child was fast asleep. As she withdrew her hand a surge of love almost reduced her to tears.

She left Laura finishing the story and closed the door quietly. The street was deserted. A gusty wind was whipping up the remains of the fallen leaves. She got into the car and put the radio and the heater on. It was starting to rain and she looked forward to getting home. As she drove to the monotonous bang of the windscreen wipers, she could still see the sleeping child. Not even the radio would move the image out of her mind.

When she got home she dropped down onto the couch in front of the television. It was eight-thirty. She put the news channel on and wondered why she hadn't chosen something else. She was quite exhausted and the news was nearly always bad, a mixture of murders, robberies and distant civil wars. When the doorbell rang she nearly jumped out of her skin. Who on earth would be calling at that time?

She walked along the hall, her legs feeling rather unsteady. She had had a busy day and she really didn't want any visitors. As she had sunk into the couch, she was looking forward to some time to relax. Instead she was scared. The television was full of the kind of dramas that frightened her. There were people out there who might have been watching the house, knowing that she lived alone and was old by young people's standards even if she didn't feel it. She was certainly at an age where people sometimes got exploited. She went to the door then illogically turned round and made her way back into the front lounge. It had suddenly occurred to her to look through the bay window. She should be able to see who was on the doorstep. She drew the curtain back and peered out. It was too dark to see much. All she could see was a shadowy figure. She went back to the front door and shouted through the letterbox.

'Who are you? What do you want?' It all sounded like a scene from a crime thriller. She wondered if she was getting things out of proportion. Maybe, but she wasn't taking any chances.

'It's me. Samantha. Can I come in?' The voice made Carole think of a whimpering child.

She opened the door, feeling nothing but a complete numbness. She knew she should be angry, furious, in fact, in the face of what had happened but she couldn't bring herself to react. It was strangely like going back in time and reliving her last meeting except that the person standing there wasn't dressed up to go out anywhere glamorous. She had the defeated look of someone who had just lost a very important race and was now out of the team.

She came in and sat down. Carole turned the television off and sat opposite, not offering any refreshment. 'Do you know the police have been looking for you for weeks? How could you do such a thing, leave your little girl with strangers?'

'She was with you. She likes you. You know what to do with children. She'll have a better life with you. I'm rubbish at babies. I suppose she's in bed.'

'She's not here.'

'Where is she? You were so good with her. I trusted you. What have you done with her?'

Carole's anger started to come to the surface. She was recovering from the shock. 'It's not what I've done with her. You can't just walk off and leave your child with strangers. The social services sent her to foster parents.'

'Why? She was all right with you.'

Carole exploded. 'You hardly know me. I could have been a paedophile for all you knew. The social worker was more cautious. I had to have a police check.'

'You took my half of the house and my mother's savings and now you're not even looking after Charlotte,' Samantha exploded, illogical in her frustration with everything and everybody. Her voice got louder and louder as her face reddened and her eyes flashed with temper. She shook her fists at Carole as though she was about to lash out at her.

Carole wished Robert was there. The woman was on the verge of being out of control. Nevertheless, she kept calm but at the same time she couldn't help being angry and indignant. 'The house is legally mine. I paid half the mortgage and a lot more. Your mother sent you money every month or have you forgotten?'

She ignored Carole. 'You didn't want her, did you? It was just like my mum didn't want me.' It was the voice of a little child.

Carole hesitated. It was a difficult area. There was an element of truth in what she said, even though Samantha was behaving like a spoilt child and the awkward silence confirmed she was right.

'It's true then? You palmed her off on a foster family just like they did with me. I trusted you.'

'No. It wasn't like that. The social services wouldn't let me keep her until my police check came through. She's been with me all day. I can't keep her permanently. I'm too old. If you don't come back and take care of her she'll be adopted eventually, probably by the foster family. Why have you done this?'

Samantha appeared to shrink into the couch like a snail retreating into its shell. 'I can't come back. I can't go back to that house.'

'Why not? You could have Charlotte back if the social worker –' She didn't have the chance to finish the sentence.

'I don't want her back. As soon as she sees me she starts.'

'What do you mean?'

'She hates me. She does it on purpose to upset me. I know. I can feel it.'

It wasn't worth arguing. There was a huge impenetrable barrier between the two women. It was obvious to Carole that it would never be crossed. Too much damage had been done to Samantha in the past. She saw the impossibility of the whole thing. The child would have to stay with Laura and would almost certainly be better off there. She suddenly remembered all the electrical goods and furniture. Another piece of the puzzle fell into place.

'What's happened to all the stuff you had in the house?' She blushed, realising that she shouldn't have said that. Samantha would know she had been round there. She'd wanted to keep that to herself but it was too late. It didn't seem to matter however. The woman seemed relieved to have everything out in the open. The charade was over.

'I've been made bankrupt. I don't have to pay for the stuff.'

Carole stared, a surge of indignation rising up. She and Paula had always paid for everything. She wondered about the companies trying to make a living. It wasn't fair. How could people like her get away with it? She took a deep breath. She just wanted Samantha out of her house. The whole thing had come to a head and that in itself was a relief. She couldn't help but be curious even though she couldn't wait to see the back of her. 'Where have you been all this time? Why didn't you get in touch?'

'I went to London with Gerry. I met him in a club. He took me to his flat. It was really posh. He was just like everyone else. He didn't want me, just some fun. It soon wore off. I had no money so he gave me the train fare to get rid of me. I didn't use it. I got a job cleaning in a hotel. There's a room thrown in. It isn't much but it's free.'

'What do you want here with me? Why did you come back?'

'I wanted to make sure Charlotte was all right with you. I'm not as bad as you think. That's why I came late. I didn't want her to see me. I hope she gets adopted by someone nice. Will you still see her?'

Carole nodded. 'Yes, I'll still spend time with her. She thinks I'm a sort of granny.'

Samantha smiled for the first time. 'That's nice. My parents won't want to know. You'll be much better. I'm going straight back now. You'll never see me again so don't worry.'

Carole winced but knew she would be glad it was all over. 'At least you cared enough to come back. Don't tell me any more. I'll have to tell the police you've been here, you know. I'll get into trouble otherwise if they find out. Don't tell me where you're living. Mind you, they probably won't bother once they know you're OK. I can't withhold information.'

'I'll go now. Tell the police to stop looking.'

Carole was tempted to give her an earful of advice but she thought better of it. What was the point? She wouldn't listen. She would have to find her own way. She let Samantha out and she disappeared into the night, like a spectre that had only existed in her imagination. As the darkness folded round her Carole suddenly felt a sense of extreme relief as if a path had suddenly opened in the darkness where Samantha had just disappeared. It was eleven o'clock. She went straight upstairs to bed, looking forward to her day out with Robert the next day. She would sleep well, knowing a weight had been lifted off her shoulders.

Robert arrived for coffee and they discussed where they would go. It was February and hardly spring but there wasn't a cloud in the sky. There was very little warmth coming from the sun and it was quite cold outside. Nevertheless, they decided to walk through the pine forests in Formby and down to the beach. As they drank their coffee in the kitchen, he leaned over and took her hand. 'You're very quiet. I kept looking at you during the rehearsal on Thursday. I wondered what was going on in your head. You seemed so preoccupied. It isn't this Samantha woman, is it?'

Carole shook her head. 'No, it isn't that. It's something else.'

Robert's sensitive face crumpled. He had let himself get involved in this relationship and Carole saw he was suddenly afraid.

She put her other hand over his. 'I'm really happy with you, Robert. It's nothing to do with us. It's just something else, something I haven't been able to talk about. Just give me some time and don't worry. It's not about you.'

He withdrew his hands, leaving hers on the still uncovered Formica table. 'Tell me in your own time. Knowing you, it can't be anything terrible. You're too nice. Let's go out and enjoy the day.'

'There is something I need to tell you straight away.'

He was half standing up ready to go. He sat down again.

'Samantha came here last night. She doesn't want Charlotte back. She was quite rude really, thought I should be replacing her as a parent. She accused me of stealing half the house again.'

'That's ridiculous. You need to tell the police then let the social services get on with it. It's all come to a head, hasn't it? It's got to be a good thing. The whole business has been hanging round your neck like a rock. Now you can get rid of it.'

Carole was tempted to tell him it wasn't quite so straightforward for her but she didn't dare. She didn't want to jeopardise their blossoming friendship. She sensed there was only so much that he could cope with. A walk down to the beach was what they needed, not a psychological workout. Besides, it wouldn't be fair to involve him in her conflicts and regrets. He only knew half the story. She would keep it like that for now. She knew he was right. She already felt as though a weight had been lifted from her but it was a good job he had mentioned the police. It had gone right out of her mind. She picked up the phone.

They went off in the car, leaving the police to deal with everything. It was a good feeling. They parked near the old church in Formby and went through the Lichgate into the cemetery. The Victorian church was surrounded by gravestones. Crocuses and snowdrops announced the imminent arrival of spring. As they wandered over the spongy grass, the ancient stones told their own story. Babies and small children were everywhere; their names engraved forever, their small bodies long gone. Some families had lost two or three babies or toddlers. Carole could almost see their little faces in the back of her mind and she shivered as the grey stones turned red. She longed to be at peace but not in a graveyard. As they walked around, reading the moss covered inscriptions, they didn't need to talk to each other. They were both thinking the same thing, realising how lucky they were to live in the twenty-first century.

The path to the beach went through the pinewoods. There was no one about. They could hear the sea in the distance. Even the birds were silent. As they walked along the path the only sound was the cracking of twigs under their feet. It might have been just one pair of shoes crunching over the fallen wood but instead there were two. They held hands, jumped over fallen tree trunks and ran up and down the hills under the trees like two carefree children, until they came to the sand dunes.

There was a boardwalk crossing the dunes, leading walkers down to the beach. The sea was far out and the beach was covered in driftwood from the recent storms. It was so quiet and lonely they could have been the last people on earth. They walked through the wet sand, leaving their footprints among the driftwood. A ferry floated noiselessly by, following the channel of deep water. It was probably going to the Isle of Man or Ireland. It didn't really matter but Carole suddenly wished that they were on the boat going away together. If only they could escape, sail far away towards the horizon, leaving their problems behind. Instead they ended up in a warm pub with a blazing fire in the grate. It was a much better idea than a trip to Ireland or the Isle of Man in February. And the concert was coming up.

It was warm in front of the fire but Carole's thoughts were straying outside the pub and far away. Robert had an uncanny way of sensing when she was thinking serious thoughts. He looked at her questioningly.

'What are you thinking about? You're miles away.'

Carole couldn't help but smile. 'I was imagining us on that boat maybe going somewhere exotic.'

Robert laughed with a certain amount of relief. 'Like a trip up the Mersey in the dark?' Suddenly he looked thoughtful. 'Why don't we go somewhere? We could go to Paris. Have you been there?'

She shook her head and a now familiar feeling of something verging on shame made her want to creep into a shell. She had never been anywhere. She was tempted to lie but she couldn't. Lying was not the way to a decent relationship and she couldn't do that to this man who was so important to her.

'No, I haven't.'

'Well, it's never too late. It's years since I was there. I've not been anywhere since Jane died and before that. She was so ill we just stayed at home then, afterwards I didn't want to go anywhere on my own. I hated the thought of eating in restaurants, just me at a table. People would have stared and felt sorry for me. But we

PATRICIA MORTON

could go any time. I know there's the concert rehearsal but there's
all the rest of the week and the weekend.' He was suddenly full of
excitement in a way she had never seen before. The crackling fire
was reflected in his eyes.

'You look like a little boy.' She giggled like a schoolgirl. 'Shall
we go now, right this minute?'

'I mean it,' he replied seriously. 'Why not? I can book on the
internet. You can sometimes get late deals, especially at this time
of year.'

A thrill of excitement ran through her. Who knew what might
happen in the future? She hoped that they would have at least the
immediate future. The distant future was too misty, too far away.

'OK. Let's do it. The rehearsal's Thursday then I take Charlotte
out on a Friday. I could change that day for once but you can't
change the rehearsal. Still, it gives you plenty of possibilities.
You'll have to see when the flights are. We have to stay
somewhere too.'

'Don't worry. I'll arrange it unless you want to do it with me.'

'No. You do it. I'll go along with whatever you arrange.'

'We may have to share a room. We can have twin beds. I'm
not trying to seduce you, you know. Of course you can do the
seducing if you want.' It was his way of putting her at ease. 'Right.
That's settled then. I'll have a look at the flights and then we can
decide when to go. How about next week?'

'What!' She was startled. There would be no time to get used
to the idea. Then again maybe that was a good thing.

CHAPTER 15

Weekend in Paris

ROBERT WAS AS good as his word. He booked a late deal and on Friday 22nd February they flew to Paris. The rehearsal had gone very well on Thursday evening. Everything was falling into place ready for the concert. Carole had kept the trip to herself but the excitement was difficult to suppress. Nothing ever escaped the attention of Valerie.

'You look as though you've won the lottery.' She laughed. 'It's nice to see you looking so cheerful. You're not getting married, are you?'

Carole's eyes widened then her face melted into a grin. 'Absolutely not.'

'Oh well, that's all right then. I thought you might have been eloping to somewhere exotic.'

Carole chuckled inwardly. Valerie seemed to have this sixth sense about things. Carole didn't tell her how close she was to the truth. They weren't getting married or eloping but they were going somewhere quite exotic as far as she was concerned.

They had both packed after the rehearsal, just enough clothes for three days. They were flying back the following Monday. It wasn't a honeymoon but to Carole it was a big adventure. She had gradually acquired a rather elegant wardrobe so she didn't have to buy anything much. The only thing she bought was a new nightdress. She had agonised over it in the shop for longer than was reasonable. It was rather beautiful, purple satin embroidered with matching purple and white flowers. As she carried it out of

189

the shop, she had almost turned around and taken it back. She had never had anything so glamorous. It was just right for going to Paris. She held it up and stared at herself in the mirror. She noticed not so much the nightdress as the lines on her face and the blond hair that was subtly gaining pure white streaks.

She flung the nightdress into the case, reproaching herself for her unrealistic expectations. What did she expect at sixty-one? There were bound to be a few lines on her face and streaks in her hair. Back to reality! There were plants to water before she left for the airport. She went outside to get the watering can. It was messy from exposure to the rain. She shouldn't have left it out. Too bad! She picked it up and filled it in the sink. There weren't that many plants to deal with, fortunately. She tried to pour some water into the pot of rambling geraniums that she had rescued from outside. The pot was quite big so she had left it in the porch on the floor. She couldn't understand why the water wasn't coming out. Perhaps there were leaves blocking the spout. She poked her finger in but didn't find anything. Bemused, she tried again. Suddenly a head poked out of the end. She had disturbed a sleeping slug. She tried to grab it but it was too slippery and she wasn't that keen on touching it. Every time she tried to grab it, it went back inside. She groaned aloud. A contest with a slug wasn't appropriate when you were going to Paris. She got a stick and poked it out onto the floor from inside the can. The indignant slug tried to escape. She picked it up with a paper hanky and threw it outside. Then she started to laugh in the empty hall. This was real life. But Paris was fantasy that was going to become reality.

They had breakfast in the airport. They were flying at ten o'clock so they had had to check in early. As they sat in the café, staring out at the planes, Carole felt as though her life was taking off, not just the fat jumbo jets. She savoured the toast and marmalade and the hot coffee. They had had to get up early and she was tired almost to the point where nothing seemed real. She didn't want to admit that at sixty-one years old she had never been on an aeroplane. They found the gate easily enough. Soon their flight number was called over a loud speaker and ten minutes later she was going down the stairs and out to the plane. The air felt cold on her face after the heat of the air terminal. The silver plane looked like an oversized toy. As they climbed the stairs she grasped her hand luggage so tightly her fingers started to hurt. They found their seats and she fastened her seat belt, making a huge attempt to look unconcerned.

As the plane gained speed and took off she held her breath. She looked round at Robert and the other passengers close by and relaxed. They were seemingly unaffected by the noise and upward motion as the plane gained height. Robert took hold of her hand. He knew she was scared. It wasn't a long flight. She had more coffee and a bacon baguette on the plane. It was hot and delicious. She was quite hungry in spite of her airport breakfast. Robert laughed with pleasure at her obvious enjoyment. It must have been like going out with a wide-eyed child.

The hotel was near the Nation metro station. They had to get a taxi. Carole was shocked by the traffic and then further shocked by the price of the taxi. She and Paula had hardly ever spent anything on luxuries. She mentally shrugged her shoulders. Nothing was going to spoil her fun. She could afford it and anyway they were sharing the cost so everything was half price. The room was small but had a new en suite bathroom. The toilet roll holder was in a rather inconvenient place in the cupboard-like bathroom. The first thing she did was scrape her arm on it. Somebody had made a design mistake. She couldn't seem to remember not to do it so the scrapes built up over the three days but it was a small price to pay.

They had got to the hotel early and had plenty of time to settle in. They had both eaten enough on the plane so they went out and had a drink in one of the nearby cafes and discussed what they would do in the afternoon. They were both quite fit so they decided to walk to Notre Dame Cathedral. It was the first item on their list. They wandered down the Boulevard Diderot which led down to the River Seine. There was a cycle track on one side of the pavement. Carole didn't notice it as she was so busy looking in the shops as they passed them. A young cyclist nearly ran over her, making her jump out of the way.

'Oh, pardon,' he shouted apologetically.

They reached the river then walked along the bank to the cathedral. Carole caught her breath and tears filled her eyes. Robert looked worried. He put his arm round her. 'Are you OK? What's the matter? Are you tired?'

She laughed through her tears. 'None of those things. I'm just so happy.'

The cathedral soared upwards into the unseasonal blue sky. The gothic towers were breathtaking. She wondered how on earth they had built it without modern technology. She looked solemnly at the gargoyles over the door and up at roof level. They didn't frighten her. They were supposed to be frightening but to her they just seemed welcoming. They joined the queue to visit the interior, listening to the voices from all over the world. They didn't have to wait too long. It was quite dark inside but the darkness was lit up by the beautiful circular rose windows in a multitude of colours. They sat down on one of the wooden pews. It had been quite a walk from the hotel to the cathedral. It was the right place to have a rest. The organist started to play. Carole clutched Robert's hand. It was the Bach *Toccata*, one of her favourite organ pieces. She started to cry for the second time. The atmosphere was almost too powerful. It was then that she resolved to tell Robert the secret that had obsessed her all her adult life. It was the right time and the right place to make the decision. She would wait for the opportunity. She would know when it came.

They had dinner in a little bistro near the hotel. It wasn't a gourmet restaurant but the staff were friendly and attentive. She had fish with rice. Robert had steak and chips. They both settled for ice cream, feeling as though they should be eating something French but not really wanting much. They lingered over the meal, drinking some house wine and drinking in the ambiance. Carole was fascinated watching people and what they ordered. It was a quite different world. They did without coffee, paid the bill and went back to the hotel for an early night. It had been a long day.

The hotel was on a busy road and Carole was woken in the early morning by unfamiliar noises outside. There were bangs and clangs, metallic sounds that she couldn't identify then the bin men arrived followed by a street sweeping machine. She lay there listening but not caring. She was in Paris. Robert was still fast asleep in spite of the noise. She smiled from under the duvet, thinking that she was going to learn a lot of new things about him during the three days' holiday. She hoped there wouldn't be any nasty surprises.

They had breakfast in the hotel. It was a quite delicious buffet breakfast that certainly made up for the noise outside. She had breakfast cereal, fruit and croissants with jam. There were cold meats and cheese but she had had enough. She wasn't used to eating a lot for breakfast. The only annoyance was the waitress who kept trying to help them. It was self-service so she wasn't needed but she obviously wanted to be important. Or did they look so old they needed help? She hoped not. They lingered over several cups of coffee, planning what they were going to do. It was Saturday so they would probably have to cope with crowds of people celebrating the weekend. They would celebrate too but where? They both had the Musée d'Orsay on their list so there was no conflict. They decided to walk the same way as the previous day but thought they would get the Métro back. It would be tiring walking round the art gallery all day.

They set off, passed Notre Dame then crossed the bridge. They hadn't realised how far it was so they stopped in a café just the other side of the bridge. There were lots of booksellers selling posters and souvenirs as well as books. They bought posters and cards. There was a gift shop nearby. Carole bought three mini models of the Eiffel Tower for Eva, Charlotte and James. She got two place mats for Valerie and Jennie. They were just like paintings. She couldn't resist getting another two, one for herself and one for Laura. The one for Laura had a picture of a mother with three children in front of Notre Dame. She thought this would be just right for her.

It was nearly midday when they got to the art gallery. There was a big queue outside. Was this going to be the first mistake? It wasn't too bad but once they had paid and gone through the door it was time for lunch. When they saw the number of floors and the queue for lunch they realised they should have come earlier.

'We should've got the Métro here,' sighed Carole as they joined the lunch queue.

'*Should've* isn't a good word,' he announced solemnly. 'Remember Edith Piaf's song – no regrets. We'll just have to pick and choose what we go to see. You can't do the whole lot in an afternoon.'

They had a quick lunch then went to visit some of the Impressionist paintings. Robert was more prepared to spend a lot of time looking. Carole knew there was a difference between them from their last visit to an art gallery. She chose one or two paintings that she really liked, read about them and stood examining them for a long time. She'd get a stiff neck and not much else if she tried to look at all of them. She began to feel very tired.

At the end of the gallery there were two circles of armchairs. She noticed a vacant one and collapsed into it. They were made of soft shiny leather and big enough to sleep in. She sank down into the comfortable depths and closed her eyes, her feet sticking straight out, making her feel like a lost doll in the enormous armchair. She was so exhausted she could easily have gone to sleep. Whoever had thought of installing the armchair circles had done a good deed. Robert came to fetch her but by then she had had enough time to relax. They stared out of the massive window at a wonderful panorama of geometrically constructed boulevards and magnificent old buildings. Carole felt totally at ease. She was getting used to being in Paris. It was so easy!

They left and made their way across the road towards the river. It was still early although people were gathering in the cafés for their aperitifs. They both decided they would do the same but first they wanted to sit by the river and watch the boats go by. It was going cold and would soon be dark. They wanted to soak up the atmosphere while it was still light. They found a bench. People waved from the boats and they waved back. A girl who couldn't have been more than twenty was sitting on the next bench. Her baby was crying in the pram. She took it out and rocked it gently. Carole stopped breathing for a moment. Robert noticed her intake of breath. He was sensitive to her reactions. He took her hand.

'Something's bothering you. Is it the baby? She's just a kid herself, isn't she? Perhaps you would've liked some children yourself. Is that what's upsetting you?'

Carole nodded dumbly.

'We all miss out on things, don't we? You try and pack so much into life but you run out of time in the end.'

She started to cry. 'I know you're right but not completely. You see,' she hesitated, 'I did have a baby a long time ago.'

It was the last thing Robert was expecting. A worried frown appeared above his eyebrows. 'What happened? Sorry. You don't have to tell me about it unless you want to.'

'Yes, I do. You might be shocked. I hope you won't.'

'I can't be shocked by you; at least I don't think so. It sounds as though you'll be a lot happier once you've got it off your chest.'

She nodded. 'You see, when I first started teaching I had a relationship with a man in the choir. It was a crazy romance and I was very young in the head. He went to Australia so that was the end of the relationship for him but not for me. I was pregnant and living at home. I couldn't tell my parents. It was a different era. The school would have asked me to leave. I didn't know what to do. I got more and more panicky as the weeks passed. I bet you're shocked now.'

Robert shook his head. 'No, I'm not shocked. I'm just sorry it was the wrong time for you. But what happened?'

The girl with the baby looked on curiously. She could see that a drama was taking place on the next bench but Carole was past caring about the impression she might be making on the banks of the Seine.

'I didn't do anything for nearly four months. I had to hide the fact that I was being sick every morning. My parents would have been concerned in case I was ill. It would never have occurred to them that I was pregnant. I was stuck in a corner with no escape. I couldn't tell the school or my parents. I literally considered killing myself. It seemed the only way out but I couldn't. You see, even then I felt protective towards my baby. I couldn't kill my baby.'

Robert's eyes dissolved into deep pools of brown. 'Oh, Carole! I had no idea. You always seemed so uncomplicated. So what happened to the baby if you can talk about it?'

'I have to.' She took a deep breath. It was like vomiting a massive amount of poison. 'When I was nearly four months, I thought I would have to tell my parents even if they threw me out. They were very conventional people. It was a terrible disgrace. The whole street would have gossiped about it and they would never have recovered their respectability. If they'd thrown me out I would have had no job and nowhere to go. There was no solution.'

'It strikes me you've never got over whatever happened anyway.'

'No. It was awful. I don't know how to tell you this.'

Robert removed his hand and put his arm around her. 'Watch the river boats going past and tell me.'

'So much time has gone and yet it's still as clear as the day it happened. I wasn't feeling well and I had to come home from school. I had really bad griping pains and I was frightened. The school thought it was just the time of the month. The pain got worse. It was so bad I thought I was going to die. I knew enough to realise I was having a miscarriage. There was so much blood and I had no one to help me. I was so terrified I didn't feel anything, not even regret. I put the whole lot in the bin in a carrier bag – yes, a carrier bag! I was terrified someone would find it and I felt like a criminal. Then the bleeding stopped so I didn't go to the doctor's. Nobody knew. I blamed myself. Somehow I'd subconsciously made it happen.'

A lifetime of tears ran down her cheeks. 'I should have buried it. I don't even know if it was a boy or a girl. I've never even given it a name. If I had it might've helped.'

Robert took her in his arms and stroked her head like a baby. 'You'll feel better now. It could have happened because you were so upset but it wasn't your fault. Sometimes the past stops you moving on in the present. Maybe it's time for both of us to move on.'

Gradually she stopped crying. The girl with the pram had gone and darkness was falling over the Seine. The boats were lit up and suddenly she felt better. It wasn't her fault. She would try to remember that. It wasn't her fault. She would stop grieving.

'It all seemed such a coincidence. I mean the business of Samantha. I couldn't believe the same thing had happened to Paula and she'd never said anything about it. We'd both kept secrets all the time we were together. It's incredible. If we'd been more honest we might have been able to help each other.'

'Maybe.'

'Then there's the business of Charlotte. I could have adopted her if I'd been younger but it's the wrong time again. I sometimes feel as though the gods up above are pulling all the wrong strings for me.'

'I know what you mean. People who have children are often not ready and make a mess of it. When you are ready you're too old. I'm afraid we just have to live with that. Jane and I didn't do such a great job with our own children but we did our best at the time.'

'I bet you were lovely parents. Your kids have done well, haven't they? Shall we go and have an aperitif? I think I could do with a drink. I don't often feel like that but I think it might help.'

Robert got up and pulled her up too. They stood like young lovers on the banks of the Seine then they started walking towards the cafés. 'I think you deserve two aperitifs. It's a special occasion in more ways than one. I don't think you'll become an alcoholic just like that.'

She laughed and it chased away the pain. 'No, I'm too happy with you to need to drink a lot but maybe two drinks might be a good idea.'

'Definitely. Alcohol can cure pain but it's not a permanent solution. We both deserve a bit of fun. Let's celebrate being alive.'

They looked at the cocktail menu. They could have had Martini but it seemed unambitious. They ordered Kir with white wine and clinked glasses like their neighbours were doing. It wasn't long before they were ready for the second one. This time they ordered Kir Royal with Champagne. The bubbles tickled Carole's nose. The first cocktail had relaxed her. She was really enjoying the prickly sensation of the bubbles and the world suddenly looked bright and shiny. Was it the Champagne or could it go on forever? She hoped it was the latter.

They decided to spend the final day on the river. The boat was a good way of seeing Paris without too much walking. They sat side by side and watched the sights coming into view then being replaced by others as the boat sailed along the banks of the river. She thought about the previous night when they had made love for the first time. She turned to look at the man she hoped to spend the rest of her life with. He was staring at Notre Dame as it came into view. How beautiful and majestic it was! He too was happy. It wasn't like it had been with Michael. They were past the flush of youth but it had been wonderful in a different way. It had cemented their relationship. It had turned out to be a honeymoon after all.

They spent the last evening in a more upmarket restaurant with a view of the cathedral and the river. They both loved the cathedral and wanted to see it lit up in its prized position on the Ile de la Cite. They ordered the Kir Royal again then ate Coq au Vin with a bottle of wine recommended by the waiter. The lights of Notre Dame shimmered on the water. There was a new intimacy between them. Carole wished the moment could last forever but of course it didn't. They walked back to the hotel and made love again. This time it was more like her first experience with Michael. They were getting to know each other in a new way.

The flight was early the next morning. They had ordered a taxi. It was Monday and the streets were full of people going to work. She sighed. This was reality. Last night was fantasy. As the driver battled through the traffic, dodging cars with big dents in their bodies, she resolved to go and see Laura that night. She had missed her day with Charlotte last week. The little girl would probably not have noticed but who knew? She couldn't get inside the mind of a small child. Maybe Charlotte was wondering where she was.

It had been an early flight. They were back in Liverpool at ten-thirty and she was back in the house at midday. Robert had gone straight to the supermarket then he was going home.

'Are you going home for a rest?' she joked, suddenly realising how tired she was. They had been walking almost the whole time in Paris apart from when they were sleeping and eating.

'Yes. I could do with a rest. I've got some phone calls to make to the kids but really I need to relax for a bit. What are you going to do? The same, I expect. You must be tired too unless it's me getting old.'

'No. It's been lovely but I am tired too. I just need to go and see Laura and Charlotte. I won't really relax until I've done that. I should have had Charlotte on Friday. I did tell Laura but I didn't really say anything to Charlotte. She might have been disappointed but she probably wouldn't have understood. She's too little.'

Robert shook his head with a certain amount of disapproval. 'You can't let go, can you? I do understand better now why not but you've got your life to lead. You shouldn't feel guilty all the time.'

'I don't feel guilty now. I feel really happy but I have a chance to make a difference. That's all.'

'I know. That's one of the reasons I love you so much.' He smiled as he got his car keys out. I'll give you a ring tomorrow. Bye.' He kissed her on the forehead, got into his car and drove away.

She made herself some lunch, watched the news on the television then got into the car and drove to Laura's. She realised she should have phoned first but she was impatient to see them and be reassured that everything was all right with Charlotte. She knew she didn't have the right to be so possessive and over-anxious about the child but she couldn't help it. She remembered the little hand in hers. She recognised that there was an element of trying to compensate for the past. It was impossible to escape. It was like a jigsaw, the pieces of the past and present all fixed together.

It took her half an hour to get to Laura's. She had to really concentrate on her driving. She felt very anxious and kept telling herself not to be stupid. This child wasn't her baby and never could be. She wondered why she couldn't be more rational about it all. Without Charlotte, she could get on with her U3A activities and maybe she and Robert might even get married. She wondered what most people would do in the present situation but the answer didn't come.

She parked outside the house and walked up to the front door. There were usually signs of activity around the house but everything was quiet. There wasn't even the usual line of washing out in the back. *They must have gone out for the day.* Then again it was term time. Laura had probably taken Charlotte out shopping before picking the others up from school. She decided to knock anyway as she had come this far. She knocked. There was a silence then she heard slow footsteps coming down the stairs and along the hall. It didn't sound like Laura.

The person at the other side was fumbling with the lock as though it was unfamiliar. It finally opened. It was Don, Laura's husband. His face was pale as though he hadn't slept. He hardly seemed to recognise her.

'Don. It's me, Carole. I've come to see Laura and Charlotte. Are you ill? You look a bit tired.'

He looked as though he was in shock. 'Laura's gone. She's in the hospital. You'd better come in.'

He shuffled down the hall in his slippers. They went into the lounge. There were no toys anywhere. Carole's body started to shake. Something awful had happened. She wanted to shout at Don to hurry up and put her out of her misery but he didn't seem able to rush. They sat down in the tidy lounge on either side of the fire.

'She had a car accident on Saturday. Susan was here. The others were in the back. She was coming back from Ormskirk market. Some idiot pulled out of a side road in front of her on the A59. It was his fault but she got the worst of it. Thank goodness the children were in the back. They had cuts and bruises but they're OK.'

Carole didn't know what to ask first. 'Can I see Laura?'

Don shook his head. 'No. She's in Intensive Care. She's unconscious. Nobody knows if she'll survive.' He put his head in his hands. 'It's funny. One minute your life's going along steadily then suddenly it's turned upside down.'

'I'm so sorry, Don. I hope she'll be all right.' It sounded so inadequate but she didn't really know what to say for the best. 'What's happened to the children?' She hardly dared to ask.

'Susan's still with me. The others are in care. The social services came and took them away. I couldn't cope. I can hardly cope with myself at the moment. I'm off work. The shock nearly killed me. If it hadn't been for Susan I think it would have but she needs me.'

Carole felt a terrible sinking feeling. They had had such a wonderful time drinking Champagne by the Seine and now it was definitely back to reality, but a reality she couldn't have dreamt of. After all that had happened to that little girl, she now had to cope with yet another change. Then she thought of the other two, George and Mary. Mary would probably shrug her shoulders rather cynically or would she? They had both been settled with Laura and now their lives had been disrupted. She knew George would be upset. He had been with Laura for a long time and saw the two of them as his parents.

'Where have they gone? Did the social workers tell you?'

'I didn't ask. I was too shocked by the whole thing. They kept the children at the hospital then took them away from there. They came to collect their things but I didn't think to ask. You'll have to get in touch with the social workers and perhaps they'll tell you.'

'Yes, I'll do that as soon as I get home. Is there anything I can do for you?'

Don shook his head. 'Thanks, but no. I'll cope. I have to.'

'Look. I'll give you my phone number. Ring me if you need anything and let me know how Laura is.'

'Thank you. I'll do that. I hope there'll be better news soon but she won't be able to look after the children. It could take months.'

'Never mind. Just look after yourself and Susan. She must be very upset. I'll find out where the children are. There might be something I can do. I'll be in touch.'

She went out to the car, feeling strangely strong. She had something to do now. She would have to find the children. She drove back and phoned the social services. She asked to speak to Jean Parkinson but she wasn't available. Carole explained the situation and got a more sympathetic response than she expected. Not being a relative meant she had little influence over anything to do with Charlotte. The person on the end of the phone told her she would ask Jean to get in touch as soon as possible. Carole put the phone down feeling helpless. There was nothing else she could do except wait. She paced about the house, wondering what to do.

She considered phoning Robert but decided not to. He had had enough of that particular situation. He would be sorry about Laura but when it came to the children, she knew very well he would tell her to leave well alone. She couldn't do that. They had had such a wonderful time all this would be like a cold shower to him. He would feel they were going backwards. Of course she would have to tell him but not straight away. She looked at the clock. It was nearly four o'clock. It was unlikely Jean would phone so quickly. She probably wouldn't go back to the office until tomorrow. She had only just resigned herself to waiting when the phone rang. She grabbed it too quickly and almost dropped it.

'Hello, Carole. It's Jean here. The secretary rang my mobile. I'm hardly ever off duty! Life's never straight forward, is it, especially for Charlotte. The children were taken to the children's home in Ormskirk. I can give you the address and phone number. There's no reason why you shouldn't go and see her. You are the only person she's at all close to now so she would benefit from a visit. Both the other foster children are understandably upset. It was a terrible accident and they're lucky to have escaped with cuts and bruises. Of course the memory of it all will last longer than the bruises.'

She took down the number and the address. She said she would go tomorrow if it could be arranged. Jean agreed to keep in touch. As she put the phone down, Carole looked around the house and accepted that she was home. Paris was over. The keyboard was standing in the lounge and she was glad it was there. It linked her to the U3A and made her feel attached to something. She sat down to have a practice. It was something to do to take her mind off the startling events. She opened the book of songs that had come with the keyboard and searched for something easy and cheerful to play. She put the accompaniment on and played 'Besame Mucho'. It had a lovely South American beat which make her think of sunshine. She needed that in the February gloom. It was going dark already so there was something a bit illogical about it but she felt better. Slowly but surely she was making progress with the keyboard. It gave her something to focus on while she waited for news of Laura and Charlotte.

CHAPTER 16

Crossroads

I<small>T WAS</small> T<small>UESDAY</small>, less than three weeks to the concert. It had been something quite enormous up to now but suddenly it hardly mattered. Something else had taken over. The problem of Charlotte had come back and made the concert seem of secondary importance. She knew the little girl would be devastated by all that had happened to her. She had lost her mum, she had lost Carole and just when she was getting used to Laura her world had been turned upside down again. Carole phoned as soon as she had finished her breakfast.

The woman on the other end of the phone seemed a bit vague. She heard a rustling of paper as though she was leafing her way through a large file. She was probably a secretary. Perhaps she was just in charge of administration. Or was the children's home so big that they didn't know the children? She shuddered at the thought. 'Oh, yes. They came in last Saturday, three of them. Is that right?'

'Yes. That's right. I'd like to come and visit Charlotte. The social worker said it would be all right.' Carole wished she didn't sound so defensive. It was like dealing with an invisible wall that wouldn't let you in. She wasn't a relative and that seemed more important than anything else to these people.

'I'm sure that will be OK. When do you want to come? Charlotte is young so she'll be here all afternoon. The others are at school. They try to keep things as normal as possible. It looks as though the three of them had a big shock.'

'I'll come round at two o'clock if that's all right.'

'Yes, that's fine. I'll make a note.'

She put the phone back then went into the lounge. The big teddy was still lying there next to the empty grate. There wasn't much point in lighting the fire. She would be out all afternoon. She was so restless it was difficult to sit still. She paced about, wondering when to tell Robert. He would be ringing later. She didn't want to tell him because he would try to influence her. She needed to make her own decision, whatever that might be. It was still early. She did some housework to pass the time and then played the keyboard to reward herself.

It was soon lunchtime and soon after she was in the car driving off to Ormskirk. As she drove down the A59 she noticed the road where the accident had taken place. Laura might have been going really fast. At the side of the road there was a big round sign with a '60' on it. If she'd hit someone at that speed no wonder she was hurt. On her way back she would be watching out for trouble. A sports car passed her then cut in, in front, causing her to brake too quickly. She looked in the mirror. There was a car just behind her. It had braked in time. Life was a lottery.

The children's home turned out to be an enormous building set in large gardens. It must have once been an elegant Victorian house. Although it had kept its elegance there were nevertheless signs of an institution. Cheap modern extensions had been added and a large concrete car park filled half the garden. A mini bus stood outside the front door probably ready to pick children up from school. Carole rang the bell and a jolly, curly headed woman of about forty opened the door. She showed Carole into a waiting room furnished with comfortable sofas. Carole explained who she had come to see and the woman nodded.

'I'll just have to go and tell Mrs Adams,' she said. 'I won't be too long. Make yourself comfortable. Have a drink while you're waiting.' She disappeared out of the large door which made her look like a dwarf.

Carole looked around, thinking of the Champagne they had drunk not so long ago. 'Have a drink' meant help yourself to tea or coffee from the machine in this case. She didn't bother. Instead she looked around the walls at pictures of groups of children going back quite a few years. They were all smiling happily but perhaps it was just an act, a pose for a photo. Ten minutes later, the door opened and the woman appeared with Charlotte and a box of toys. The little girl looked pale and tired. When she saw Carole her face lit up and she ran across the room and into her arms. The reaction hadn't escaped the notice of the woman with her. She smiled and nodded.

'Just ring the bell when you're ready to go or if you want anything. By the way, I'm Karen Collins. Mrs Adams would like to have a word with you before you go.'

Carole nodded. Karen negotiated the large door again, leaving the two of them together. Charlotte wouldn't let go of her. She didn't take any interest in the toys, just kept saying 'Carole' and playing with her scarf. It wasn't anything special but Charlotte seemed to like the tiny flowers that formed a border all the way round. She took it off and tied it round Charlotte's neck. This seemed to help, as though having something belonging to Carole gave her a sense of security. She let go of her hand for a moment and caught sight of herself in a long mirror on the wall.

'You look pretty like that,' Carole told her, hoping she would show some interest in the box of toys but she didn't. She came straight back to sit on her knee. She hadn't said anything at all. She began to wonder how they were going to pass the time. She could see their reflection in the mirror. They were like any typical mother and child.

She tried to get her to play with the toys. She picked up the box with difficulty as Charlotte was glued to her. Inside there was a small teddy that looked like a mini version of Samson. She picked him up and tickled Charlotte's face with him. 'Do you like him? He looks like Samson's baby brother.'

The child didn't respond, just cuddled him. Then suddenly out of the blue a little voice said, 'Me home Samson.'

Carole looked down at the little girl. It was only three words but her meaning was clear. She had arrived at this enormous building without any real thought about what she would do. She was fairly powerless anyway as a non relative but she made her mind up once and for all. If they would let her take Charlotte she would do it regardless of any reaction from Robert. She was sure they wouldn't let her adopt the child. She was too old but she would be better at home with Carole until an adoption could be arranged. It suddenly seemed much clearer.

'I can't take you home today. You must be patient.' Even as she uttered the words, she knew it was meaningless to the child but she didn't know what else to say. She rang the bell.

Karen arrived almost immediately as though she had been just outside the door. Maybe she had been. Carole didn't care too much whether she had been eavesdropping or not. She had nothing to hide.

'Mrs Adams wants to see you. Have you got time to have a word with her? She's very keen to discuss Charlotte.'

Carole got up, putting Charlotte down by the toys. 'I'll come back soon to see you. I'll bring Samson.'

Her words had no effect whatsoever. Charlotte saw what was going to happen and started to scream, clinging on to Carole. It had all happened before and she remembered.

'Can I take her with me?' she asked, not seeing any other solution.

'Well, we'd better leave the toys here and you can carry her if that's OK.'

Carole picked her up and they went along to an office down a long corridor. As she walked she noticed the coved ceiling with mouldings adorning the walls. It was still a beautiful building. She wondered how she was going to have any sort of conversation with a heavy child round her neck a bit like one of the heavy plaster Victorian mouldings. They came to yet another enormous door. Karen knocked and a voice shouted for them to come in.

Amanda Adams was sitting behind a large desk filled with paperwork. Carole felt a bit sorry for her. She hated the administration jobs that Paula used to tackle but which were now her responsibility. The amount of paper on the table made her jobs seem minute but of course this was Mrs Adams' profession.

At least she got paid for doing it. The job obviously involved a lot of paperwork. The face behind the paper and wire baskets was friendly but Carole got the impression that she wasn't someone to get on the wrong side of. *She must be around fifty,* Carole estimated. Her blond hair indicated a recent trip to the hairdresser. She also looked as though she worked out at the gym every day.

'Charlotte, would you like an ice cream? Karen's got some strawberry ones in the freezer for special little girls. Can she take the scarf with her?'

Carole nodded and amazingly Charlotte and Karen went off to get the ice cream without any fuss.

'I'm Amanda Adams.'

'Carole Peters. Nice to meet you.'

They shook hands quite formally then Amanda came out from behind her desk and pointed to two armchairs on either side of a large Victorian cast iron fireplace. There was no fire but the central heating was on so it wasn't cold. A coal fire would probably have required a maid, Carole mused, and such things didn't exist in this day and age or if they did they would cost money.

'Do sit down. We need to talk and time is short. I'm afraid the ice cream won't last very long.'

She wondered what was coming. Amanda Adams gave her the impression that decisions had been made and she was now to be informed, even though she wasn't a relative. Amanda's face was serious. She looked as though she had only limited time to say what she wanted. She kept looking at the large clock on the wall as though she was playing a game of 'Beat the Clock'.

'The truth is that the social services have tried to get her relatives to take responsibility for Charlotte but they have been unsuccessful.'

Carole noticed how objective she remained. If she did feel angry with Samantha's parents she was certainly keeping it well hidden.

'She was bonding with the foster mother but that's over, given the circumstances. The other two children will be fostered together and this will give them some stability but Charlotte wasn't there very long. You appear to be the only person she has had a relationship with apart from Laura. It's obvious she has an attachment to you. We wonder if you could foster her for now to give her some security. She's had a very bad time.'

'Yes. I can.' There was no hesitation in Carole's voice. She wasn't intimidated by Amanda. The decision had been made the moment she had seen the child.

Amanda looked astonished. 'I was expecting you to think about it. Are you sure?'

'Yes. Don't imagine I haven't thought about it. I'm one hundred per cent certain that it's the right thing to do. She seemed to have settled and Laura even talked about adopting her. It all appeared to be working out so well but now things have changed. Of course she's not my granddaughter but her mother was my friend's child. We were friends for thirty years. We were probably closer than a lot of sisters.'

'Yes. It isn't always blood ties that count. It can be other things.'

'There's only one thing I want and it's not for me, it's for Charlotte. I'm sixty-one. I can't be a parent to her. I want her to be adopted eventually for her sake. But I would like her to be adopted by a family in the area so she can continue to visit me. As she gets bigger I'll tell her that she will get a new family but she won't lose me. I want that put in her notes.'

To Carole's relief, Amanda agreed with a certain sadness. 'I'm sorry you can't adopt her but you have to realise that she's only three and you're sixty-one. As she grows up she would realise the age gap. Ideally she needs a person or people young enough to be there for her until she grows up.'

'I will, as long as I can. I understand perfectly. My own mother was forty-four when I was born. I knew she was old as I grew up. I was scared my parents would die and leave me on my own.' She took a sharp intake of breath. Why was she telling Amanda this? She had hardly ever admitted it to herself.

Amanda smiled wryly. 'Life's a lucky dip, isn't it? Sometimes not so lucky! You don't always get what you want at the right time but if you've got any sense you make the best of it. You obviously have.'

Carole didn't contradict her. What was the point? She was tired of hearing about life being a lottery or a lucky dip. It seemed a superficial image given the seriousness of some of the situations. 'So what happens now?'

'I'll have a word with the social worker who contacted me – Jean Parkinson. I still think you need some time to consider what you've decided. Do you realise it's a huge commitment? It's going to change your life. You won't be free to do what you want. You need to be able to change your mind. We won't say anything to Charlotte at the moment. I'll get things moving and if you still feel the same you can probably take her in a couple of weeks but only if you're sure. I won't think any the less of you if you change your mind.'

Karen came back and Carole braced herself for the inevitable scene. She bent down until her face was level with Charlotte's. 'I have to go now. I'll come back tomorrow and I'll bring Samson. Would you like that?'

Charlotte looked confused. Carole knew very well that the only reality for the child was the fact that she was going and leaving her. Any promises were a waste of time but she had to make them, more for herself than for Charlotte. She gave her a kiss and a hug then turned towards the door. Karen held on to her while Carole departed. The bitter crying was something that she had heard before. It was a repeat performance but it still hurt just as much. She wouldn't change her mind.

She had only been in the house for half an hour when the phone rang. Robert wanted to come round and spend the evening with her. She had several hours to work out what to tell him. Would he want a partner with a child in tow at his age? She dreaded the thought of losing him but she wasn't going to change her mind. Somehow she would fit in the choir and the keyboard. Her mind went round in circles, examining the limited possibilities. Jenny would help and perhaps Valerie. She started to get the spare room ready for Charlotte. A new duvet cover and curtains would liven it up immediately. She needed a design that would appeal to the child, probably flowers. Charlotte liked flowers.

It was only two weeks to the concert and Robert arrived keen to discuss the last minute details. Carole was waiting for a gap in the conversation to tell him the news. She tried several times but he just kept talking. Of course he was preoccupied by the ticket sales, whether the soloists were in good health and many more small details involved in organising a concert. Carole knew her part and would simply pick up her uniform black skirt and white blouse and go and sing. Robert stopped to take a breath. She finally told him what had happened to Laura.

There was a look of discomfort on his face as he listened to how the accident had happened. 'I'm so sorry. I've been talking about the concert. It's really trivial considering what's happened. Is there anything I can do to help?'

She took a deep breath. 'They've asked me to foster Charlotte. I've said yes although they want me to think about it for a while but I've made up my mind. I know it will affect our lives but I can't refuse. The child has nobody else. And I want to do it for her, to give her some quality of life.' She stopped, running out of breath as though she had been dashing up a steep hill. She waited for his reaction.

He looked at her questioningly, his face a little sad. 'Is there room for me in all this?'

'I was dreading telling you. Of course there will be room for you. I thought perhaps you wouldn't still want to be with me the way things have turned out.'

He smiled gently, holding her hand. 'I hereby take you and Charlotte under my wing. Will that do as a promise?'

His reaction took her breath away momentarily. She had been expecting all kinds of reasons why she shouldn't be doing it and he had just agreed that it was the right thing.

'You seem surprised. A few months ago I had nobody in my life. Now I've got not one but two people. Do you think I'll make a good granddad?'

'Of course you will.' She couldn't believe what she was hearing.

'It won't be easy, you know. You'll be tied up all day and in the evening. How are you going to have a life? And what about the concert?'

'Don't worry. I'll find a way. I wouldn't miss the concert for the world. I could bring her and get someone to look after her. My friend Jenny might do it.'

Robert looked relieved. 'I'm sorry to be going on about the concert but it's only two weeks away and it's my responsibility. It has to be right.'

'Of course it has and it will. I'm so glad you approve of what I'm doing. I didn't want to lose you.'

'Well, you won't.'

They watched the second half of a film they'd seen before, cuddled up close on the sofa. *Surely nothing else could go wrong!* Then she remembered Laura, fighting for her life in the hospital.

Carole went every day to see Charlotte. She took Samson with her the first day. Karen opened the door and the look on her face made Carole blush. Well, she did look a bit silly with the large animal. You could hardly see Carole behind the mound of fur.

'Well, hello, teddy. Have you come to see Charlotte?'

Carole laughed from behind the mass of yellow fur. She knew Charlotte would be happy with the teddy so she had braved the stares and smiles. She suddenly remembered that when she had first got him he was in a bin bag. She had been in such a hurry she hadn't thought of that. She still had the bin bag. She could have put him in it. She wouldn't have looked quite so conspicuous. She'd just dumped him on the back seat and driven off.

Charlotte still loved the big teddy. He was a link with the past and Carole hoped if she left him there with the little girl he could be a replacement for her until she could take her home. It worked to some extent and Carole found herself going home each time without feeling so bad. There were still tears but Samson saved

PATRICIA MORTON

the day! Several times Amanda Adams had cornered her and asked her if she had changed her mind but she was adamant. She would take her as soon as it could be arranged. She wasn't sure when that would be but assumed it wouldn't be too long.

She had spoken to Valerie after the rehearsal and told her what was happening. She was very supportive if a little surprised at her decision. She was wearing another rather glamorous top that Carole guessed had come from the charity shop. She had obviously had blond streaks added to her hair and the red necklace that she was wearing suited her perfectly.

'I hope you're doing the right thing, Carole. It could be long term, you know.'

'I know. I'm assuming it will be. It depends if they find somebody to adopt her. I don't know how easy that is but I know it takes a long time. I intend to enjoy every minute of it while she's with me. It's quite a privilege, you know, to be able to help a child to have a better life. I know that sounds a bit sentimental.'

'No, it doesn't. I know what you mean. Don't forget how you helped Mark. I think you're becoming a saint! There's a definite halo round your head.'

Carole laughed. 'No chance of that.'

'Well, if you need some help just ask. I could look after Charlotte sometimes to give you a break.'

'Thanks, Val. I might take you up on that. She can go to the nursery some days so I won't be completely housebound. I want to keep going to the keyboard group. I'm really enjoying it. I'll make some arrangements, don't worry. By the way, I'm sorry I haven't seen you lately. I'm so busy considering I'm retired! And I do like your top and necklace.'

Valerie smiled with pleasure. Carole didn't tell her she'd been to Paris with Robert. It was the end of the rehearsal and the cleaner was waiting to close up the hall.

On Friday night, she phoned Jenny and told her what had happened. She impulsively asked her round for a meal then realised she hadn't got anything in to eat. She drove to the supermarket and bought a lot of buffet food and some nice bread

214

and fresh fruit. She added a few sweets to make goody bowls. The children loved them and she didn't want to disappoint them. They enjoyed the buffet then the children watched some television while they talked about the new situation.

'I'll help,' Jenny said immediately. 'You've got the concert soon. I bet they'll let you have Charlotte before the concert. If we all come to the concert I can look after Charlotte while you sing. James and Eva will be OK. They don't need so much looking after now. They'll enjoy watching you and the orchestra. It'll be good for them.'

Carole heaved a sigh of relief. She hadn't wanted to ask Jenny to look after Charlotte. It was much better that she had offered. She had been worried about what to do about the concert. She was sure she would have Charlotte by then. At least she knew Jenny. Everything seemed to be falling into place. The bedroom was ready. The new curtains and duvet cover gave the room a new lease of life. She wished she could have painted it and perhaps put up new wallpaper but there wasn't time. She thought she might get a decorator to do it at some point but at present she had done enough. It was after all the relationship that mattered, not the décor.

'Where's Samson?' Eva demanded, appearing in the kitchen doorway.

'He's staying with Charlotte at the moment,' Carole replied. 'She's coming to live here.' As she said it she felt a warm ripple of excitement.

'Wow! Is she staying for ever and ever?'

'No. Probably only for a time but we don't know how long. She needs a new mum and dad.'

'I've only got a mum,' Eva retorted, as though she thought Charlotte was being too demanding.

'I know. But she's a very good mum, isn't she? She cooks nice meals for you and makes sure you have lots of fun. You can come here and play with Charlotte if you like.'

James looked a bit reluctant. He hadn't forgotten the last time and what she had done to his Lego model. Eva had a shorter memory and looked delighted.

'Can I come tomorrow?'

'Well, she isn't here yet, is she? When she comes I'll invite you round, maybe not straight away but soon. She'll need a bit of time to get used to being here. It'll be new because she's been at Laura's.'

'Who's Laura?'

Carole sighed. This conversation wasn't going away any time soon.

'She's the lady she was staying with. She's had an accident and she's in hospital so she can't look after her any more.'

To distract her Carole got out the glass balls and gave one to Eva. It worked. She stopped asking about Laura and started asking about the Eiffel Tower. She began to realise that she should do as much as possible during her week of freedom next week. If Charlotte started asking questions like Eva she would be exhausted all the time.

Jenny laughed, obviously catching on to what Carole was thinking. James came in and Carole gave him the other ball. She spent another ten minutes explaining about The Eiffel Tower while Jenny relaxed, enjoying a bit of peace. Carole gave her the place mat. It was such a lovely souvenir of Paris, even if it was made of plastic. Then she felt unhappy as she realised she still had Laura's with the picture of the woman with the three children in front of Notre Dame. It no longer seemed an appropriate present. She would probably never foster children again. The picture might be an unwelcome reminder of that. They all went home promising to keep in touch on the phone. Carole lit the fire and sat down to play the keyboard. Things were turning out well, she thought. Little did she know what the next day would bring.

CHAPTER 17

Endings and Beginnings

SATURDAY DAWNED FULL of hope. The daffodils in the garden were swelling, poised ready to burst into flower. Snowdrops were already blooming in green and white clumps. Weeds were also starting to grow but Carole didn't care. She would get out there and do some gardening with Charlotte. They could grow some vegetables. Messing around with soil was not much different to messy cake mixes. It was all hands-on stuff that a toddler would enjoy. She had her breakfast staring out at the sunny garden, her mind full of plans. After breakfast, she would go to the charity shop and see if she could find some more books and toys for Charlotte. Jenny kept passing her things too so she wasn't short of playthings for the little girl. She knew it was more for her than for the child. Maybe she was going backwards to childhood herself. She smiled at the thought then mentally denied it. No, she was just having some fun.

The phone rang. That would be Robert. They were going to a concert that evening. He would be ringing to make sure she could still go then he was going to stay overnight. Things had certainly moved on in her life. She cast her mind back to how glad she had been sometimes to talk to the cold callers. Looking back now, it had seemed rather pathetic. Soon after she had come back to the house the postman had knocked with a parcel. He was a cheery man with kind brown eyes and a rather untidy beard. When she opened the door he had looked so delighted to see her.

'Miss Peters! I'm Ken. I've been delivering your post for months and I've never seen you. I'm so glad to meet you. Are you OK?'

It had been hard not to cry. She wasn't OK but this man had made her feel better. It was just a bit of human contact. A kind word had made all the difference. She wouldn't forget his kindness or how her life had changed. She picked up the phone. The voice on the other end spoke in nothing more than a whisper.

'It's Don. I'm just ringing to tell you that Laura died last night.'

Carole froze. It couldn't be true but she could tell by his voice that it was. 'Oh, Don, I'm so sorry.'

It all sounded so inadequate but there was nothing she could say that would have sounded right. 'Have you got anyone with you? Have you got family there?'

'Yes. My sister and brother-in-law are here. I just wanted to let you know. You asked me to.'

'Look, Don. If there's anything I can do just let me know.' She felt as though she was reading the dialogue out of a book. It sounded just like something from a melodrama on the television. It felt so inadequate but she was helpless. It was too late.

'Thank you. I'll keep in touch and let you know when the funeral is. Bye.'

She sat down, looking miserably at the cold remains of her toast. Why on earth did these things have to happen? She thought of Susan. She would be devastated by the loss of her mum. Laura had been so happy and positive. She thought maybe she could invite Susan round to help her with Charlotte then had second thoughts. That might not be a good idea. It would remind her of her mum. In any case, she couldn't get involved with yet another problem situation. She decided not to volunteer unless Don asked her for help. Then she wouldn't be able to refuse.

She resolved to get on with her life. She would go shopping for toys then go to the concert with Robert. What was the point of sitting in the house brooding? She threw her cold tea down the sink and made herself another cup. She caught sight of the place mat with the three children in front of Notre Dame. A desperate wave of sadness came over her like a storm cloud gathering momentum. Her new life resembled a variable period of weather that just wouldn't settle. She would keep both the place mats now but Laura's would always be a reminder of what had happened to her. She looked solemnly at it, noting the cafés and the ancient black wrought iron street lamps. There was so much life in the picture. It was an amazing souvenir of Paris and a reminder that life is precious and perilous.

Robert rang as promised and arranged to pick her up at seven o'clock so that they could get to the concert at seven-thirty. She didn't tell him what had happened. She instinctively felt that the bit of news about Charlotte was enough for now. She would have to tell him that evening but face-to-face would be better than over the phone. He had his own concert to cope with on the 16th. She didn't want bad news to upset their blossoming relationship. She resumed her position at the window while she finished her tea. She noticed the cherry tree's buds were already swelling with new life. It was early spring. Laura would not be there to see the spring. She put her coat on and made her way down to the shops.

She went straight to the charity shop. It had become a way of life. Buying in proper shops had become difficult as she was used to things being cheap. She found some more jigsaws and books then went to say hello to Joyce. She hadn't been in for quite a long time so it was nice to see her. Joyce never looked any different, neither older nor younger. She was pleased to see Carole, whom she considered to be a friend after all her visits and purchases.

'Hi, Joyce. Are you all right?'

She nodded. 'I'm fine, well just the same as usual. The usual aches and pains but I'm not complaining. How about you?'

Carole hesitated. She didn't really want to start making Joyce's life a misery. She told her about Paris and her face lit up.

'Well, you're getting about, aren't you? I've never been out of the country. I've seen it on the television. I think that's enough for me. I'm a bit of a home bird. I can't speak French either. I wouldn't be able to ask for anything and I might get lost.'

'As long as you're happy I don't think it really matters where you are. To be honest, you don't need to speak French in Paris. Most people speak English. I did French at school but I don't remember much. As soon as you try to say something they start speaking English. To tell you the truth, it's a bit humiliating. You'd think they'd just pretend you were French but it doesn't seem to work like that.'

Joyce listened solemnly. Some people would have laughed but she didn't. She was well out of her comfort zone talking about Paris and French. She'd probably left school at fourteen without ever learning a foreign language. Not that it had done Carole much good when she was in Paris but she had at least had the experience. Joyce changed the subject.

'There's a white blouse just come in. I haven't had time to price it but it's really nice. It's a very good make.' She laughed. 'It's from someone who's got more money than sense. I bet it cost a fortune and it's brand new. It looks as though it would fit you.'

Carole couldn't resist. She was intrigued. Joyce went into the back room to get it. When she saw it she gasped. It was beautiful quality cotton trimmed with delicate white lace and brand-new. The label told everything. It would have cost a fortune in the shops. It was the right size. She went to try it on. As she stood in front of the mirror she realised it would be ideal for the concert. They had to wear a black skirt and a white blouse. Jewellery could be any colour. She bought it and a black ceramic necklace to go with the skirt. Looking good would surely help her to sing well. Good clothes gave you confidence, even if they had come from the local charity shop.

She said goodbye to Joyce and wandered along the pavement to where she had parked the car. She could have walked but she had planned to go to the shopping centre if she couldn't get anything in the charity shop. She had got some toys so there was no reason to waste time wandering round the town centre. She went home and spent the afternoon practising the keyboard. She practised most days and Barbara was happy with her progress. She was actually better than some of the people who had been in the group for a year or two. A few of them found this depressing but she always insisted it was because she could play the piano. It gave her a huge advantage. Her life was full of children and music. She was so happy then she thought of Laura and the thought of her lying in the mortuary modified but didn't destroy her happiness. Life had to go on.

She went to the concert wearing her new blouse. She had decided to try it out before Robert's important concert on the 16th. He was obviously impressed.

'You look so young in that blouse. It's really beautiful. Where did you get it from?'

She told him and he couldn't stop laughing. 'You would be an easy person to live with. We'd never get into debt with your way of shopping.'

'It's just the way you're brought up, isn't it? My parents were careful with money then when I lived with Paula she never spent anything. Mind you, that was probably because she was paying money to Samantha.'

With a shock she realised she had put Samantha completely out of her mind but nevertheless she couldn't help wondering if she would end up coming back to plague her. She turned her attention to the concert. She had let Robert choose what they went to. He was the expert but she'd got the impression that he'd chosen for her rather than for himself. Music was his life and he knew so much more about it but the concert was just right for her. He knew she found symphonies difficult so he had avoided them.

'I hope you haven't come to this concert to please me,' she questioned, feeling a bit uncomfortable. She wanted him to enjoy it too.

'I looked for a programme that would be nice for both of us. I wouldn't have enjoyed it if I thought you weren't happy. It's a lovely programme and it's quite unusual. You don't often get a choral work and a piano concerto together.'

Carole looked at the programme. Elgar's 'The Music Makers' was one of her favourite pieces. She had sung it when she had belonged to the other choir. The Rachmaninoff Third Piano Concerto was new. She would just enjoy it because she loved his music. She particularly loved the second one as it had been featured in the film *Brief Encounter*. She hoped the third one wouldn't disappoint her. As she listened to the choir in the first half, it took her back to her youth and Michael. She wondered what had happened to him. He was probably married and now a grandfather. The thought shocked her. Time passed so quickly and if you weren't careful you didn't notice it happening. The awful sensations she had experienced had almost gone away since her confession to Robert. All the built-up guilt and regret had flowed out of her like blood from an open wound. The wound had healed now. It was a wonderful feeling of relief.

After the break, they settled down to listen to the pianist. Piano music always inspired her. It made her want to keep practising even though she would never be a real pianist. It was too late and in any case she didn't have the talent. It didn't matter, however. She had learnt to enjoy music for its own sake. She was hardly going to be a concert pianist but she would try. The concerto started and she sat back prepared to be disappointed. It couldn't be as beautiful as the second one. Every time she heard 'Rach Two', as it was affectionately known, she felt that same loss as the main character in the film. Her beloved had gone off on the train for the last time just as Michael had gone to Australia. Their love affair had been very similar in some ways.

After the break the pianist started to play the Third Piano Concerto in D Minor. She settled down to listen. It was new so there were no images of the heartbroken characters in the film or of her own regrets. She could enjoy it for itself. As the pianist ran up and down the piano, the theme recurred several times and she memorised it. They had good seats and she could watch his fingers. He was amazing. In the past she would have been jealous, somehow imagining it could have been her up there. Now she just enjoyed listening. At the end there was a climax involving the piano and the whole orchestra in an outpouring of emotion that was almost unbearable. Tears ran down her cheeks, tears of raw emotion and joy. The feeling was beyond explanation. Their mutual love of music was such a privilege and united them in a very special way.

Time was running out. Carole had had a phone call telling her that she could take Charlotte home on Friday 8th March. She went to the keyboard group on the Wednesday, aware that the next session would be a problem. She would have to get someone to look after Charlotte or take her to the nursery. Barbara gave her lesson then they all had a practice while she came round to see them individually. Carole had been playing 'Carolina Moon'. She was very fond of country music. She had found an organ sound on the keyboard and she was thrilled. It sounded really good. As she played she imagined she was in the Tower Ballroom in Blackpool. She told herself firmly that there was nothing wrong with fantasy as long as you didn't get carried away!

It was time for the play-around when anyone who wanted could do a solo. Carole was quite happy to play for herself with the headphones on. Barbara had other ideas.

'Have you got something to play for us?'

She blushed uncomfortably. 'I don't think I'm good enough to play in public yet.' It was a bit like going back in time to when she was asked to do the solo at the choir.

'Have a go,' Sam said out of the blue. 'We're not the public, just the group. Go on, have a go. We're all in it together, you know.'

Carole wasn't quite sure what he meant by 'all in it together' but she gave in as she had at the choir. 'OK. I'll try.'

She took the headphones off and resolved to concentrate on what she was playing and not think about the audience. It was what she did at the choir to stop herself from being too nervous. The music was more important than the impression she was making. She tried to remember that as she got started. At first, she was nervous and her fingers were sticky. Gradually she gained confidence and realised how good the organ sounded. It was almost like the real thing even though the little keyboard that Sam had lent her was fairly basic. It just showed what you could do with even a cheap instrument. She hardly made any mistakes, thanks to her piano experience. She finished with an ending provided by the keyboard. It was great. All you had to do was press a button and it did it for you. Everybody clapped. It was the next best thing to playing Rachmaninoff! Barbara seemed impressed.

'That was very good. You haven't been coming long and you're doing really well. Are you practising a lot?'

She nodded. 'I do try and practise a bit every day. That seems to work well for me.'

'That's the best way, little and often. Keep it up and you could be one of our star performers!'

'Oh Barbara! I don't think so. I've got a long way to go. There's so much to learn and not enough time.'

'Well, we just do what we can. It's supposed to be fun.'

'Oh, it is. I'll keep going and see how far I get.'

She was considering buying a new keyboard but she didn't tell Barbara. She would reward herself if she kept making progress. Then she could give the other one back to Sam. She felt like pinching herself to make sure all this was real. Sometimes she thought she might wake up and realise it was only a dream. It seemed too good to be true. When it came to Friday, she would know it wasn't a dream. She hoped it wouldn't turn into a nightmare.

CHAPTER 18

Home

IT WAS FRIDAY and the sky was a leaden grey. Carole stared out at the cherry tree. It looked black against the grey sky and reflected her mood. While she was happy that the great day had finally arrived she was nevertheless nervous. She wondered how Charlotte would react when she got into the house. She hoped she wouldn't turn into a resentful little monster. It was a strong possibility given what she had had to cope with. There was bound to be a reaction. Carole had all the new toys laid out ready and she had vacuumed and dusted the bedroom so everything was immaculate. There was nothing more she could do except go to collect her. She went out and got into the car trying to ignore the rocking and rolling going on in her stomach. So much had gone wrong. Surely they were both entitled to some peace.

She drove down the now infamous A59, taking care with her driving. It was still difficult to believe what had happened. As the bushes in the middle of the two-way road flew past, she caught a glimpse of the exit where the accident had taken place. Paris seemed so far away. Of course she still had the two place mats to remind her that it was actually real. So much had happened to her in such a short time she found herself doubting the reality of some of it.

She pulled into the car park and walked up to the door. The place looked just the same but she knew her life would never be the same again. She knew it but she was ready. When it came to life, she would give as good as she got. She rang the bell and the big door opened like a magic door into the future. It was Karen again, almost like reliving her first visit, except that she had been there so many times lately that it wasn't quite like that. She knew which way to go to get to the lounge and sat down stiffly while Karen went off to get Charlotte.

'These are the last minutes of my life as a free person,' she told herself rather melodramatically. She wasn't changing her mind. She was just becoming aware of the reality of the situation. It was only now that she could really feel the weight of responsibility that went with her decision to take the child. The door opened and Karen came back. She didn't have Charlotte with her. 'Mrs Banks wants to see you first. There are papers to sign.'

Carole had been expecting this so she wasn't surprised. 'OK. I'll go and get it done so we can go.'

Amanda Banks was waiting for her behind the usual mound of wire baskets and files. She didn't get up to go and sit by the unlit fire this time. Instead she produced some forms to sign. She looked long and seriously at Carole. 'Well, you've had quite a time to think about this. Are you really sure you want to do it? You could still change your mind, even now.'

'No. Of course I won't change my mind. I've been here most days spending time with Charlotte. I've come to take her home with me. I know it won't be easy. I'm not under any illusions but I'm prepared to do it for her.'

'OK. That's settled then. Just sign the papers and you can take her. You will get an allowance for her. I suppose you know that?'

'I hadn't really thought about it. Of course the money will come in useful. I'm living on a pension and there will be things to buy for her. I'm not doing it for the money, you know.'

'No. I know you're not. I wasn't suggesting anything like that. I'm just doing my job. That's all. Jean Parkinson will visit you. If you have any problems get in touch with her. She's very experienced.'

'Yes. I will. She's very nice. I hope there won't be too many problems. Charlotte's had an awful lot to cope with considering she's only three.'

'That's what concerns me a bit. I know you were a primary teacher so you are experienced but this situation is a bit different as she'll be at home with you as the sole carer. She might feel the need to test you. You'll have to establish boundaries and stay firm.'

'She's done that before so I know what to expect. She used to do it with her mum as well so I saw what went on. I'll just have to brave it out until she settles.'

'She probably won't believe she's staying with you after so many changes.'

'I'll just take it a day at a time.'

'Good luck then. If Jean's not available and you need help just give me a ring or call in. There's always somebody here to help.' She passed a small card over to her.

'Thank you. You've all been very kind. I hope I won't need your help but it's nice to know it's there in an emergency. I'd like to take Charlotte now unless there's something else that has to be done.'

'No. The formalities are over. Take her and I hope you can make a difference. That's what fostering's all about.'

Carole nodded. She wanted to get out of this building and back to normality. Real life wasn't about form filling and well-meaning lectures about what life might be like with an unhappy child. It was time to get on with the job.

Amanda accompanied her back to the lounge where Karen was waiting with Charlotte, a small case and an oversized teddy. When she saw Carole, Charlotte ran into her arms, confirming the bond that had developed between them. It seemed such a happy scene and yet Carole instinctively knew that there would be trouble. How much she couldn't estimate but there would be some.

'Come on, Charlotte. We're going home.'

It was difficult carrying the case and Samson. Charlotte wanted to hold her hand. In fact she would have liked to be carried as well. It was impossible. She hadn't got out of the door and already she was having problems.

Karen came to her rescue, looking more than a bit amused. 'Here, I'll carry the case and the teddy. You carry Charlotte.'

So that is what they did and it worked. The child was heavy. She wanted to be a baby but she wasn't a baby. She probably weighed the equivalent of twenty-eight bags of sugar if not more. By the time they got to the car, Carole was exhausted and her back was aching. She put Charlotte into the car seat and strapped her in. Fortunately she didn't make a scene. Carole didn't want to look inadequate in front of Karen even if she felt it. She sat Samson down beside Charlotte and thanked Karen for her help. They had all been very pleasant but she felt as though she was being assessed. She put her foot on the accelerator and drove off with a lurch, thinking it was a good job she wasn't doing her driving test.

The main road was full of traffic as she drove towards home. It was Friday. She thought is shouldn't be so busy so early. She knew Friday afternoon would be busy as people got out of work early but it was still the morning. She made quite slow progress and didn't get home until lunchtime. She left Charlotte in the seat while she took the case and the teddy into the house. She thought that was the right way round as she didn't want to leave Charlotte in the house by herself. When she got back, the child was screaming and tears were running down her cheeks. Perhaps it should have been the other way round after all.

She took her out of the seat and led her into the house then sat her down on her knee. 'It's all right. I had to take Samson in first. He didn't want to be left in the car either. I thought you would be OK for a few minutes. Look. I bought you some new books and a game with dolphins. Shall I show you what to do?'

Charlotte nodded silently, wiping a rather grubby hand across her face. Carole got the game out and showed her how to put the little coloured balls into the slots. Then you had to press the lever and the ball jumped out of the dolphin's mouth and into the basket. She was fascinated by the game and all went well. She had been successfully distracted for at least a short time. Carole went into the kitchen to get the lunch when she heard a thump. She went back into the lounge and Charlotte had disappeared. Forty small plastic balls were scattered everywhere. The little girl was behind the sofa waiting to see what she was going to do.

Carole had been expecting this kind of behaviour but perhaps not so soon. The dolphin game had lasted precisely five minutes. She took hold of Charlotte's hand and tried to pull her from behind the couch. Charlotte refused to come out and Carole didn't want to drag her so she gave up. She was already beginning to realise that she was going to need the wisdom of Solomon to deal with her. They'd only been in the house for ten minutes. She was already emotionally exhausted.

'I'm hungry. I'm going to get something to eat. If you come out you can have a sandwich and some fruit and cake.'

There was silence. A battle of wills was taking place. She wondered how long Charlotte would keep it up. She had to give in, in the end, surely. Carole started to eat her sandwich, wondering if she had done the right thing. Teaching infants had been different. They didn't go behind furniture and refuse to come out. Neither had they ever deliberately thrown toys around to annoy her. This was a different relationship. She would have to work through all this again as she had the first time. The trouble was that this time it could be worse because Charlotte had been traumatised. Carole resolved not to tell her about Laura. She wouldn't understand anyway. She was too young.

Carole put the radio on for company. She listened to *Desert Island Discs*. She liked the programme as it combined some interesting music with the biography of the celebrity. She enjoyed being a fly on the wall in somebody else's life. She hoped it might give her some inspiration. The woman being interviewed was talking about her own children. Carole listened. She wasn't that interested because she was feeling stressed. The voice was at least some company. Suddenly she pricked up her ears.

'I've always had my own life,' the woman was saying. 'My children saw me doing things. I used to sing and play the piano. I had to practise for my performances. The children had to accept that. They ended up enjoying it and now they play instruments. You can't spend all your life focusing on what the kids want to do. It isn't good for them.'

It was as though the advice had come out of nowhere. The woman was right. Why should Carole pander to Charlotte? She would enjoy her lunch and maybe play the keyboard afterwards. The child would probably enjoy that, once she had stopped sulking behind the couch. Of course she would get her to help to pick up the balls but she would wait until she came out herself. It would be bad if she lost all her confidence and let Charlotte rule the roost. She felt better and enjoyed the rest of the programme, mentally thanking the celebrity for her well-timed advice. She finished her sandwich quite peacefully.

As the programme came to an end, she sensed a small presence behind her. She started to peel an orange rather casually, not turning round. As she divided it into segments a small hand shot out to take a piece. 'No. You have your sandwich first then the orange and a piece of cake if you want.'

Charlotte looked quizzically at the sandwich then at Carole. She was obviously weighing up what she could get away with. Finally she sat down and ate the sandwich, then the fruit and cake with a drink of fruit juice out of the fridge. She looked as relieved as Carole. When she had finished Carole broached the subject of the mess. 'Now we have to find all the plastic balls. We can't leave them all on the floor. We can't play the game without them and we might slip on them.' She gave her a plastic bowl and took one herself. 'Let's see who can find the most.'

The little girl's face brightened. Carole gave herself a silver star. She had succeeded in turning a confrontation into a game. The mental star was only silver, not gold, as she wasn't sure it would work. Also, she didn't know how many more confrontations there would be. They went into the lounge and started picking up the plastic balls. It went very well and she made sure Charlotte had more than her. It was quite fun looking for them under the furniture and behind the long curtains. Finally they finished and Carole counted the balls. She had made sure Charlotte won but strangely there were still some missing.

'You've won, Charlotte, but there's a problem. There are still four missing. We'll have to keep looking until we find them or the game'll be spoilt.'

They kept on looking for so long that Carole got really frustrated. They were bright colours and they just couldn't have disappeared. She had checked the number when she bought the game. They kept looking until she felt they just had to give up but she didn't like mysteries. Inanimate objects just didn't take themselves off somewhere. She spent another half hour feeling down the sofa in case they had gone down behind the cushions but she still didn't find them. She had wasted a valuable hour and a half looking for four plastic balls. She felt like having a temper tantrum. She could have been playing the keyboard. At sixty-one, time flew much more quickly than when you were three. She gave up then remembered what the woman on the radio had said about not concentrating all the time on children.

'The balls have gone. I don't know what's happened to them. Perhaps we'll find them later. I'm going to do my keyboard practice now. You can play with the game but be careful. Don't spill them like you did last time or we'll have to pick them all up again.'

There were lots of other toys dotted around so Charlotte would have a choice. Carole started practising a new piece of music. She had bought a book with lots of famous pop songs. They weren't too hard. She had decided on 'A Whiter Shade of Pale'. It had always been one of her favourites and she already knew how to use the organ style but it was quite difficult. She tried a bit at a time, leaving Charlotte to play.

The little girl came to listen for a while then wandered around, not really playing with anything. Carole watched her out of the corner of her eye in between her efforts. She came back and tried to sit on her knee.

'I can't play with you on my knee. You can sit by me if you want.'

Charlotte didn't want and went off the play with the remains of the plastic balls. Carole tried to concentrate but it was difficult. *So much for the woman on the radio!* It wasn't going to work in this case. She then came back down to earth. It would take ages before Charlotte settled again. She mustn't expect too much. She would have to practise when she was asleep, assuming she did sleep. Carole felt as though nothing was now certain in her life with Charlotte. How on earth would Robert cope if she continued to disrupt everything? She decided to take her out.

'It's a nice day. Would you like to go to the park? I've got some bread. We can feed the ducks.'

The child's face lit up.

'But first we'll have to tidy up the game.'

The balls were all over the carpet but fortunately they weren't under the furniture. She had simply dropped them all near the game. They used the bowls and picked them up again. Carole couldn't escape from her years as a primary teacher. It was second nature to count them to make sure that at least the remaining ones were all there. It was also good for Charlotte. It would help her to understand what counting was all about. They counted the yellow, blue and green ones. They were all there. She hadn't realised that it was the pink ones that were missing. They counted them. They were all there. The missing ones had mysteriously reappeared.

Carole looked at Charlotte. Her face didn't register any emotion. Her mysterious blue eyes stared, expressionless, at her new foster mum. The child had deliberately hidden the balls, probably in her pocket. Carole was really angry. She had wasted half the afternoon looking for them. Why had Charlotte done it?

She wondered if it was to test her once again or was it to keep her attention. She probably didn't like her playing the keyboard. It had certainly succeeded.

She pointed to the pink balls. 'Why did you hide them? You let me crawl around looking for those pink balls when all the time you had them in your pocket.'

She realised that there wasn't any point in asking her why. Was she really expecting an extended explanation from a child with very little language? Her mother would have slapped her. Carole had more self control but she was experiencing the kind of behaviour that Samantha had found it so hard to deal with. Her mum was still a child herself. *She does it on purpose to upset me.* She remembered her very words. She also remembered that Charlotte's behaviour had improved when she was with her. The trouble was she had had more bad experiences and Carole wondered if she would ever settle. Then she might be adopted and that would be another trauma for her. She had known what she was taking on but she experienced a rush of fear. Life had started to be so good. If she had to live with a child who needed constant attention and reassurance how was she going to have a life with Robert?

She doused her anger with a cold douche of realism. It was only a small incident. The child had only just arrived. She was sure she would settle eventually. She looked Charlotte in the eye and told her that they had spent so long looking for the balls they could only go to the park for a short time. 'There won't be time to feed the ducks,' she added. 'We'll have to do that tomorrow instead.'

It was a kind of punishment but also a way of showing her that her behaviour had consequences. She put her coat on and they went off to the park. It was only down the road so they walked. It didn't take long to get there. As she stared at the bank of trees memories came flooding back. She would make sure Charlotte didn't run into the trees. They went through the gate. There was a winding path leading down to the lake and also to the swings.

As soon as they got through the gate, Charlotte was off like a greyhound in a race. She seemed to have no fear or awareness of danger. Carole was forced to run after her just like last time but in a different direction. Thankfully she was reasonably fit and soon caught up with her. She grabbed Charlotte's hand and stooped down to her level. 'You have to stay with me or you might get lost. If you run away again I'll have to hold your hand all afternoon. Do you understand?'

Charlotte looked at her very solemnly. Her mouth turned down as though she was sulking.

'Are you going to stay with me? Can I let go of your hand?'

She was twisting to try to get free. Carole let go of her and this time she stayed close. The half hour went by without any more incidents. Robert was coming the next day. She was dreading it. It was so soon and she knew there was bound to be some sort of scene. He would be a lot more disturbed by bad behaviour than she was.

When they got home, they had an uneventful meal. A tin of ravioli and a bowl of fresh fruit was not exactly a gourmet meal but children liked that sort of food and Carole was too tired to think about cooking. Charlotte watched a bit of television then Carole read her a story and took her up to see her renovated bedroom. The little girl was entranced by the flowery duvet and curtains. After giving her a quick bath and helping her brush her teeth, Carole settled her into bed. As she lay there under the duvet she looked like an angelic statue in the middle of a garden full of flowers. Carole sighed. Perhaps the statue was a hidden gargoyle like the ones on Notre Dame. The next few weeks were certainly not going to be an easy ride!

CHAPTER 19

Unresolved Problems

S URPRISINGLY, CHARLOTTE SLEPT through. Carole was prepared for a broken night. It didn't happen so she was wide awake when Charlotte came into her. It was seven o'clock and still dark outside. She had left the landing light on and could see the little girl standing in the doorway. She put her arms out of the duvet and beckoned to her.

'Come in and have a cuddle,' she called from the warmth of the bed. 'You've been a good girl. You slept all night.'

Charlotte beamed and ran into the bedroom and into bed with Carole. She was carrying the little teddy that had once been on the Christmas tree. Carole played a running game with the little bear, making him run along the duvet and tickle Charlotte's neck. She giggled. 'Again,' she demanded, so many times that beams of light started to come through the curtains. The day had started very successfully but it was time for breakfast.

She and Robert were going to take Charlotte out to the Liverpool art gallery. There was a children's room with lots of equipment where small children could have fun painting and cutting and sticking different materials. The nearby museum was also interesting. They would play it by ear and see how things went. Carole had been reluctant to invite Robert so soon. She didn't like to admit it but she was a bit scared. She wasn't totally in control of Charlotte. She didn't know what she was going to do next and didn't want to look inadequate in front of him. Still, he had suggested the outing and obviously wanted to start straight away in his new role.

Thanks to Jenny, Charlotte had quite a wardrobe of clothes so it wasn't difficult to find something for her to wear. At this point Carole made her first mistake of the day. She let Charlotte choose what to wear from the clothes hanging in the wardrobe. She chose a summer dress. It was very cold outside so it wasn't suitable. She didn't want to wear the smart navy tights either. There was a terrible screaming match leaving Carole in a quandary, not wanting to give in but realising that this particular battle was about to be lost. Finally she negotiated. 'You can wear that dress but you must wear the tights. It's cold outside. When you're ready we'll have a drink and a snack before we go out. I bought some nice biscuits with faces on them.'

She knew it was bribery but she was at the end of her tether. The biscuits worked, the tights went on and she made herself a coffee while she waited for Robert. She wouldn't make that mistake again. There were undoubtedly lots of others waiting to torment her! Next time she would give her two choices, not the whole wardrobe. She had learnt something but she wondered what her next mistake would be. Childcare wasn't as easy as people imagined. How could such a little child cause so much trouble? It was quite incredible.

She thought back to her own childhood. Those memories stayed with you for life. She remembered her mother working at the sink, washing dishes and cooking. She had been good at practical things. She washed and cleaned but she couldn't remember her ever playing. A sense of terrible loneliness came over her, remembering the isolation of the only child. She had been lonely for the whole of her childhood. Her father was a taxi driver who worked long hours. He had had an old-fashioned approach to marriage. Children were women's work. He brought in the money. She thought bitterly that he probably didn't know that she was so lonely. He was hardly ever there.

Her mother only went out to the shops, dragging her along, first in the pushchair then on foot as she got older. Sometimes they passed the park where there was a playground. She didn't ask to go. There wasn't any point. Nobody ever came to the house, none of the happy mums with little children that she sometimes saw in the street or in the shops. She remembered seeing two women laughing together while the children danced around their feet. Primary school might have been a break in the cloud of the daily routine but it hadn't turned out that way. She had been a misfit from the start. She didn't know how to make friends and rapidly made enemies. The bullies had quickly singled out the isolated awkward child who couldn't make friends and looked scared stiff in the playground. Looking back, she knew it had somehow been her mum's fault. It was all a long time ago but still fixed in her memory like an ever present sore.

She knew who had saved her. It was her piano teacher. Strangely, the woman who'd had no time for her nevertheless sent her to piano lessons. It was the thing to do in those days. Looking back she almost laughed out loud at the poor piano teachers who probably cursed the fashion for children's piano lessons. It was a miracle that she succeeded as well as she did. Mrs Griffin was an old lady making a bit of money to supplement her pension. Carole remembered her mum shutting her in the front lounge where the piano stood in state. Piano lessons were something she could understand. You paid and the child played. It was the child's business, not hers. She got on with the housework. That was her job. Carole couldn't remember any time when either of her parents had come in to listen. It was just what you did with children, something tangible that made more sense than other aspects of child-rearing.

Most children would probably have reacted badly to the enforced piano lessons but Carole had been different. The truth was that Mrs Griffin became the nearest thing she had to a proper mother. She smiled a lot, let Carole try her walking stick and always produced either cakes or biscuits halfway through the lesson. Sometimes she patted her on the head or on the back and something akin to love grew between them. Carole longed for the day she went for her lesson and every night when the door banged and she was left to play she practised. It was a way of feeling as though Mrs Griffin was there. She sometimes talked to her quietly and when she wasn't talking she spoke to her through the music. She was sure she could feel the teacher's hand on her back every time she played.

The lessons had continued until she was eleven. Several times her mum had tried to stop them as money was always short but she had begged to go on with them. Both parents were quite surprised, wondering where their daughter got her love of music. Neither of them was interested in the kind of things she played. They were too busy watching game shows and comic films on the television. She was heartbroken when Mrs Griffin died and the piano lessons came to an end. At secondary school, she had played the violin in the orchestra but it was all more impersonal and she had never liked it the way she had the piano. There was no Mrs Griffin to inspire her. She had spent a lot of time staring at the piano, standing silently in the front lounge, but she had had never played again until she joined the choir. She was still living at home and the piano was in its usual place. She had started to play and the old pleasure was still there as she hit the somewhat faded black and white ivory keys. Whenever she sang in the choir or played the piano she could feel Mrs Griffin smiling. She resolved to include the old lady in her thoughts when she sang the Fauré Requiem.

The prospect of dealing with Charlotte suddenly took on a frightening aspect. People who had had a happy childhood made good parents. She had learnt the theory at college but it was only now the reality came to plague her. She had written about it in essays and got good marks. How strange that you could write about something so convincingly when you only understood it intellectually? This was reality. Her stomach turned over and ripples of fear made her heart thump. A terrible question was taking shape inside her. Did she have the skills to bring up a child? And if she didn't could she learn them?

When Robert arrived at eleven o'clock he found Carole a bit subdued. 'What's the matter? You look as though you've had a bad day and it's not eleven o'clock yet. The sun's shining and we've got the whole day to have some fun. I've never used my bus pass.' He grinned. 'It's quite an adventure.'

Carole felt instantly better. Maybe she was getting things out of proportion. After all, they'd only had one bit of conflict over the dress. In the end she'd done quite well over the wretched dolphin game. It was better to be positive.

Charlotte was staring curiously at Robert. He was wearing jeans, a red check shirt and a fur lined jacket. He didn't look out of the ordinary but she stared and stared. She had seen him before but they had never been out together with her.

'We're going to Liverpool on the bus. It'll be fun. Would you like to go upstairs? You can see more then.'

'Bus,' she repeated, looking very serious. Her blue eyes flipped from one to the other, full of questions.

He smiled at her, then whipped out a piece of paper and drew a bus with three people staring out of the window. Then he drew a dog that appeared to be laughing.

'I didn't know you could draw that well,' Carole said, admiringly.

'I've got hidden talents. You've seen nothing yet!' He stroked the little girl's hair and then passed her the drawing.

She took it and started to jump up and down. She pointed to the people, one at a time, repeating their names. When she came to Robert she looked a bit confused.

'That's Robert,' Carole said helpfully.

'Robert,' Charlotte repeated slowly then moved on to the dog and the wheels.

'It's the song – "The Wheels on the Bus". That's what she's trying to tell us. I sang it with her when she was here before. She's remembered.'

Robert went over to the piano and played it. Carole envied the way he could play anything without music. They sang one verse and Charlotte joined in the part where the dogs barked. Anyone being a fly on the wall would have seen a happy family having fun. Carole felt better. Perhaps you could learn parenting at sixty-one. Then she remembered that she had played games with the little teddy, making him tickle Charlotte. She wasn't such a bad person after all but she still had an uneasy feeling that the day wasn't going to be straightforward.

They walked down to the bus stop and stared at the timetable. They didn't know what number bus went to the town centre so they had to check. It wasn't long before the bus came. The small pushchair folded up and everything appeared to be going well. Carole went first with Charlotte while Robert carried the pushchair. The driver looked as though he was going through the motions like a puppet. He actually had to wake up a bit when Carole informed him that she didn't know what to do with the bus pass.

'Put it down there,' he almost groaned, pointing to a small metal square and not making eye contact with her. She felt sympathetic. After all, he was trying to do two jobs but it wasn't a reason to be rude. First she'd been angry with Charlotte, now she was angry with the bus driver. The day out wasn't starting out very well.

Robert had been so busy folding up the pushchair and carrying it onto the bus he hadn't noticed what she had done with the card. Carole was now several paces away from the ticket machine.

'Excuse me. What do I do with my card?'

The driver stared at him through bleary eyes as if he was thinking: *Haven't I just explained that? What's the matter with these people?* His eyes were heavy and sunken in a mass of wrinkles as though he smoked and drank too much. He looked Robert up and down wearily as though he was some kind of alien armed with a push chair. Carole chuckled to herself. Perhaps he thought she'd had IVF and that Charlotte was their daughter. Anything was possible these days.

They went upstairs. The little girl thought it was a great adventure, especially as they got the front seats. Robert looked quietly amused. His blue eyes were twinkling and his mouth was slowly turning up in a grin. 'I think the driver thinks we're a bit peculiar. Has he never seen grandparents with their granddaughter? Or maybe he thinks we are very old parents.'

'Just what I was thinking a minute ago! Maybe he doesn't like his job. He looks bored stiff. I don't think he's got the energy to think about us. He's probably just waiting for the end of the shift.'

'Oh. I expect you're right. Let's just enjoy the ride.'

It was quite a long way to the town centre but it was fun. Charlotte and Carole pretended to drive the bus and the time passed. They went straight to the art gallery where there was a café. They tried to discuss the coming concert. It was only a week away and there was only one more rehearsal. Jenny had offered to babysit for the Thursday rehearsal. Carole was very grateful as she had nobody else to ask. She didn't want to send Charlotte to Jenny's as she was only just settling in. Consequently, Jenny had had to get a baby sitter for James and Eva so it was quite a feat of organisation. Jenny was coming to the concert so she would look after Charlotte on the Saturday. It was very difficult to have a conversation. Every time they started to talk, Charlotte would interrupt with her limited vocabulary. They both got quite frustrated.

'I don't remember my grandchildren being so demanding,' Robert said quietly as they got up. 'Perhaps she'll be better doing some craft work. They look as though they've got plenty to keep her busy for a bit.'

'Let's wait and see,' Carole replied rather cynically. 'She just wants to feel safe, I think. She's had a lot to put up with.'

Robert looked as though he was about to say that they were having a lot to put up with but he kept quiet.

They made their way to the craft room. There were a lot of little children there and plenty to do. Charlotte made a beeline for the painting table. There was a space for her to sit down. She took a large piece of paper and started to paint. Carole and Robert looked at each other. They were both thinking the same thing – peace at last! The only trouble was that it didn't last. As soon as they started talking she stopped painting. Carole sat with her for a while but as soon as she went back to Robert she was shouting for attention. Carole put her foot down and refused to get up again. After all, they were only a few metres away from the painting table.

All the other children were quite happy painting while their parents talked but Charlotte wasn't happy. As they talked she tore her painting into little strips then tipped all the pots of paint over. Fortunately they were spill-proof pots but the other children couldn't use them as they were all rolling about on their sides. There was a paint brush in each pot so that the children didn't mix the colours. Some of them rolled onto the floor. The paintbrushes fell out of the pots still on the table and rolled onto the other children's paintings, making a mess. There were cries of protest from the other children. The parents came running and looks of disapproval were directed at the three of them.

Carole was mortified. Robert looked bemused but philosophical as he apologised and cleared up the mess. Charlotte looked very pleased with herself. Everyone was focusing on her. They made her pick up the paint containers but she had got what she wanted. Pleasing them didn't seem as important to her as getting their attention. They began to realise that the only time they would get together would be when she was in bed.

They went to the museum, relieved to leave the art gallery behind and escape from the critical gaze of the parents and attendants. Charlotte had made the kind of scene that left them looking like rather inadequate parents, even though they were neither parents nor grandparents. They shuffled into the museum, resolving to keep a close eye on her this time. They looked at various prehistoric animals and some creepy-crawlies. Charlotte liked them best. They walked round with her, talking about the various exhibits. She wasn't any trouble because they were concentrating on her all the time. They both had the same feeling that something wasn't right about the situation but they couldn't quite put their finger on what it was. One thing that was obvious was that Charlotte was in charge of them instead of the other way round!

It was time to go home. It was difficult to know who was the most tired but Carole was convinced she won the exhaustion prize. She was tense because of Charlotte's attention-seeking behaviour but she was also feeling rather helpless. The child was going to rule her life and she wasn't sure that she wanted it. She *had* wanted it but it suddenly looked like trying to climb a high mountain without any experience or walking boots.

They went back to Carole's house and she put Charlotte to bed then went into the lounge. Robert was sitting in one of the armchairs near the fire, reading the paper. Carole collapsed into the chair opposite. They were like two old cars that had run out of petrol.

Robert looked up rather wryly. 'I expect you're beginning to wonder what you've taken on.'

'I'm sorry, Robert. I hoped it would be a really nice day out for us. I bet you hated every minute.'

He shook his head. 'No, I didn't hate it. For heaven's sake, she's only been with you for one day. Apart from what's happened to her recently, you don't know what sort of life she had with her mum. A health visitor once said something that stuck in my mind. She was talking about children who had had a bad start. She said they could take as long again to recover. What I mean is Charlotte is three years old. It could be another three years before she recovers. Of course, it might not. Don't panic. I'm just making you realise it's early days. Give her time. I don't mind. Let's work at it. Once the concert's over on Saturday, I'll have more time. I'll help you. It's worth it.'

Carole wanted to throw her arms around him but he was too far away on the other side of the fire. She had worried so much about how he would react yet here he was coping better than her and the concert was only a week away. She didn't want to tell him about her unhappy childhood. He was really together as a person. He was so right for her. He had talked a bit about his parents and his childhood. He took for granted the warm stability he'd grown up with. His own children sounded similarly together although she hadn't met them. It was like an old-fashioned scale. His side was weighed down with so many advantages that he had never even thought about. Her side was too light. He didn't notice but she did and it made her feel bad. She kept telling herself that the past had gone. It was the present that mattered. But the past was encroaching on her present. She was threatened by the child. She remembered what Samantha had said. *She does it to upset me.* Children had hidden antennae. They knew when adults were vulnerable. Was that why Charlotte behaved like that? Was she, Carole, so different from Samantha?

Jenny came on Thursday as she had promised and Carole went to the final rehearsal. As they sang through the programme she thought about Laura. It had been her funeral two days ago. She hadn't been because she couldn't leave Charlotte and she couldn't take her. She hadn't mentioned anything about Laura to Charlotte. She was too young to understand what dying really meant and she didn't want to remind her of what had happened in the car. It was better not to go. She had phoned Don and explained then sent a card. It was all she could do.

They sang through the Fauré, *Carmina Burana* and Schubert's 'Ave Maria'. Robert was very pleased. The orchestra was as well prepared as the choir. It was all as good as it could possibly be. Carole suspected that he thought too much time had elapsed and that they would be stale but she didn't think so. They had practised so much that they were all very confident. She was sure the whole thing would be a great success. The tickets had gone well so they would have a fairly large audience.

Chapter 20

Requiem

I T WAS SATURDAY 16th March, the day of the concert. The daffodils were coming into flower. The spring was really coming into its own. Carole had had a difficult week with Charlotte. Jenny had come early to babysit on the day of the rehearsal and Carole had had time to confide in her. After all Jenny had two children of her own and had a lot of first-hand experience. She explained how the little girl needed constant attention and didn't seem able to be left even for five minutes.

Jenny looked thoughtful. 'It could be because she's missed out on some baby stage and she constantly needs to go back to it. I did a child development course and I remember being told about the different stages. If you miss out on one you want to go back to experience it then you can move on.'

Carole was both impressed but also alarmed by her friend's explanation. 'Perhaps that's why some people are so childish. They're stuck in a previous stage of development.'

'Yes. That's probably true. But I suppose most people don't have idyllic childhoods. You're lucky if you do. It just has to be good enough according to the psychologists.'

'What if it isn't? What if Charlotte never escapes from her past?'

Jenny shrugged. 'She'll have to find a way of living with it like most people. Are you really worried about it?'

'Yes. It's hard living with ambiguity. I have to have a life of my own. As she grows up, she'll have to go to school and I won't be there to hold her hand all day.'

Jenny laughed. 'No, you won't. If I were you I wouldn't wait until she goes to school. Let her go to the nursery down the road. Perhaps not yet but I think you'll know when she could cope with it. You have to think of yourself, not just Charlotte. If you crack up you won't be any use to her or Robert.'

Carole nodded. She knew Jenny was right and it put a ray of hope in her day. Carole would continue to surround Charlotte with love and reassurance but at some point she would contact the nursery. They would probably give her priority because of her situation. 'Thanks, Jenny. You've made me feel better.'

She had gone off to the rehearsal feeling a new sense of freedom. She wouldn't be using the nursery to get rid of the child. She would use it to give herself a break and a chance to be with Robert without constant interruptions. She hadn't told Jenny her fear about her lack of parenting skills. She resolved to keep it to herself and just do her best. She couldn't get the picture of her mother washing dishes out of her head. She felt the first wave of affection she had ever felt for her. She had paid for the piano lessons and fed and clothed her. It wasn't enough but she had done her best. Carole would do the same.

Robert was going early to coordinate with the conductor of the orchestra. Carole had agreed to drive there with Charlotte and meet Jenny inside. She had tried to get the little girl to sleep in the afternoon but it hadn't worked. Children on the continent had a sleep then stayed up late. It wasn't worth trying to explain that to her. She was tempted to give in once again then she had an idea. She decided it was worth a try otherwise she would be tired by the time they arrived, never mind later.

Jenny had given Carole a lovely dress for Charlotte. It was a yellow party dress covered in sequins with had a wide sash round the waist. Charlotte hadn't yet had the opportunity to wear it. She got it out of the wardrobe and sat down on the bed with it. The child's eyes were round with astonishment at the glittering sequins and the shiny blue satin sash. Carole set about explaining that they were going out in the dark that evening to a very special concert. Jenny and Eva and James were going too. They were all having a sleep so they wouldn't be tired. 'When you wake up you can wear your lovely dress.'

Charlotte listened solemnly, her eyes drifting from the dress to Carole then back again. Carole could almost hear the little girl's mind ticking over. She was amazed at how complex children were even when they were only three. She thought back three years, trying to remember what she had been doing when Charlotte had come into the world. She had been at school she supposed but she couldn't remember exactly. It was hard to realise that before that time Charlotte hadn't existed. She realised it was once again a form of bribery but if she didn't sleep she might cause a scene during the concert. She hastily put the thought out of her mind. The horror of it was unimaginable.

She left the dress on the chair hoping Charlotte would sleep and wouldn't do anything crazy such as throwing the dress out of the window or ripping it. There had been all kinds of bad behaviour during the week, leaving her with little confidence. She had no real choice. Jenny had wanted to come to the concert and all the other people she knew were in the choir so there was nobody to leave Charlotte with. Carole also thought it would be good for her to come and watch the orchestra. If she could just get her to sleep she would probably be all right during the performance.

Silence reigned upstairs. Had she succeeded? She didn't dare to go up to investigate in case she disturbed her. She rewarded her effort with a cold orange juice. She would rather have had a glass of sherry but she couldn't afford to start drinking. She would need her wits about her to do the solo while watching for trouble from Charlotte. She half wished it would be dark so she wouldn't be able to see her but she knew they would all be in full view.

Carole felt as though she had won a gold medal. There was no noise from upstairs. After half an hour, she couldn't control her curiosity any longer. The fearful side of her worried that Charlotte might have found something interesting to do to pass the time! Her mind ran round in circles, imagining an overflowing bath or talcum powder sprinkled in interesting patterns. Similar activities had occurred during the week. She tiptoed upstairs and put her head round the door. Charlotte was fast asleep holding the tiny teddy that she loved so much. Carole felt like dancing down the stairs but she was too afraid of making any noise or falling head first!

Charlotte slept for an hour and a half, enough time to allow her to go to the concert without being too tired. For once that week, the day was going in the right direction. Carole laid out her black skirt and the blouse that Joyce had found for her. She had quite a lot of jewellery. It was one of things that Joyce always drew her attention to when she went in. People seemed to change their necklaces fairly often and Carole found it hard to resist when she saw something that she liked. She chose a black one. Each glass stone was like a raindrop and encircled with stainless steel. It wasn't expensive but it looked wonderful to Carole. Black was just right for the Fauré Requiem. She added a pair of black earrings that didn't match but looked as though they went with the necklace. The outfit was complete.

She started to get her music ready when she heard a noise upstairs. She dropped everything and ran. She didn't trust Charlotte. She was scared she might decide to do something nasty to punish her for making her sleep. Or maybe the child would be angry that she had lost the battle and fallen asleep. She went in and then felt ashamed of herself. Charlotte was lying peacefully in bed singing to herself.

'Charlotte. You've been such a good girl. You've had a good sleep. You won't be tired at the concert tonight. You'll have fun with Eva and James.'

She pointed to the dress. 'Dress,' she said firmly.

Carole was tempted to point out that it was hours to the concert but she thought better of it. As she looked at the dress she saw it in pieces then blinked. It was in one piece. She was getting neurotic. It wouldn't do.

'Come on then. I'll get you ready.' She didn't go into the fact that it was still hours to the concert. Charlotte was only three after all. Time was still a mystery to her.

Charlotte leapt out of bed and Carole put the dress on her. It was just the right size. She fastened the sash and took Charlotte into to look at herself in the long mirror. She looked very serious then twirled around like a ballet dancer.

'You look lovely. I'll put my skirt and blouse on after tea. Let's go down and have something to eat.'

That always worked with Charlotte. She seemed to be always hungry although she didn't eat that much when she was at the table. Eating filled the time. Charlotte found time something of a problem. Carole put an apron on her so she didn't get dirty then they played the dolphin game. This time they didn't lose any of the pieces although she could tell from Charlotte's face that she hadn't forgotten. Charlotte gathered up the balls at the end of the game and pulled at her straggly blond hair as they put them away. Her blue eyes expressed a certain emotion but just what she was thinking was a mystery only known to Charlotte.

While she was watching children's television, Carole got her music ready, checking carefully that she had everything. After a traumatic week with Charlotte she had visions of standing up to sing the solo then realising she hadn't got the music. She was more nervous than usual about everything. The little girl was having a bad effect on her. A big black cloud was forming in her mind. It was far away but it was menacing. She couldn't help wondering what was going to happen to her if Charlotte didn't settle. How long could she go on before she had a crisis?

The concert was due to start at seven o'clock. She left home at six-fifteen with Charlotte looking very smart in her party dress. She had let Carole brush her hair and wash her face without any squirming about. This was unusual. Perhaps it was a good sign. The brushing had turned her usually tangled, messy hair into something quite acceptable. Tiny blond curls encircled her little white face and reached down in a curly fringe above her questioning blue eyes. Carole's mood kept fluctuating according to Charlotte's behaviour. She knew it wasn't a good situation but she couldn't help it.

They arrived at six-thirty. There were already a lot of cars in the car park. She hurried into the hall as though she was late. Jenny was already there with James and Eva. They were very excited, particularly Eva. 'Carole. We'll be going home in the dark. It's getting dark now.'

They had never been to a late concert. The prospect of going home in the dark interested Eva more than the instruments being set up by the players.

'Charlotte. You look really nice. I do like your dress. It really suits you,' Jenny exclaimed.

'I had one like that when I was little,' Eva remembered, forgetting about the dark.

'Yes, you looked nice in yours too.'

Eva smiled happily and there was no more talk of dresses, new or second-hand.

Carole bent down to talk to Charlotte. She pointed to the stage. 'I have to stand up there and sing. Look, there's a seat for you next to Jenny. She's going to look after you while we sing.' Once again, she felt a sinking feeling. What if Charlotte wouldn't stay with Jenny?

Jenny seemed to sense Carole's dilemma, especially after their last conversation. She took over. 'Look, Eva's saved you a seat next to her. I've brought some sweets to share. You can have one now then some in the interval, that's when people have a rest and go and have a drink.' She passed a sweet to Charlotte. She put it in her mouth and sat sucking and looking round. 'When people have a rest you can have a red one.'

Charlotte nodded and settled peacefully next to Eva. Carole went to find her seat next to Maureen. The hall started to fill up. Most of the tickets had been sold so there would be a good audience. The orchestra started first with the *New World Symphony*. It was one of Carole's favourites and the title seemed very appropriate. The present world was a new world for her. As they were just listening she was able to watch Charlotte. She was sitting mesmerised by the music and the orchestra. It was quite strange as she wasn't in any sense the centre of attention yet for once she seemed happy. Carole relaxed. Perhaps she was going to be musical.

It was a long symphony. It was astonishing that Charlotte sat all that time without any objection, in fact quite extraordinary. After the symphony the choir sang excerpts from *Carmina Burana*. It was very loud and lively. She could see Eva and Charlotte giggling at the noise from the orchestra accompanying them. They had Jenny's sweets during the interval then drinks and biscuits in a big room off the hall. The first half had gone really well.

After the interval, it was the choir's main piece, the Fauré Requiem. Carole thought Charlotte would be either asleep or squirming after sitting for the whole of the first part. She was surprised. The little girl continued to listen. Robert raised his baton and the orchestra played a chord then they all came in. *Requiem aeternam* – Grant them eternal rest. Carole was filled with a deep sadness. This Requiem Mass was for Laura but also for her own baby. She didn't even know if it was a boy or a girl. She would sing now for her baby. It was time to move on. There was another baby down there at the front, a living child who needed her. But she would still sing for the child she had lost, the mother that she might have been.

It was soon time for her solo. She stood up and stared down at the music. The 'Pie Jesu' was a plea for eternal rest for those who had died. As she prepared to start, a grief so profound filled her that she thought she was going to choke. She looked at Robert and he nodded and smiled at her. She somehow felt that he knew what was going through her mind. His kind smile gave her the courage to sing. Her voice soared up to the rafters of the old hall as she sang for the baby she had lost so many years ago. She sang to Charlotte too and the little girl's eyes were round with emotion. She hardly blinked. Everyone in the hall had a sense that something extraordinary had just happened. The atmosphere was electric. They finished with *In Paradisum* – May the angels lead you into Paradise. As they finished Carole felt a kind of release. This Requiem had been for a special purpose and now she would leave it all behind and go forward.

They finished with Schubert's 'Ave Maria'. She loved the piece and sang it for Mrs Griffin who had been so kind to a lonely child. She could still feel her hand on her back as though it had settled there for life. The music was very beautiful and she could see Charlotte trying to join in. Could music be an answer? Time would tell. As the final chords of the 'Ave Maria' died away Robert and the orchestra conductor bowed with a certain amount of relief and satisfaction. They motioned to the orchestra to stand. As they all stood up, the applause began. Almost everybody got to their feet and gave them a standing ovation. Charlotte and Eva and James were clapping and jumping up and down with excitement. Carole wondered how much such an experience would stay with them for life. It would certainly stay with her. She thanked Jenny, hugged James and Eva and promised to contact them soon. Then she drove home with Charlotte.

Robert arrived in his car and together they put the sleepy child to bed. As Carole kissed her goodnight two little arms went round her neck. Then she and Robert went to bed. As she lay there in his arms, she felt the years flying backwards like a film in reverse. They were still alive. It was a second chance and this time she wouldn't waste a minute.

21798522R00154

Printed in Great Britain
by Amazon